Arthur's
Soul Adventure

JOHN HUNT PUBLISHING

First published by O-Books, 2010
O-Books is an imprint of John Hunt Publishing Ltd., No. 3 East Street, Alresford
Hampshire SO24 9EE, UK
office@jhpbooks.com
www.johnhuntpublishing.com

For distributor details and how to order please visit the 'Ordering' section on our website.

A CIP catalogue record for this book is available from the British Library.

Design: Stuart Davies

UK: Printed and bound by CPI Group (UK) Ltd, Croydon, CR0 4YY

Arthur's Soul Adventure

Brian R. Chambers

BOOKS

Winchester, UK
Washington, USA

CONTENTS

This book is dedicated to my father,
Arthur A. Chambers (1923-1995) who always had something
good cooking on the stove and whose boundless love made this
book possible.

Acknowledgements

I am deeply grateful to my beloved wife and tenacious editor Suzanne Phelps Chambers whose love, support, and magical edits brought this story to life. Her son Dennis William Weir, whose youthful nature helped me to create the many humorous escapades of the main character Arthur, has been a source of my inspiration. I wish to thank my delightful mother-in-law Rev. Catherine C. Gibson who was my first reader, and our friend Ellen Johnston who helped refine the early manuscript with her expert edits. I also wish to thank our other family members and many friends who read and commented on the manuscript in various stages, including my sister Carol Dever, as well as Richard Deraney, Khadijah Brown, Paula Wood Dyer, Mary Beth Hritz, Brian Summers, Kathryn Phelps Summers, Susan B. Mills, Anne Nichols, John C. Wright, Clare Alice McManus, John Harrington and his family, especially his daughter, Kristen Marie, John Fitzgerald, my hiking buddy Jack Madden, and even my lifelong friend Michael McDevitt who refused to believe I could actually write, yet, who now humbly concedes. Special thanks go to Rhys Thomas, and all of his healing students who read my manuscript in various stages and were an endless source of encouragement in bringing this book to life. My friend, Rick Parastatides, provided creative, technical expertise in adapting an oil painting by Peter W. Phelps (1936-1990) for the cover art. To Robin Allen, who believed in my dream, and always knew this book would happen, I am grateful. My love goes to my uncle, William Del Jenkins, who has been an eternal source of inspiration to me by encouraging me to believe in the impossible with his nearly mythical vigor and ageless wisdom. And lastly, I wish to express my thanks to John Hunt of O Books for taking a risk on an unknown voice from Savin Hill, Massachusetts.

Brian R. Chambers

Chapter 1

Tracks

Arthur's eyes followed the bend of the railroad track as he scanned rows of open boxcars for a sign he had been there. Sometimes he'd see a shadow pass by an open door, and his heart would start beating quickly. He'd run ahead only to find a sleepy drunk swinging a brown bottle or a flock of pigeons, and he would sink down into that empty place inside of himself until he could push it aside again. The last time he saw his father he was wandering down the tracks and suddenly disappeared into a boxcar. Each night in his dark bedroom, just before going to sleep, he would rehearse the words he would say when he finally found him. "Why did you leave us? Why did you leave, and never come back?"

Everyday after school, Arthur would go down to the tracks to find coal. It was the one way he could help his sister and brothers. He always thought maybe today would be the day he'd see him. Sometimes he swore his father was around the corner. He could feel him there. And then, there was silence. Maybe tomorrow he'd find him.

Walking along the track, he picked up pieces of coal left behind by trains that had passed through Boston the day before. Sometimes he would find a piece as big as his fist, but usually only small ones, bits and pieces shaken off by the rumbling trains. Arthur threw the coal on top of his school books inside a satchel his sister Alice had made for him. The burlap potato sack with "Maine" boldly displayed in red block letters hung across his back. He was proud that Alice could depend on him to keep the coal stove burning in their cold water flat. His best friend Tommy followed behind him, coaxing Arthur to hurry up. The snow was falling heavily, painting their shoulders and their Irish caps with crystal icing. Arthur reveled in the simple joy of walking in virgin snow. Like an explorer discovering arctic lands, Arthur insisted that they investigate every protrusion in the snow for their elusive quarry. Tommy sighed impatiently.

"Tommy, over there. See it on the side of the track? That's got to be a good piece."

He kicked the powdery snow where Arthur was pointing to find only an empty beer bottle.

"Nothing here," Tommy replied.

It was at that moment that Arthur saw it. The pyramid of snow rising up from the ground looked like a sandcastle waiting to be knocked down.

Arthur started to walk toward it when Tommy complained, "Can't we just go home? Come on we're not going to find anything."

"Wait a minute. I think this is a good one."

Arthur brushed the snow from the intriguing protrusion to reveal the largest piece of coal he had ever seen. He estimated that this find was the size of a small melon, yet resembled the shape and cut of a huge black diamond.

"Over here! Look at this one," Arthur shouted.

Arthur held the extraordinary piece of coal between his two hands, gazing upon it as a jeweler would a prized diamond. He was flabbergasted by its incredible beauty, and he was convinced that he held the "Holy Grail" of coal.

"Art, let's go! I can't stand it. My toes are going to fall off they're so cold."

"Okay, help me open my coal bag so I can drop this one in, and then we'll go."

Just then, Tommy noticed something in the distance sitting on the tracks through the fog of quickly falling snow.

"Look at that! What the heck is it?" Tommy asked.

Arthur turned his head and blinked rapidly through the white haze.

"Oh my God, it looks like a real castle," Arthur said.

"It looks like some kind of fancy train car."

"Let's go over and look at it."

They quickly shuffled through the snow toward the mysterious train car. As they approached, the two boys slowed to admire its fine craftsmanship and colorful paintings that adorned all four sides. The train car was painted bright yellow and red, surrounded by ornate gingerbread carvings framing its windows. One end of the car had black wrought-iron railings leading to a carved door shining with new varnish.

"Let's see if it's open," Tommy said, jumping up and over the railing, and jiggling the glass doorknob.

"It's locked!" he declared with disappointment.

Arthur stood at the side of the car admiring the colorfully painted advertisements. Across the top of the boxcar, the faded title "Buffalo Bill's Wild West and Congress of Rough Riders of the World" illustrated a pitched battle between a group of quick shooting cowboys and wild Indians.

"Hey, come over here, and give me ten fingers so I can look in the window," Arthur said.

Tommy jumped down off the back platform of the car, weaved his two hands together, and grabbed Arthur's right foot to lift him up. Arthur looked into the window with wide- eyed amazement. Inside the car, he saw cowboy hats, Indian head dressings, fancy riding saddles, and a pearl-handled pistol sitting in a decorative holster hanging from a wooden peg.

"Art, what do you see?'

"Real cowboy and Indian things. And Tommy, I can't believe it. There's a pearl-handled six-shooter in there!"

"You're fooling me. There's no such thing."

"See for yourself."

Arthur stepped down from Tommy's ten-finger assist.

"Give me a hand up so I can see," Tommy impatiently

demanded.

"I can't lift you up with my sore hand. I won't be able to hold you."

"Huh? This is the first I've heard of your sore hand. What are you talking about?" Tommy said.

He impatiently walked around to the other end of Buffalo Bill's train car to see if there was a way inside so he could see the tantalizing treasures for himself. He noticed right away that the back of the car was much different than the front. A large metal ramp folded up onto the back of the car, and behind it there was a large, unlocked door.

"Art, come here and look behind this iron ramp. This looks like a way we can get in."

Arthur walked over and peered behind the metal ramp as a strange but powerful feeling of impending doom came over him. He stepped back a couple of paces, sensing they might get into trouble for trespassing or something.

"I don't like it here. Why don't we take off?" Arthur said.

"Come on, will you? You have me out here all afternoon searching for boring pieces of coal, and now we discover something really neat and you want to go home? No way!"

Tommy inspected the ramp to discover its inner workings. It was hinged at the bottom and secured with heavy metal pins at the top. Arthur watched Tommy fiddle with the hinges of the ramp, feeling an odd sense of dread, but he also knew there was no stopping him.

"I've got a bad feeling about this. We shouldn't be here. I know it. Please, let's go!" Arthur warned again.

"Come on, you chicken," he replied, pulling a large metal pin from one side of the ramp, "I think that should do it. Help me pull the ramp down. Then we'll both take a real good look at that six-shooter."

Arthur's curiosity now had the better of him as he grabbed the side of the ramp. In unison, they pulled down on the ramp.

"It's not moving, Tommy."

"There must be another pin on the other side. Can you see it?"

Arthur looked and noticed an "L"- shaped pin protruding from the upper-right corner of the ramp.

"Yes, I see it," he replied.

He reached for the big pin slowly and then, hesitated. For only a split second, he thought he saw out of the corner of his eye – a flash of black cross the snowy sky.

"Hey, let's go! Pull it out so we can lower it down," Tommy commanded.

"Okay, here goes!" Arthur shouted as he mustered all his strength to pull the pin from its placement.

The heavy, black ramp crashed down out of the white sky. Like a sudden flash from Arthur's memory, the massive iron ramp swung down with such speed and force that it gave the boys no time to move. It slammed into the left side of Arthur's head with a violent force. His young skull caved inward, leaving it cracked and broken. Only a step behind him, Tommy felt the edge of the ramp swoosh past his nose, ripping the buttons off his coat, slicing through the leather belt around his waist, and violently pulling him onto the icy ground.

Arthur crashed down with such incredible force that he felt his body bounce up a foot or more into the air, but what happened next he thought was quite odd. Instead of falling back down to the ground along with his wounded body, he hovered in the air, watching his body fall back onto the snow-covered ground. Arthur floated above Tommy's motionless body, and was perplexed as to why his own was still lying on the ground below. As he watched his lifeless body in the blood-soaked snow, Arthur wondered strangely if he might be dead. Arthur noticed that his new floating form felt like it had substance, but when he looked down, he saw he had no feet. He held up his right hand in front of his face and was amused that his sore hand felt fine. It appeared to be filled with a flowing light that moved through his fingers guided by some unseen force. The thought that he may be dead was of no real concern to him, and he began to realize that he could move his new weightless figure in any direction just by thinking about it.

"Hey, Tommy, wake up! Come on, Tommy, this is really fun. See, I can fly!"

Arthur tried to communicate with his friend as he floated several feet above him.

He started to circle above the accident scene like a soaring eagle moving higher and higher. He swooshed downward, hesitated, and waited for Tommy to join him. He no longer felt the bitter cold. Almost warm, the fluffy snow swirled around his tingling body of light in a loving caress. Arthur became aware that a bright light in the distance was moving closer to him, and becoming larger. The apparition was a cylindrical shape that emanated pure beams of light that made his eyes feel comfortable as he gazed upon it. Arthur turned away from the light and instead was drawn back to Buffalo Bill's train car. He thought about what it might be like to be inside, admiring the pearl-handled six-shooter. Almost instantly, he found himself inside the train car looking at the intricate silver inlay on the gun's smooth white handle. He ran his hand of light over the leather carvings on the gun's holster. Awed by this quick travel propelled by mere thought, Arthur realized he could not only move among and around things like a soft wind, but through them as well. He could travel anywhere effortlessly just by thinking about a place he wanted to be. He thought, "What a blast! This is fun. Why won't Tommy join me?"

He began to think about what his older sister Alice might be doing and he instantly found himself standing behind her listening to her hum a simple child's lullaby as she washed the dishes. At 13, she was just three years older than Arthur. She was pretty with dark hair that fell over her small shoulders, and she had kind, brown eyes that contrasted with her white skin, but he always thought she looked too skinny. He moved toward Alice, wrapping his light-filled arms around her in an embrace of profound love. Arthur felt a bowl suddenly slip from Alice's hands that smashed into countless shavings of glass, filling the kitchen with shafts of brilliant green.

Immediately, he felt an odd shift like an open window slamming shut. He was instantly transported back to the train car. He found himself hovering over the accident scene again. He peered down on his own ice-cold body and watched Tommy struggle to his feet. The opening of light that Arthur saw earlier in the distance had now moved near the head of his earthly body, glowing with embers of tantalizing beauty. Arthur was transfixed by the swirling light that emanated from its center. Drawn to its tender gravitational pull, a profound sense of peace came over him, and he moved closer to the light. Arthur began to feel like one single drop in a limitless ocean; he was connected to every other drop by an all-encompassing force. He drifted closer and closer to the light. Two graceful angelic figures emerged from its center like shimmering butterflies. These beings had softly-colored auras that sparkled as they floated nearby, hovering with him at the light's outer edge. Arthur paused. What was at first a hazy understanding slowly came into focus. He began to recognize them, instinctively. The beings before him were his earthly mother and father in the full flower of their youth, complete and happy in every way. Their serene presence made Arthur feel safe, completely loved. They pointed toward the light and softly said together, "Arthur, it is time to go."

The persistent pull of the divine light felt so familiar that he nodded to his mother and father to take him home. Arthur turned back to look one last time at his physical body. His friend Tommy was gasping. In shock, he was standing over Arthur's lifeless body watching the snow run red. Tommy fell to his knees beside his body, and begged, "Please Art! Wake up! You can't die now. Not now! Wake up!" he cried hysterically as he shook

Arthur in vain trying to stir him. He wept in panic.

"What about Alice, Art? You can't leave Alice. She needs you! I need you."

Tears poured from Tommy's eyes, which were wide with horror. They fell into the snow, mixing with Arthur's crimson blood and melted the snow into pink puddles. Tommy realized that Arthur was not going to wake up, and he knew his friend was hurt very badly. He shook off his state of frozen panic, and knew he needed to act and fast. He leapt into action. Tommy started to run wildly to find help as he yelled out in agony at the plight of his friend. Not sure what else to do, he ran down the track through the heavy snow towards Arthur's house. He slipped and fell, sobbing and landing hard in the icy snow once, and then again. He cried and gasped. Tommy got up, and continued to run.

He felt like his legs were in slow motion as he yelled out into the darkness, "Please God, not Arthur!"

Chapter 2

Alice's Premonition

Alice stood at the kitchen sink wondering why Arthur was so late coming home from school. It was unlike him to be late. "This never happens," she thought. She leaned against the sink to steady herself when a sudden wave of anxiety strangely rose up within her. She trembled. A sharp bolt of fear shot down her arms, forcing the bowl she was washing to jump from her hands. For an instant, the glass bowl hung in the air defying gravity before it slammed down, shattering into pieces at the bottom of the gray soap-stone sink. Through the deafening silence that followed the crash she could feel the ticking of the kitchen clock pulse through her veins. It sounded like the slowest noise she had ever heard. In the pregnant moments that continued to hang like a death knoll between the tick-tock of the clock, somehow she sensed something was wrong. With an unimaginable dread, Alice took two steps back from the sink and stood paralyzed by a mounting sense of fear that seemed to come from nowhere. She couldn't push away or dismiss the uncomfortable premonition that her brother Arthur was in some lonely place, perhaps hurt somehow and in need of help. Something was wrong with Arthur. She knew it.

Alice threw open the door, raced down the three flights of stairs into the street and yelled "Arthur!" into the thick wall of snow. She wondered if she was crazy, but somehow she couldn't stop herself. She had no sense of where she was running to, or whether anyone could actually hear her desperate calls out to her brother. Nonetheless, she ran as fast as her thin young legs could carry her. She heard her own voice inside her head saying, "Go to the railroad tracks."

She ran past endless rows of three-decker tenements that lined the street leading to the railroad tracks. A feeling of impending doom cast a shadow over her as she ran with a growing sense of uncertainty. "What am I doing? Have I lost my mind?" she asked herself. She felt the sharp wind and the cold sting of wet snow hit her bare arms as she slowed down, and then began a fast walk to catch her breath. Through the descending darkness, Alice suddenly saw Arthur's friend, Tommy. He emerged from a veil of snow, running as if he had seen Lucifer himself. As Tommy came closer, Alice noticed that the front of Tommy's coat was torn and the belt on his trousers was cut through and hanging off to one side.

As he ran wild-eyed up the street, he would have passed right by her without even noticing her if she hadn't yelled out, "Tommy! Where's Arthur?"

The high-pitched sound of Alice's voice sliced through the fog of terror that surrounded him as he came to a sliding stop directly in front of her.

"Tommy, have you seen my brother, Arthur?" Alice frantically demanded.

In shock, he said nothing.

"Have you seen Arthur?" she shouted again.

Tommy partially awakened from his nightmare, rapidly started to nod his head affirmatively as he pointed down the street toward the railroad tracks.

"What's wrong?"

"Art's hurt bad, real bad!"

Alice trembled at the alarm in Tommy's voice, and she screamed, "Oh, my God! Where is he?"

"He's down on the tracks right before the tunnel, behind a red and yellow train car."

"How could you leave him there?" she asked.

"I had to run and get help. He's not moving."

"Run right now to the fire station to get help. Tell them where he is," she commanded.

Alice began to run with all her might toward the place Tommy had pointed. The street bordered a snow-covered field that led over to the railroad tracks. The driving wet snow penetrated her blue gingham dress as she ran, chilling her frail bones. The voice of her mother, telling her one cold, snowy night that she would rather go to bed hungry than cold, echoed through her mind as she neared the tracks.

It was dark on the track, and the swirling snow stung her eyes, and made it difficult to see. Alice's heart was racing with a pounding fear as she slowed down. She ran along the tracks looking for some sign of Arthur's whereabouts when she began to make out a red and yellow train car through the white haze. She made her way quickly toward the car. The cold, dark air hung over everything, the train yard felt like a place of death. Her young body started to tremble with dreadful anticipation. The howling wind was her only companion in the terrifying silence. The brightly painted walls of the train with the banner along the side proclaiming, "Buffalo Bill's Wild West and Congress of Rough Riders," caught her attention. She knew instantly that Arthur would have found this train car irresistible. Arthur loved stories of cowboys and Indians and was fascinated by anything having to do with the Wild West. She cautiously made her way along the side of the car, calling out Arthur's name into the muffled wind. Looking down, she noticed that the snow appeared to be undisturbed along the side of the car, and she wondered if Tommy was making up all of this. She decided to check around the back of the train car just to be sure, when she saw something dark protruding out of the undisturbed snow. She moved closer and recognized the object to be Arthur's brown shoe. She ran to his side and peered down on the snow-covered body of her ten-year-old brother. She fell to her knees and brushed the snow from his blue-tinted face, whispering softly to him, "Everything will be all right," as she held back a gasp.

She straightened the collar on his jacket and reached down, pulling his icy arm from the snow to make sure that his wool mittens were on his hands when she noticed that his hands were ice cold. She grabbed the collar of his jacket pulling him upward, saying sweetly, "Come on, Arthur. Get up. It's time to go home."

Frightfully cold and limp, Arthur lay cradled in Alice's arms. She rocked back and forth softly, whispering a familiar song that she often sang to her cherished play dolls that lined her bedroom walls. Her eyes filled with tears. Alice thought back to the first time that she had held her little brother in her arms.

Many years back, their mother Mary had been deathly sick, and they were waiting for the doctor to arrive. Alice had been told by her mother that she was much too young to hold Arthur, yet he was crying in his crib while their mother lay still in her bed. Alice couldn't remember exactly how she did it, but she managed to climb up onto his crib. She carefully picked him up, and carried him down to the floor. Meanwhile, the downstairs neighbors discovered their mother nearly dead in her bed. They spotted young Alice sitting at the foot of the bed gently rocking baby Arthur in her arms to the lullaby she softly sang to him now. Their mother never fully recovered that day. And her young brother had become Alice's responsibility. She doted over him endlessly and worried about him collecting coal along the tracks since she knew he could get hit by a train. Alice was afraid of the roaming hobos she had heard lived in boxcars, scoundrels who traveled around the country robbing and drinking whiskey. She feared they might jump poor Arthur. It just seemed such a dangerous place for a ten year old boy. Nonetheless, Arthur insisted he collect coal daily for the struggling family. He had managed to scrounge enough to store a large pile in the back hall for use during the winter months. Alice's cold bare hand held Arthur's left shoulder as she felt something warm and wet covering her fingers. She turned her brother's head slightly, and saw a large gash that was streaming blood from the side of his head. She panicked, praying this was just a nightmare. Bolts of raw fear pierced her heart. The frigid reality of what was happening began to crash down upon her. She lowered her head so that her cheek touched his to be startled by his icy skin. Alice began to shake and cry. Her soft tears and tender embrace slowly turned into violent sobs of grief as she realized that her younger brother lay mortally injured in her arms. Finding it impossible to withstand the unfathomable depth of her loss, towering waves of grief crashed down upon her. She cried out, "No, God, please, please send him back to me. I need him so much. I never told you how much I need him. Please, God, don't let Arthur die."

Alice brushed away the remaining snow from Arthur's jacket, and noticed a large piece of shiny black coal sticking out from his coal bag that was half buried in the white snow. In the numbing cold, she gently rocked her young brother to the soft sounds of her tender love. She did not think about how all this might have happened, but only about how loyal Arthur had been to her. The image of her brother walking along the icy tracks in search for coal made her realize how much her brother loved her. Her grief began to chill and immobilize her. She couldn't move. Alice was frozen to Arthur's body with the horrible realization of what had come to pass. An avalanche of emotions made her soul quake. Her young voice cried out mournfully with the heavy grief that boiled up within her to fill the sky with a primal cry of utter loss. Alice looked up into the dreadful night and from the seat of her soul, she pleaded to God, to Jesus, and to all her angels to return her brother to her. "When would help come? Where was Tommy?" her thoughts screamed. She begged God for one more chance to show Arthur how much she loved him.

Meanwhile, unaware of the tragedy below, Arthur floated peacefully toward the light that continued to fill him with an expanding sense of love. His mother and father stayed by his side guiding him into the light. Arthur felt that there was no difference now between his light-filled presence and the wondrous, expanding light that beckoned him onward. A profound feeling of calm relief washed up over him as he realized that his earthly life had ended, and that he was now returning home to a place of tranquility. With no anxiety or even concern about what had just happened to him on the tracks, Arthur felt an ever-increasing sense of knowing that gently encouraged him to keep moving further and further into the light. The light swirled and spun magically in a marvelous dance of white energy that reached out for him in waves. The light moved through his body with a loving caress as he became aware that a community of love beckoned him home. The light was both his source and his destination. A river of creation that flowed through humanity completing the circle of life beckoned him. Arthur was becoming part of that circle. He was beginning the journey home.

His mother and father's loving presence followed him into the light as Arthur began to sense a change. A vibration deep within the core of the light began to herald a message that Arthur instinctively understood was meant for him alone. He felt the message instantly move from the core of the light that connected him to an infinite source of knowing. His progress forward into the light stopped momentarily as he looked back to the place where his earthly body lay motionless in the snow.

His sister Alice was bent over his cold, lifeless body pleading to God that she be granted one more chance to show Arthur how very much she loved him. Arthur thought this seemed odd since he clearly knew how much she loved him, and he found it difficult to understand the intense feelings of grief conveyed by his sister. "I have never been so happy. I am finally going home. Why is she so sad?" he thought.

The loving light that swirled around him seemed to be asking for an answer to a question. Arthur looked to the angelic figures of his parents for help in understanding what the light might be asking for. They moved toward him to convey to him the nature of the question from the light. They let him know that he was being asked by the light to make a decision. He could continue on into the light to return to his true home, or he could go back to his earthly life in answer to his sister's prayer. The decision was his alone. The light would not interfere.

Arthur looked back at the lifeless body that was once his own, and he saw his sister Alice bent over, gasping with suffocating grief. He thought about how very sad she seemed kneeling by his side, and felt touched by her tender care. Arthur watched as she brushed the snow from his face and straightened his clothes like she would before he went to school each morning. Her sisterly love felt like rays of sunlight holding him in a soft embrace. He watched as his sister's petite body heaved with grief. He felt the depth of her pain and wished he could help her.

Arthur felt a rumble coming from the center of the light like a giant rogue wave hitting an unsuspecting ship floundering at sea. The wave crashed through the emotional fabric of his soul, transporting him back onto the turbulent sea of his sister's grief. He tried to navigate the depths of her sadness, but was overwhelmed by its enormity. Pushed by the winds of loss, Alice seemed to drift away to a place of no return. The loss of both her parents, and now her beloved brother, was too much for her young heart to bear. She lay on the dark, snow-covered tracks holding tightly onto Arthur's dead body screaming and crying out into the dreadful night for help.

While Arthur floated near the outer edge of the light, he watched his sister drown in grief. He turned to face the light. With a single powerful intent, he communicated to the light, "I want to go back to help my sister."

Within the immeasurable split of an instant, he was abruptly transported back into the trap of his ice-cold body. Arthur was shocked by the heaviness of his body as bolts of electrifying pain surged through his bones. The light, warm loving feeling vanished. He felt irreversibly imprisoned within his shattered and broken body.

With Arthur cradled in her arms, Alice rocked rhythmically back and forth to a soulful prayer-song for her brother's return. She refused to believe he was gone. Her loss and the depth of her sadness were unbearable. She tried to shelter Arthur from the blowing snow with her small body. Numb from the cold, she couldn't even feel her arms under her frozen dress.

A suffocating need to breathe began to build inside Arthur's body. He gasped violently to fill his lungs with life. Alice clung desperately to him as she started to feel a monumental change beginning occur. She was overcome with a tingling sensation of relief when she realized that her prayers had been answered. Almost imperceptibly at first, she began to feel Arthur's lifeless body move in her arms. His lips parted to make a swooshing sound as air poured into his lungs. Alice's entire body trembled with relief and gratitude as she realized Arthur was still alive. As quickly as she felt the wave of relief rise, it came crashing down again into despair as she thought about her brother's grave condition.

"Why aren't they here yet?" she thought with panic.

If help didn't come quickly, she knew she would lose him for good.

Chapter 3

The Rescue

Tommy barged through the fire station doors as if he was knocking down a lineman on his way to a touchdown. He had run as fast as he could through the snow and ice just as Alice had commanded. Now, he stood in an empty fire engine bay, bent over in exhaustion trying to catch his breath. Tommy surveyed the first floor of the fire station. Seeing nobody there, he cuffed his hands around his mouth, and yelled into the quiet building, "Hey there, anybody home?"

Tommy heard the echo of his own voice bounce off the old wooden beams that braced up the Columbia Road Firehouse. A sickening feeling began to rise up from the pit of his stomach as he yelled, "Is anybody home? Please, there must be someone here."

Just then Tommy heard staggered footsteps coming from just above him on the second floor, and he yelled out again, "Hey up there, please help. Someone is hurt real bad!"

"Who's hurt?" someone responded through an opening in the ceiling surrounding the house fire pole.

"Art Chambers. He's hurt real bad. He needs help!"

"Well, there iz no one here that can help eh him. Everyone iz out zat fire cross town," the anonymous voice slurred through the ceiling hole.

"Please, Mister! If you don't help, he's a goner."

"Go-zz away kid eh there's no help here," the drunken voice from above mumbled.

In a panic, Tommy yelled back up through the hole, "My father knows Chief Kennedy, and if you don't help me, he'll tell the Chief that you're drunk, and if anything happens to Art, you'll be in big trouble, mister!"

With that, one shaky leg appeared through the hole in the ceiling, and then another, as the inebriated fireman fell down the pole, landing in a heap right in front of Tommy.

Looking up from the deck of the fire station bay, Fireman Murphy extended a hand up to Tommy saying, "I iz at your ser-service and we'll ke-keep the little drinking ting to ourselves. Er uh got that eh?

"Okay, but let's get going now!" Tommy demanded.

"Where-ere iz the uh, zee uh injured partee?" Murphy slurred.

"Down on the tracks behind the Sears warehouse," Tommy said swinging open the door to the fire station ladder truck, and climbing up inside.

"I ca-can't drive zat truck kid. We have to take zis one," Murphy said, pointing to an old firehouse pick-up truck.

"You're a fireman that can't drive a fire truck?"

"I uh fix fire-eh alarm pu- pull stations, and this er is my tr-truck."

"Does that small truck even have a siren?"

Noting Tommy's disappointment, Murphy said, "Well, er, would you pro-fer to wa-wait for some eh body else?"

"No, let's go, mister, now!" Tommy pleaded.

Murphy crawled behind the wheel of the truck, and fumbled for the keys before finally starting the engine with a loud rumble. Tommy was seated beside him, and anxiously stared through the windshield waiting for the truck to move.

"Come on will you? We don't have all night!"

"Hold-da your hersess- horses youn- young man, eh we'll git there in due-eh time."

"There is no time! My friend is dying on the tracks. Now move it."

With that order, Murphy forced the clutch into gear with a grinding screech, and the truck lurched out of the fire station and slid onto the snow-covered street. Within a few seconds of

Murphy's erratic driving, Tommy was certain they would not make it to the railroad tracks in one piece. He was dead drunk. The slippery, snow-covered roads and Murphy's inebriated state made it nearly impossible for him to keep the truck between the curbstones. Swerving from one side of the road to the other, Tommy was certain they were going to crash at every turn of the wheel. Murphy unintelligibly mumbled something as his drink-filled head pulled his chin down onto his chest.

Tommy yelled, "Look out for the- -"

Murphy was startled awake, and jerked the wheel to left, but it was too late. The truck careened wildly off the street, crashing into a deep snow bank. Tommy sat silently stunned, but he wasn't hurt. He tried to coerce Arthur's rescuer from his drunken stupor by pulling his heavy head up off the steering wheel – to no avail.

"Come on, stupid, wake up! We have to get out of here," he pleaded in horror.

Murphy momentarily lifted his head up off the steering wheel, looked at Tommy, and said, "So-rry, am drunk-ka as uh billy goat!"

The fireman's head fell back onto the steering wheel; he passed out from the day's heavy drinking.

Tommy was in a complete panic. "How can I get back to Arthur and Alice now?" he mumbled in confusion.

He stared into the bright glare from headlights reflecting off the snow, shocked by the realization that he had failed Alice, and let down his best friend when he was most needed. As his face fell into his hands, he began to think about Art alone on the tracks. He imagined Alice finding him there when he heard a soft tapping on the truck window.

Charlie Chambers felt grateful that he had worn his good boots as he walked home from work through the heavy snow. The collar of his thin blue jacket was pushed up around his neck in a feeble attempt to ward off the sting of the blowing snow. He couldn't remember the last time he felt this chilled or hungry as he measured the weight of the chicken wrapped in newspaper he carried under one arm. He was pleased with himself that he had managed to talk the local butcher into selling it to him for only twenty cents. The chicken had been around the shop for a few days, but hadn't yet gone bad. He looked forward to a steaming, hot roast with his family on this bitter night. Charlie had been somewhat surprised when he learned from the butcher that Alice hadn't even stopped by the shop earlier in the day after school. The butcher always looked out for them and had called Charlie in off the street about the unsold chicken. He rounded the corner onto Bay Street, and he noticed up ahead the flashing red lights of a fire truck. As he got closer, he realized that the truck had slid off the road and was stuck in a snow bank. Charlie walked quickly toward the truck, wondering if someone was still inside. He tapped on the passenger side window, and noticed that the driver was slumped over the wheel.

"Hello, is everyone all right in there?"

Charlie peered through the frosted glass. The passenger side window slowly rolled down, and he heard, "Yup, I'm alright, but he's as drunk as a billy goat."

Charlie recognized the familiar voice coming from the truck. "Tommy Laucka, is that you?"

"Yeah, the last time I checked it was," he wisecracked.

Tommy stuck his head through the open window to see a familiar figure outlined in the snow.

"Charlie is that you? Is that really you?"

"Yes it's me! What are you doing here?"

Tommy frantically started to crawl out the truck window, and lurched forward to grab   Charlie's coat, yelling, "Art's hurt! He needs help."

Surprised by Tommy's hysterical plea, Charlie took a step back, and pulled Tommy through the truck window with both arms onto the snow-covered street. Tommy tumbled onto the ground, and struggled to his feet, shaking from the cold and fear.

"Just calm down, and tell me what is going on," Charlie said.

"Art is hurt bad, real bad."

"What do you mean Arthur's hurt real bad?" Charlie angrily demanded, shaking Tommy to force out an explanation, "You tell me what's going on here, Laucka. Or I swear to God, I'll punch you so hard – your mother will cry."

Overwhelmed by his fear and scattered thoughts, Tommy began to nervously cry out, "Art is on the tracks behind the Sears warehouse. Alice went to find him."

"What's wrong with him?"

"He fell and hurt his head real bad."

"Where on the track is he?" Charlie demanded as he realized Tommy was in shock.

"Before the tunnel, by the red and yellow train car," Tommy answered.

"What's wrong with that guy?" Charlie asked, pointing to the man slumped over the steering wheel of the truck.

"Oh, that's Murphy the Fireman. He's drunk."

"Some fireman!" Charlie shouted as he walked over to Murphy trying to revive him.

"Hey, come on, buddy. Wake up!" Charlie commanded as he lifted Murphy's head off the steering wheel and then let it fall back down, which made the horn go off loudly. The sharp honk startled Tommy who was shuffling his feet on the ground as he tried to gather his jumbled thoughts.

"Charlie, he can't drive. He's too drunk. We need to get Art. We're wasting time."

In agreement, Charlie reached into the cab of the truck and grabbed the collar of Murphy's jacket, and pulled him out and onto the street.

"Tommy, get over here, and help me swing him into the back of the truck. Grab his legs and on the count of three, we'll lift him into the back," Charlie instructed.

Tommy secured his grip as Charlie rhythmically sounded out "One, two, three, and up!"

Murphy's drunken heap swung up through the air and landed in the back of the truck with a muffled thump. Charlie jumped into the driver's seat of the fire truck and turned the ignition key, and to his dismay heard the engine cough to a stall.

"Damn it! Come on, start," Charlie yelled as the haunting image of his helpless brother and sister stalked him. He turned the ignition key again to no avail while Tommy stepped up onto the running board, and announced, "It won't start because it's still in gear."

"Oh, gotcha!" Charlie put the truck's gears into neutral and started it with a roar, then slammed it into reverse as it labored back onto Bay Street.

Tommy balanced on the running board and clung to the side of the truck as it slid to a stop in the snow. He yelled at Charlie, "Wait! Not so fast, I'm coming with you."

"No, you're not. It's too dangerous, and you've done enough. Now, jump off!"

"No way, I'm coming with you," Tommy shouted back.

"Have it your way, but hang on tight," Charlie said.

He accelerated down the street, hastily putting the truck through its gears, forcing Tommy to hold firmly onto the truck's side to keep his balance. Charlie was having trouble navigating the snow-covered street as the truck fished-tailed, forcing him to slow down.

"Faster, Charlie, faster!"

Tommy's feet were firmly placed on the running board of the truck, and his hands gripped tightly to its side. He yelled, "Arthur is hurt bad. We need to get there now!"

Charlie quickly looked out the open window of the truck at Tommy, nodded and said,

"Hold on!"

With the gas pedal held firmly to the floor, the truck shot

forward through the snow toward the railroad tracks with Fireman Murphy sliding around in the back.

Charlie slowed down as he drove the truck around the bend of the track. The snow ahead covered everything with a smooth white surface that reflected the headlights. Charlie thought about how his young brother would wake up early after a snowstorm to be the first to walk in newly fallen snow. His random thoughts quickly gave way to the present reality. Art and Alice were alone. There was no telling how bad the situation was. The snow in front of the rescue truck lay undisturbed just as Arthur would have liked it, but it suddenly made Charlie wonder if anyone had actually been down this way after all. He comforted himself by thinking how Art's friend tended to exaggerate.

"Tommy, are you sure that Alice came down here this way?" Charlie yelled through the window.

"This is where I told her to go," he answered.

"And you're sure this is where you saw Arthur?"

"Yes, straight ahead by the tunnel."

The truck's headlights reflected off the swirling snow making it difficult to see in the dark. Charlie peered carefully through the snow-covered windshield. He thought he saw something up ahead as the truck rocked grudgingly forward along the uneven railroad ties.

"Hey Tommy, is that where they are up ahead?"

"Yeah, that's it."

Tommy heard the sound of his own voice drop off as he was jolted by the sight of the red and yellow car again.

"Well, I can't see anyone," Charlie complained.

"Art was at the back of that train."

Tommy tried to look forward into the snow. Just then, Charlie thought he saw something move at the back left corner of the train car.

"Tommy, is that them? At the back?"

"Alice!" Tommy yelled as he jumped off the truck, slipped in the snow, and ran toward her.

Covering her eyes with one arm, Alice looked up into the bright truck lights to see Tommy charging toward her. The truck came to an abrupt stop. Charlie jumped out and ran to his sister's side. Alice was shivering and half frozen, clinging to her gravely injured brother as she still prayed out loud to God. She stopped abruptly when she saw her oldest brother emerge out of the light and snow.

"Alice, are you all right? What happened?" Charlie asked as his eyes moved down upon Arthur who lay in his sister's arms with a frightening gash running down the side of his head.

"Oh my God, Alice, we have to get him to the hospital," Charlie stammered as he reached down to touch his brother. The icy feel of Arthur's skin shocked Charlie. He ran the back of his bare hand down across Arthur's face, and felt the cold sensation of possible death. Charlie was frightened now beyond anything he had ever known. His sister appeared to be nearly comatose from the cold as she continued to pray like someone possessed with tears streaming down her face. Arthur lay so close to death that they could sense its awful presence. Charlie knew there was no time to waste. He bent down, gently picked up his brother in his arms to carry him to the truck, and slowly placed him onto the front seat.

"Alice, get in the front with him, and place his head on your lap. Use this rag to press against the wound to keep more blood from spilling out. Press hard. I'll be driving fast so try to keep his head from moving around. Keep him as still as you can. Hold tight. We need to be strong."

Charlie jumped behind the wheel of the truck. Tommy stood off to the side with his arms hanging down, his shoulders bowed, and his head bent toward the snow-covered ground.

"Hey, Tommy! Thanks for everything. We'll let you know what happens," Charlie shouted out the window as he started the truck.

"Okay, Charlie. Make them help Art," Tommy yelled back over the roar of the engine as he wiped tears away, beginning to sob as they started to pull off. Something didn't feel quite right to Charlie as he put the truck into gear. It seemed disloyal to leave young Tommy behind after all he had done to help his brother.

"Do you want to come with us to the hospital? I think we might need your help," Charlie asked Tommy through the truck window.

Tommy wiped his eyes, and noticed Arthur's coal bag. He picked it up out of the snow and ran to the truck.

"Why don't you jump in the back and keep an eye on that Murphy? Don't let him cause any trouble and hold on," Charlie commanded as he started to drive the truck along the railroad tracks and onto the dark street toward Boston City Hospital.

Cradled in Alice's arms, Arthur laid across the front seat of the truck. His badly injured head rested upon the lap of her dress. Warm air flowed from the truck's heater that brought comfort to Alice's frozen feet and legs, but the warmth may have started to make Arthur's head bleed faster. The blood oozed from his wound at an alarming rate, spreading all the sticky warmth all over Alice's dress. The sickening smell filled her with a mounting sense of terror. Arthur was dying. There was nothing she could do to stop it.

"Alice, where is his hat?" Charlie asked.

"I don't know. Who cares about his hat now? He was like this when I found him. Charlie, drive faster. We have to get to the hospital now. Arthur is bleeding more and more. I'm scared he's not going to make it. "

Alice thought she felt Arthur move slightly in her arms. Feeling him stir even just slightly reassured her. She clutched him a bit more and softly whispered, "Arthur, it's all right, we'll be at the hospital soon. Everything is going to be okay, Arthur, I promise."

She looked into his round face and was sure she saw his eyelashes quiver. With disbelief, she watched as his lips parted slightly in what seemed to be a gentle smile.

"Charlie, I think he's trying to say something," Alice said as she lowered her ear to his lips.

"I can fly! I can fly! It's so beautiful!" he mumbled.

"Is he talking?" Charlie asked.

Alice listened closely and said, "I think he is, but it doesn't make any sense."

"What's he saying?"

"I'm not sure, but I think he said it's beautiful and he can fly," she said.

"He said he could fly? What could he mean by that?"

"I don't know, Charlie. His head is starting to really bleed now. We have to stop talking and get to the hospital fast."

Dark thoughts of the very last time she had held Arthur in her arms like this flashed before her. It was only last year that Arthur laid across her lap as he wept silently to the slow, depressing sound of the funeral horse and cart as it pulled away from the old cemetery. Their father had been gone for several years and now their mother was dead. They were all alone. Her thoughts had pressed against a future so bleak that her young mind could not even bear to imagine it. Instead, she had softly whispered to Arthur not to worry. She had promised him everything would turn out to be fine, but she had overheard the talk about what might have to happen. She hadn't understood all the words that were being said back then, but through the whispers she came to know that children without parents couldn't stay together, and had become vaguely aware of something called the Depression that made families unwilling to take on extra children. So she was greatly relieved when Charlie, at only 18 years of age won legal custody of the family. Sympathetic families and friends in the neighborhood would leave food and hand-me-down clothes quietly on their back porch stairs. Alice never knew who had left these things for them, but she was glad for their kindness. As Arthur lay gravely injured in her lap now, Alice could feel their lives coming apart all over again.

Arthur drifted in and out of consciousness. His body was heavy with the painful sensation of life. It seemed to Arthur as if his whole body had fallen asleep. He wasn't able to move his limbs. His body tingled with a numb, prickly sensation. He wasn't sure where he was, but he knew that the light-filled sense of peace he enjoyed earlier was gone, and his world was now dark and painful. He kept thinking that he could see Alice, but he didn't understand what she might be doing here with him. He was becoming confused and frightened, and wanted to go back to the other place filled with light. He thought of trying to bounce out of his body the way he did at the train car, but couldn't. He felt stuck in the pain-ridden tomb of his dying body, with no way to escape. He concentrated hard on trying to bounce up and out of his body, hoping to fly high among the white puffy clouds. Again, nothing happened. His eyes opened briefly, and he could see a blurry vision of Alice's face. Suddenly and without warning, he sensed a movement of energy within him like the deep tumbling sensation of a great waterfall that instantly popped him out of his body.

Arthur was hovering just above Charlie and Alice in the front cab of the truck. Arthur worried that he was blocking his older brother's line of sight, but he seemed to see right past him as he continued to drive. Confused by his new predicament, Arthur tried in vain to speak with them.

"Hey you guys, it's me!"

He watched as Charlie and Alice just stared straight through him with intense, fearful faces. Arthur looked down at his earthly body, lying motionless in his sister's lap. He noticed a new look of horror on his sister's face as she realized that he was no longer breathing. He heard her say, "Charlie, he's not

27

breathing! He's not breathing anymore. Hurry, please!"

Panicked by his sister's screams, Charlie pushed harder on the gas pedal and raced through Edward Everett Square. He swung wildly onto Massachusetts Avenue toward Boston City Hospital. Arthur saw them becoming hysterical and tried to calm them down.

"Hey, I'm alright! I'm right here. Can't you see me?" he said, floating just above their heads near the ceiling of the truck.

Then Arthur began to feel something very strange. It felt like the same sensation of rushing energy that had pushed him out of his physical body was now mysteriously making him shrink. Arthur was becoming smaller and smaller. The sucking force reduced his presence to the size of a tiny field mouse. He had gone from filling the entire ceiling of the truck's cab to being perched way up high, on one side of the rearview mirror. He looked down upon his grieving sister and his terrified brother as they frantically tried to get him to the hospital to save his earthly life. Arthur strangely understood that he had to return to the cold darkness of his body below to fight for his life. "I can't stay out here. I have to go back," Arthur thought. No sooner had this notion crossed his mind than he felt himself, once more, being painfully sucked back into his physical body below.

Chapter 4

The Emergency Room

Charlie barreled into the parking area reserved for ambulances when he saw the yellow incandescent light illuminating the large red block letters pointing the way to the "Boston City Hospital Emergency Room." He was greatly relieved that he had actually gotten there, but he wasn't sure he had made it in time. Arthur lay next to him in the front seat of the truck looking ghostly pale and motionless. He didn't appear to be breathing and the skin on his face under the streetlight seemed a ghastly shade of pale gray.

Charlie jumped out of the truck and told Alice, "Stay with Arthur. I'm going for help."

"Okay, but please hurry! I'm so scared."

Charlie remerged seconds later with a young emergency room physician and two attendants carrying a stretcher. The doctor reached into the truck and felt Arthur's wrist to check his pulse and quickly inspected the injury on Arthur's head. Alice saw the look of concern pass over the physician's face as he yelled to his assistants, "Quickly, take him straight to X-ray and start preparing him for surgery. I'll clear the operating room. Bring him to 'Bay Four' after the X-rays. I'll meet you there."

The doctor turned to Charlie and Alice and said, "My name is Dr. Frances Ingram and I'm the attending physician for the emergency room this evening. The injuries to the young boy appear most serious. I assure you, we'll do everything we can for him."

"Thank you, doctor," Charlie replied.

"What is the relationship between both of you and the boy?" the doctor inquired.

"His name is Arthur Chambers. I'm his brother, Charlie, and this is his sister, Alice."

"Where are his parents?" Dr. Ingram asked.

"He doesn't have any," Charlie replied.

"He doesn't have any?"

"No."

"How is that?"

"Dead. They're both dead. Now, all this won't mean much if Arthur dies too. Will it, doctor?" Charlie said impatiently.

"Who's that over there in the back of the truck? Is he injured too?"

"No, he's just drunk," Charlie answered.

"Well, this is all mighty odd, but I don't have time for this now. We'll continue discussing this after I attend to your brother. You can both wait inside," Dr. Ingram said as he swiftly walked through the emergency room doors back into the hospital.

"Boy, that really steams me up. No one ever believes that I'm the head of the family,"

Charlie complained, shutting the truck door, "Let's go inside and get out of the snow." Tommy jumped out of the back of the truck, still holding onto Arthur's coal bag, and the three of them headed toward the hospital entrance to await the fate of young Arthur. As they walked away, a voice from the back of the truck rang out, "Hey, what's this all about? What am I doing back here?" Fireman Murphy staggered to lift himself up before falling back down again.

Charlie reached into his pocket to pull out the keys to the truck. He tossed them in Murphy's direction in the back of the truck and Charlie said sarcastically, "Thanks for the rescue, Mr. Fireman. You saved the day."

Arthur's head was wrapped in a thick white bandage. He passed in and out of consciousness as he was wheeled back in from the X-ray room. They put him in Bay Four of the emergency room as the doctor had ordered, right next to an elderly man named Joe Robinson who had just suffered a minor heart attack. Joe watched as the nurse rolled Arthur into the area next to him.

Joe said to the attending nurse, "It's one thing for an old coot like me to be in here, but it's quite another for a young boy. That poor, young kid."

"The boy has a very serious head trauma," the nurse replied.

"Hey, kid, what's your name?" Joe asked.

"Art," he weakly mumbled.

"What did he say?" Joe asked the nurse.

"He said his name is Art, Arthur A. Chambers to be exact," the nurse replied, looking at his medical chart at the end of the bed.

"Arthur A. Chambers, now that's a proper name if I ever heard one. I'm glad to meet you, Mr. Arthur A. Chambers. My name is Joe Robinson."

Too weak to respond, he tried to lift his hand slightly in polite acknowledgement.

"Well, Art, I'll let you rest. I'm sure glad you're here now since it's been pretty boring with no one else to talk to. My wife is out in the waiting room, but they won't let her back in here to see me," he complained.

"I can fly," Arthur said in a faint voice that was barely audible.

"What did he say?" Joe asked the nurse.

"Hmm... he said he could fly. That's all he's been saying since he woke up. He's most likely a little confused because of his head injury," the nurse commented.

"Fly? Well that's something! Maybe you could teach me how to do that too, Arthur A. Chambers, and we could both fly out of here together," Joe laughed loudly.

"Now that's enough of that, Mr. Robinson. Both of you need to relax and rest," the nurse cautioned.

Joe placed his head back and closed his eyes.

"It would be good to sleep. It's been a long day," Joe thought as his head sunk into the starched hospital pillow.

Charlie, Alice, and Tommy sat anxiously in the waiting room, hoping to hear from Dr. Ingram, but time just seemed to drag on. Alice fidgeted nervously in her chair as she watched an old woman who was sitting across from her pray under her breath. Her delicate, wrinkled hands moved rhythmically through a strand of rosary beads. Every few minutes she would pause momentarily to raise her eyes to search for her husband's doctor. She sat all alone with empty chairs on both sides of her. Her white hair was neatly pulled back into an expertly-woven bun. She sat perfectly straight against the metal chair despite her age. She was wearing a finely embroidered dress and her shiny black shoes were placed neatly together with the toes pointed outward toward the center of the room. Alice found her calm, dignified demeanor somehow comforting. She imagined, "Wouldn't it be grand to have a mother who is so elegant?" Alice's thoughts drifted back to the time when her mother was still alive. Her mother would never have allowed anything bad to happen to Arthur. Alice blamed herself for letting Arthur pick up coal on those dangerous train tracks. He had insisted on helping out that way, but she always knew nothing good would come from it. Alice looked up at Charlie's tired face, his wet, dark hair made him appear even older. She took his large hand in her own, and she said gently, "I'm so sorry. This is all my fault! I let him go down on those tracks. I should have never allowed him to go there."

"No, Alice, this is not your fault. We all let Arthur collect coal on those tracks because it was what he wanted to do. Gathering coal helped him to find a way to live with all that has happened. It helped him to believe in himself. It gave him purpose. What happened today was just an accident, plain and simple. It's no one's fault."

Charlie started to say something else, but stopped.

"What is it, Charlie? What were you going to say?" Alice

asked.

"It's nothing. It can wait until later."

"No, tell me Charlie. Is it about Arthur? Do you know something about Arthur that you're not telling?" Alice asked.

"No, it's nothing about Arthur. It's just not the time to bring it up that's all. I shouldn't have said anything."

"Charlie, you're scaring me. I want you to tell me," Alice cried.

Charlie looked down, rapidly tapping his shoe on the waiting room floor. He took a deep breath. His hand moved down across his face, casting a quick shadow. He paused.

"I had a talk with the landlord. We have to move again."

"No, we can't move. We just got there. I won't do it. You just tell him we can't."

"He says he has a family that wants the place who can pay three dollars more a month."

"Well, you'll just have to pay what he's asking. This isn't fair, Charlie."

"Alice, you know we can't even afford the place now. We can't pay three more dollars," Charlie replied.

The worst thing about moving was that they tried to hide it from Arthur until the last possible moment. Ever since their mother had died, Arthur had become quiet and withdrawn with all the changes. They would put off telling him as long as possible. Alice thought about how Arthur hated to go with her to the moving picture show. She didn't want to have to take him back there again. She hated pretending that nothing was happening. It felt like lying to her, and she knew that she couldn't fool Arthur again anyway. He had told her once that he hated going to the picture show because he knew what it meant. Whenever Alice announced that they were going to the Saturday afternoon matinee at the Strand Theater in Upham's Corner, Arthur knew they were being forced to move again. They'd walk in uncomfortable silence until they reached the swinging doors with the swirling frosted glass. Each time, Arthur would buy the smallest box of popcorn with hot melted butter for both of them to share. He would say nothing. They would walk under the twinkling chandelier in the grand hallway and under the archway and down to the rows of cushy, high-backed seats that lined the theater. Alice relished the excited chatter and laughter before the theater lights dimmed, and Arthur liked the darkness. It made him feel like he was invisible. He would sink back into the deep leather seats hiding from a past he could not bear to remember and avoiding a bleak future he could not dare to imagine. He dreaded the moment the show would stop, the light would go on, and they would have to leave.

It was like a re-occurring nightmare. Arthur loathed the silent walk home from the Strand more then anything else in his small world. He never doubted that the fateful corner would soon appear. What really bothered him was that he never knew exactly where it would be. It could happen at any place during the walk back home. Arthur would turn left, or right, or walk straight ahead, and suddenly Alice would grab his arm and pull him back, saying, "Not that way, Arthur. We live this way now."

Arthur would stumble along beside his older sister until they came to the new place. It would always be smaller and dingier then their last. Arthur never liked the smells in any of the new apartments. Each place reeked of the people that used to live there, and he couldn't seem to wash the odor off no matter how much soap he used. Yet always, Arthur wanted to know just one thing about each new place. Did it have a coal stove?

Arthur lay motionless in the bright light of the hospital emergency room as he passed uncomfortably in and out of consciousness. He battled to banish the terrifying blackness. The dark, rectangular object from his dreams seemed to be falling out of the sky again, and it was crashing down toward him with an inescapable and suffocating doom. The approaching blackness was about to overtake him when he was suddenly awakened from his dream by the unsettling sound of mad chaos. Nurses were noisily moving past him; doctors were shouting instructions. Through Arthur's haze, he began to realize that they were trying to save Mr. Robinson.

"Doctor! He has no pulse," the attending nurse told Dr. Ingram.

Arthur turned to look at Joe Robinson – he was astounded by what he saw. While the doctor worked feverishly to revive Joe, he sat straight up in the bed, looked over at Arthur, and calmly smiled. They continued trying to resuscitate him as Joe gently slid off his bed and floated over to the side of Arthur's bed. It seemed as though Dr. Ingram and the nurse weren't able to see Joe doing this, but for some strange reason, Arthur could. Joe rose up toward the ceiling and floated back down again, and said to young Arthur, "Arthur A. Chambers, I see what you mean. I can fly too!"

Joe slowly floated around the hospital room and watched as the doctor tried to save his life. Arthur gazed in wonder as Joe floated downward and stood right at the end of Arthur's bed.

"It's no use, you know. They can't save me. I'm not coming back. It's my time," Joe said peacefully as he floated and hovered nearby.

"For you, it's different. It's not your time yet," he informed Arthur.

Arthur was unable to speak, dumbfounded by what he was witnessing. Joe seemed to be in a meditative state as if he was listening to a song that no one else could hear. Joe smiled and opened his eyes. Arthur knew Joe had something important to say.

He looked intently at Arthur as if he was trying to emphasize the importance of his coming words, and he said smiling, "There is nothing to worry about!"

Arthur expected a more profound message, and he remained silent and confused.

"There is nothing to worry about. I spent my entire life worrying about everything. And there is absolutely nothing to worry about," Joe repeated again.

Joe began drifting up toward the ceiling as it suddenly changed into a bright swirling array of colors. A portal of white light began to grow from its center. As Joe started to merge with the light, he paused momentarily. He said to Arthur, "Learn not to worry, Arthur. We did not come here to worry."

Dr. Ingram walked down the hospital corridor toward the waiting room and hesitated halfway down the hall. "I'll never get used to this part of the job," he muttered under his breath, turning the corner into the room. Alice was the first to notice him, and she straightened up against her chair and poked Charlie. The old woman was still clutching her rosary beads, and she visibly trembled as she stood up to greet the doctor. Her beads dropped to the floor.

"Mrs. Robinson, we did everything we could to save your husband, Joe, but his heart just gave out, and there was nothing we could do in the end. I'm sorry to have to tell you this, but your husband passed away a few minutes ago," Dr. Ingram said.

Alice watched sympathetically as the old woman's upper lip quivered while she held out her trembling hand to the doctor.

"We were married for 52 years, doctor. How can I go on now? My poor Joe," she asked.

"I'm so sorry, Mrs. Robinson. Do you have any family that can help you?" Dr. Ingram inquired.

"No, my Joe was all I had. We have no children. It was just us," she replied.

Her face was wet with tears. She retrieved her gray wool coat and black leather gloves from the nearby chair.

"I'm truly sorry for your loss, Mrs. Robinson. I wish I could have done more," he said.

"I know you did your best, doctor. My dear, sweet Joe. What will I do without him?"

Mrs. Robinson stood at the edge of the hospital waiting room completely lost. It seemed as though she didn't know if she should turn left or right. She watched Dr. Ingram walk over to the group of children who had been sitting across from her. Her mind was spinning in a numbing spiral of grief and fear. Dr. Ingram's nurse noticed her standing motionless, confused, and alone.

"Mrs. Robinson, are you all right?" she asked.

Betty Robinson looked up and sadly smiled at the nurse, replying, "Yes, dear, I'm going to be fine I suppose. I just can't seem to move my old feet."

Her knees started to tremble as she began to sense the dark emptiness of her life.

"Here, please, sit down and rest for awhile," the nurse said sweetly, pulling up a chair for Betty.

"Thank you, dear," she coughed, with tears streaming down her solemn face.

"Can I make a phone call to someone, or help you get a cab to take you home?" the nurse asked.

"No, thank you. I'll just sit here for a while to catch my breath. It's been such a very long day," she replied.

"Yes, of course. I'll be right over there," the nurse pointed to a small wooden desk several yards down the hallway.

"Thank you, my dear." .

She noticed the young girl with the long dark hair and threadbare dress who had been watching her earlier while she prayed. She thought about how she seemed like such a sweet girl, but she wondered where her parents might be at that late hour. Betty's attention was then drawn to the other two boys sitting next to the girl. She was distracted from her feelings of grief and fear by the scene that was now unfolding before her. She was oddly aware of her own peculiar sense of mental clarity despite the fresh shock of her own husband's death. She continued to watch as the doctor walked over to speak with the children across from her.

"You're Charlie Chambers, right?" Dr. Ingram asked.

"Yes, I am," Charlie replied as he stood up to greet the doctor.

"And are you Arthur Chambers's brother?"

"Yes, sir, I am," Charlie responded.

"Have your parents been told about the situation yet?" Dr. Ingram asked.

Charlie sighed, "There aren't any parents. I'm his legal guardian."

"What do you mean there aren't any parents? Surely, he must have a parent," Dr. Ingram asked.

"No, our parents both died."

Charlie's face began to redden with anger as he impatiently reached into the back pocket of his pants to retrieve his raggedy wallet.

"Here!" Charlie declared as he pulled out an official, yet worn, looking piece of paper, and handed it over roughly to Dr. Ingram. In response to his hostile manner, the doctor paused, slowly looked Charlie in the eyes as if to reprimand him, and then gazed down at the wrinkled document.

"Well, Mr. Chambers, yes, I am sorry for this misunderstanding. You must know that it is indeed a bit unusual to see a head of household who is, well, so young. And just how old are you to be exact?" Dr. Ingram asked.

"18," Charlie quickly retorted.

"Well, I guess that's fine then. Let's not waste any more time, your brother is in a most grave condition."

"This is my sister, Alice, and this is Tommy Laucka, my brother's friend," Charlie said.

"I am pleased to meet you both," the doctor said, nodding his head and shaking their hands and then asked, "So, would someone please explain to me what has happened here?"

"Nothing happened, really. It was just a big accident. We didn't mean it," Tommy said, jumping up onto his feet.

"I always did say that the guilty need no accuser. You didn't mean what, young man?" the doctor inquired.

"Arthur was playing on the railroad tracks down the street from our house and he had an accident," Charlie quickly replied.

"How did the accident happen?"

"It was just an accident. We're not really sure," Charlie said, avoiding the doctor's gaze.

"Listen to me, Mr. Chambers. Either you tell me what happened, or I'll call the police. Maybe you'll feel more comfortable telling them," Dr. Ingram warned.

"Okay, okay, hold your horses. I don't want to get anyone in a twist here. I just don't want Arthur to get in any trouble over this," Charlie explained.

"Well, if there's no foul play involved, no one will get in any trouble," Dr. Ingram said.

"Arthur and Tommy were both down on the tracks behind the Sears warehouse in Savin Hill. Arthur was looking for loose coal to heat our apartment as he does every day. He climbed up onto a train car, and the back cargo ramp came loose, which then hit him on the head. That's all I know," Charlie quickly confessed.

"I see. Well, that is really all that I need to know. Thank you, Mr. Chambers. It makes sense, whatever hit him in the head was very heavy, and a train cargo ramp is certainly that."

"Is Arthur going to be okay?" Alice softly interrupted.

"That's difficult to say right now, miss. Your brother has epidural hematomas with associated hemorrhaging," the doctor explained.

Tommy whispered to Alice under his breath, "Jumping Jupiter! What's that?"

"Oh, what is that again?" Alice asked.

"He has a very serious head injury that will require extensive surgery. There may be permanent brain damage or paralysis. We'll have a better idea of his status after the surgery," the doctor said.

"Precisely how long was he outside in the snow?" Dr. Ingram asked Charlie.

"I don't know, sir. Alice, how long do you think Arthur was down there?" Charlie asked.

"Almost an hour I think," she replied.

"That may be what saves him in the end," the doctor said.

"Why is that?" Charlie asked.

"It's good he was out in the cold. The cold slowed his system down. Cold temperatures preserve tissue and will dramatically slow blood loss. If this was summer, well then, your brother may not have made it this far," Dr. Ingram replied.

"I noticed that his head bled more when he warmed up in the truck," Alice added.

"You're lucky it was a short ride to the hospital," the doctor said turning, "We'll do everything we can to save your brother. I'll be back to give you an update as we learn more."

Betty Robinson sat silently on the other side of the waiting room trying not to listen to the private conversation between them, which she felt oddly drawn to. Her husband of 52 years had just passed away. Now, here she was eavesdropping on a privileged conversation between a young family and their doctor. She shook her head at herself and tried to clear her racing thoughts. "What is wrong with me?" she wondered, her eyes and ears focused intently on the conversation across the room. She sat motionless as she strained to hear what was being said. Then strangely, a gentle voice from within her mind began to utter something. It was barely audible. She recognized something like a powerful urge that stirred from a place very deep inside her. She instinctively knew the source of the vibration and her eyes welled up with tears again. She felt the familiar voice was her only fortress of love and strength. It seemed to rise up from the pit of her being. Betty felt dizzy again as she thought that she might be losing her mind. She suddenly and clearly heard Joe's booming voice inside her head.

"Help the young boy, Betty. Help Arthur A. Chambers."

She was shocked by the sound of her dead husband's voice. She shook her head, lightly tapped her temples, and blinked her eyes rapidly. This must be just some sort of craziness. I need to get myself together. I must stand up and go home right now. I need to get out of here," she thought, pushing herself up and out of the chair with her cane. She stood, hesitating. Once again, her attention zoomed back with crystal clarity onto the conversation across the room that she had found herself eavesdropping on earlier. Betty sat back down again, and she continued to listen.

"We're preparing Arthur for surgery. I'm hopeful that every-thing will turn out favorably, but the operation could turn out to be a lengthy and complex procedure. Your brother may require several hours of surgery, as well as many weeks of recovery and months of rehabilitation," the doctor continued.

"Rehabilitation? What do you mean by that?" Alice asked.

"Well, there's really no way to tell right now, young miss, but a brain trauma of this severity often has lingering side effects. Your brother may lose the ability to speak or to think clearly. He may also have temporary or even permanent paralysis of one or more of his limbs. There is also a chance that he may not survive the operation, but I have every confidence that he will. His age and overall good health are in his favor. As I said, he may have to spend some time here recovering and then possibly, a more lengthy stay in a rehabilitation hospital. We won't know anything until he regains consciousness after the operation."

Hearing the doctor's grim words, Charlie fidgeted with the small change in his pocket and then wearily asked, "This doesn't sound very good, doctor, but we know he's badly hurt. I am wondering how much all this is going to cost?"

"It's impossible to predict with any certainty right now, but I would expect the cost of his care and potential rehabilitation will be a few thousand dollars or thereabouts."

Charlie knew the doctor was talking to him, but he seemed

unable to focus on his words. He felt a bolt of fear come up through his legs, a sudden wave of nausea, and he sat back down again. He was stunned.

"Did he just say a few thousand dollars?" Charlie thought to himself, horrified. It felt like a bail of hay fell out of the sky and landed right on top of him in the middle of the waiting room.

"Did I hear you right, Dr. Ingram? Did you just say the cost for all this would be a few thousand dollars?"

"Yes, I think that's a fairly accurate estimate on the final cost," he answered.

"Just how many thousand is a few thousand?" Charlie asked.

"Somewhere between three and five thousand I would say," Dr. Ingram replied.

Charlie quickly started to do the math in his head. He thought, "I make $38.50 a week. $38.50 times 52 weeks that should be $2,002 a year. $2,002! I would have to work for over two years to pay for this and there wouldn't be any money left for anything, not even food or rent." Waves of panic rolled over him and he could barely respond.

"Do you have any medical insurance?" Dr. Ingram asked, sensing the answer.

"No, I don't. I don't have any insurance. We can't afford this," Charlie mumbled.

"That's unfortunate," the doctor replied, "Do you have any other relatives that could help pay?"

The nurse approached Dr. Ingram to tell him that his patient Mr. Chambers was now ready, and he was being taken down into the operating room.

"Yes, well, we'll talk about all of this again after Arthur is better," Dr. Ingram said as he turned down the corridor toward the operating room.

Charlie fought back tears while shouting down the hall as the doctor disappeared, "You give Arthur your best work. We'll find a way to pay you whatever it costs. Save our brother!"

Alice felt paralyzed by the sickly, antiseptic smell of the warm hospital air, but it helped to thaw her chilled, slender bones. Her dress was still slightly damp from the melted snow, and her thin legs had a purple tinge. She felt the crushing weight of the events of the afternoon press upon her as she glanced across the room. The old woman across from her was still sitting in her chair. Their eyes met for an instant. The kind look in the old woman's soft brown eyes made Alice wish that her mother were still alive to hold her and to take their troubles away. The old woman smiled gently at Alice before she stood up assisted by a cane, to put her coat on. She stopped again just before leaving the waiting area, turning around to stare at Alice one last time with a look of concern.

Betty walked slowly but deliberately, down the hospital corridors, looking for the main exit where she could find a cab to take her the two miles to her home. An incandescent glow emanated from the lights that hung from the hospital ceiling in a perfect row. The corridor was washed with an eerie light that made her feel like she was slipping into a dream after the long night at the hospital. She wished that none of this was happening, and that she had just dreamed that Joe had died. She mumbled to herself about how hot it was getting. She wished she had waited to put on her coat as the hot air rose up from the tile floor. Beads of sweat began to roll down off her forehead as she quickened her pace. The ghostly voice from the waiting room haunted her like an imaginary echo. She knew it had been Joe's voice, but she also knew she had to be crazy to believe that. All she wanted to do was to get out of the hospital and into the cold night air so she could breathe some cool sanity into her tired lungs. No sooner had she had that thought when the same inner voice she couldn't escape earlier relentlessly pursued her again.

"Betty, help the young boy! Help Arthur A. Chambers! Betty, help the boy. Go back and help the boy!"

She couldn't stand the haunting voice any longer, and she

began to feel like she was suffocating. She put her hands over her ears, trying to block it out. The lights above her seemed to vibrate and sway. Betty felt a vague spinning sensation as she leaned her body up against the corridor wall. She thought that she must have been dreaming because when she opened her eyes she saw the brilliant image of her husband, Joe, standing right in front of her. It was him. He was standing in the middle of the hallway several feet away from her trembling body, glowing with the most spectacular light Betty had ever seen.

"This is my husband," she proudly thought as she gazed upon him in awe.

"Betty, this is the most wonderful thing you could ever imagine. It's so brilliant and forgiving. It's like I'm a new slate cleaned off by a brilliant love. Betty, I'm so happy here." Joe spoke to her through his radiating light.

Betty was absolutely overwhelmed by what she was witnessing, and she leaned further back against the wall to steady herself. She felt a strange electrical feeling surrounding her trembling body.

"Joe, why are you doing this? You're scaring me. Oh, Joe, why have you left me?" Betty said.

"I want you to help the young boy. Please. Help him, Betty. He needs our help."

After he communicated these words, his image shimmered down the hall, and then collapsed into a single point of light, which instantly disappeared altogether.

Betty was still bracing herself against the wall as she searched the corridor for a chair to collapse into. She thought, "I must be really crazy, but my Joe seemed so real. That was his voice. He sounded so clear, so strong, like he did when he was young. That was him. I saw him. I know I did." She shook her head trying to clear her thoughts.

"Ma'am, are you alright? What happened here? Did you faint?"

Betty looked up at the nurse who had quickly run to her side as Betty fell into the chair.

"No I didn't faint. I'm okay, nurse. I'm just having trouble steadying myself. The bright lights are hurting my eyes."

"Maybe you should come with me to the nurse's station to sit down. I'll have the doctor take a look at you just to make sure," the nurse offered.

"No, I don't think so. Thank you, miss. I'll be fine. I'm on my way to the waiting room. I'll sit and rest there. Thank you for your concern," Betty said, turning to walk back toward the young family.

As Betty turned the corner into the waiting room, she was visibly shaken from her bizarre encounter in the hospital corridor. She wasn't sure if it was her imagination, or if she actually met her dead husband Joe. Whatever happened back there, she felt an overwhelming desire to help the young family who had been sitting across from her.

Alice looked up to see the old woman who had left earlier marching straight toward them. She felt slightly unnerved by the intrusion. Betty came to an abrupt stop within only a few feet of them.

She said in a shrill voice, "Pardon me, I couldn't help but overhear you talking to your doctor earlier. Oh, excuse me," she stopped herself, realizing she had not even introduced herself. She placed her hand out to shake Charlie's and added, "My name is Betty Robinson and my husband Joe just passed away. When I was sitting here next to you earlier, I couldn't help but hear the conversation you had with your doctor. I was wondering, well, if I could possibly be of some help to you."

Charlie politely shook her hand. He replied, "Thank you, ma'am, but I think we're all set here. I'm sorry for your loss."

"I understand. I just thought you might be in need of some help, especially with the young boy not having any parents and all. The hospital is very expensive, and well–" Mrs. Robinson stopped just short of offering money.

At that moment, Alice instinctively understood why the dignified-looking woman was trying to help them. The realization that Mrs. Robinson understood how little money they had made Alice's eyes water. Alice looked at her softly and took her hand. In a strange way, Alice understood that the old woman also needed their help somehow. It was possible that she needed their help every bit as much as they perhaps needed hers. Alice wasn't completely sure about what kind of help the old woman might need from them, but she could sense the loneliness surrounding her. As Alice looked at her now, she was certain that the elderly woman was meant to be there for their mutual benefit. She had always possessed a way of sensing unspoken things about people, even total strangers. Acts of sympathy from others were an everyday occurrence in their lives. She and her brothers wouldn't have survived without strangers leaving food and clothing for them. Often those who generously helped seemed slightly embarrassed and uncomfortable with giving to them openly. Alice felt this same uneasiness coming from Mrs. Robinson, and she gently took her old hand again.

"Thank you so much for coming over to ask if you could help us, Mrs. Robinson. That's very kind of you. This is my big brother Charlie Chambers, and my younger brother's best friend Tommy Laucka, and my name is Alice Chambers. Arthur is our brother. They just took him into the operating room."

"May I sit down next to you, my dear?" Betty asked, pointing to an empty chair next to Alice.

"Yes, please, ma'am. I would like that."

"Well, I must say that I am impressed with your family. This must be a very frightening time for all of you," Betty Robinson offered.

"Thank you," Charlie replied, "The doctors don't seem sure about how the operation will go."

"I am really impressed that you are all here on your own

taking good care of your brother, and to have such loyal friends too," she said, smiling at Tommy.

Betty knew that they wouldn't accept her help directly and she decided that she would go down to the billing office to handle it without their knowledge before she left the hospital. Joe wanted her to help them, and she would do it.

Arthur watched the flickering lights on the ceiling above him dance by as they rolled him into the operating room. The sweet smell of ether hung thick in the air as the doors to the operating room swung open to reveal a large circular room. The unfamiliar frenzy of sounds and bright lights unnerved Arthur. The operating room was buzzing with organized chaos. While his injured head was held firmly stationary, his tired eyes moved around the room watching a blurry vision of white masks and starched uniforms. A nurse with a kind face appeared above him and gently comforted him.

"Arthur, here are some warm blankets to make you feel better."

She reminded him of his school nurse, Mrs. McMahon. She gently laid the blankets over Arthur's chilled body, and he felt grateful as the soothing warmth drifted down into his bones. All he could think of was sleep. He tried to thank her, but he couldn't speak.

"She's so pretty," he thought.

A man framed by the incandescent lights of the operating room stood over him, and loudly announced, "Arthur, my name is Dr. Ingram. You've had a pretty good bang on the head that I'm going to fix up for you. I don't want you to worry. Everything is going to be fine. The nurse is going to put a mask over your nose and mouth. You'll smell something sweet and fall off to sleep, and when you wake up, everything will be back to normal."

One drop and then another of the liquid potion fell into the mask, suffocating him with its anesthetizing sweetness. The lights on the operating room ceiling began to spin as Arthur felt his flimsy grip on consciousness slip away.

He felt a shockwave run through his entire body. It began simultaneously at the tip of his toes and at the top of his head. The sudden energy wave shook through the awkward space between dreamy thought and wakeful recognition. It erupted out of the center of his body into an amazing kaleidoscope of brilliant color that pushed him high up into the corner of the ceiling of the operating room. He floated up above the busy scene below, and he was glad to be released from the painful confines of his physical body on the table. He noticed the worried look Dr. Ingram had as he anxiously worked to revive his body.

"Doctor, his blood pressure is dropping and he's not responding."

Arthur floated down near the operating table, and tried to communicate with the doctor and the nurses.

"Hey, it's okay! Don't bother trying to get me back. I don't want to come back this time," Arthur instructed.

Arthur received no response. They were ignoring him.

"I mean it. I'm just fine. You don't have to do anything." Frustrated that that no one could hear him, Arthur started to fly around the operating room, while he curiously viewed the activities below.

"Dr. Ingram, his blood pressure is dropping rapidly now. I think we're losing him."

Arthur floated high above the operating room, listening to the conversations between his doctor and nurse. He felt vaguely relieved that they did not seem to be able bring him back this time. Arthur loved the new way of being that enabled him by mere thought to transport himself anywhere. He thought it would be fun to soar high in the sky among the puffy, clouds he always gazed upon when he was sitting in the classroom. He was instantly transported high above the Earth where he peacefully drifted along with the lazy clouds. Arthur felt as though the clouds beckoned him on; he was one of them, a cloud himself.

He floated back down near his earthly body while he calmly observed the extraordinary measures being taken to save his young life. Arthur watched the doctor and his medical team work frantically to revive him, when he noticed a white light begin to form over his body on the operating table. The light grew in intensity as Arthur began to feel the overwhelming power of love emanating from its center. The growing light had a beautiful cylindrical opening, which radiated a comforting energy that felt like overwhelming love to Arthur. The image grew in size until it filled the room with a pure light. The radiance was soothing to his eyes and comforting to his soul. Arthur began to drift toward the light as its pull strengthened, and his desire to become part of the light increased. He had no fear, anxiety, or discomfort as he drifted toward the brightness. Arthur's eyes were transfixed upon the unfolding beauty rolling out from its center in a circular wave of stunning light that cascaded down and rolled back in upon itself again. He felt an expanding sense of joy as he drifted slowly toward its opening. The angelic figures of his mother and father reappeared on either side of the entrance as Arthur drifted happily past them into the portal of light. As Arthur peacefully floated further down what appeared to be a tunnel of light, he was immediately mesmerized by a delightful explosion of multicolored vibrations. They filled every cell of his body with a brilliant energy. Becoming one with his surroundings, Arthur was transformed into a being of love, and gradually he realized that he was one with everything. He was part of all that had ever been and all that would ever be. Arthur traveled joyfully through the tunnel of light, listening to the hum of the vibration of all things merged into one glorious song of creation.

Chapter 5

Arthur's Heaven

Arthur opened his eyes and was astonished. He stood upon glimmering tracks of gold, which weaved endlessly among triangular mountains of shiny, black coal. Wide-eyed, he looked to his left and then to his right, surveying coal piled as high as the ancient pyramids of Egypt. They were layered with perfectly-shaped pieces of huge coal, stacked in magnificent rows, one on top of the other, leading toward a towering pyramid off in the distance. Everywhere he looked there were enormous, beautiful chunks of coal. Not knowing which way to go first, he was mesmerized and confused by the unbelievable abundance in front of him. He picked up a large piece by his feet, and held it up near his face, amazed. Strangely, the chunk was as light as a feather as he spun it around slowly in both hands, running his fingers across its smooth surface. Arthur brushed the coal against his lips, declaring it to be the finest piece he had ever held. He glanced at the coal bag hanging from his neck, and thought, "I need a much bigger bag for all of this." Then magically, his bag doubled in size, and several empty wheelbarrows appeared from nowhere on either side of him. He started to bend down to gather the coal. The pieces were so light that he tossed them into the bag almost effortlessly. He looked up from the growing pile of coal and noticed ahead of him, off in the distance, a man approaching along the tracks.

"Hello there, Art!"

The familiar voice vibrated as if the greeting was being sung instead of spoken. Arthur felt his arms and legs begin to quiver with an odd sensation. He fell back dumbfounded when he recognized the youthful figure now standing in front of him, and he asked him timidly, "Dad, is that you? Is that really you?"

"Yes, Art, it really is me. It's good to see you, son."

Arthur looked away. His head fell down, and his eyes began to water. An odd blend of joy and deep sadness gripped him, and he felt like he could not move. The words he might say back to his father clung deep inside his throat, but his mouth wouldn't open, and the words wouldn't come. Countless times back home in his room, he had spoken those words to his father, over and over again, but now they would not come out. He was silent. Arthur was unable to look up at his father.

"What's the matter, son? Aren't you happy to see me?" his father asked.

"How could you leave everyone? How could you leave us, and not come back? How could you do that to us?" Arthur whispered flatly. He looked quickly at his father, and then back down at his shoes.

"Well, I understand why you're angry with me. I don't blame you. I can tell you, my son, that I lost my way. Yes, I was quite lost back then. And I made some mistakes, some big mistakes. I was wrong. I'm sorry for the pain I caused, Art. I understand why you must be sore with me. I wish I could do things over again."

Arthur paused, and felt the hurt start to slip away.

His father continued, "I'm sorry, son. Can you perhaps find a way to forgive me?"

Arthur stood up slowly. His eyes were filled with tears as he wrapped his arms around his long-lost father.

"Sure, I can. I can forgive you. No problem. That's easy for me."

"Arthur, you have a kind heart, a forgiving heart. I am grateful, son."

"But, Dad, I'm confused. What are you doing here?"

"The same thing you are," he said, tossing another piece of coal into Arthur's bag.

"What's that? What are we doing here? What is this place?" Arthur asked.

"It's whatever you want it to be. It is always just what you want it to be, but there's plenty of time to find that out. Don't worry! One thing you learn here is that there is never anything to worry about. Not one thing!"

Arthur again scanned the limitless valley of silvery black with awe. "There's enough coal here to keep my sister's stove going forever," he thought as he quickly filled the bag up to the brim. He held another piece in his palm, admiring its rough-hued beauty. Its smooth, black-mirrored surface with perfect facets seemed to have been cut by an expert jeweler's hand. He tossed the coal into the air, estimating its size and shape as it whirled above him, and thought, "I could look forever back on the tracks in Boston, and I would never find a piece of coal this perfect. And there are millions of them here - just like this one."

Arthur drew the heavy, pungent odor into his lungs, and sighed with pleasure. He looked off into the distant horizon again, not to admire the pyramids, but to find an exit. He wanted to know the way back home to return with his newly found treasure. His sister Alice would be amazed. Along with finding the way out, Arthur wanted to make sure he could also find his way back to this incredible place. He needed to be able to get back here again to bring home more of the fine coal.

"Dad, I'd like to stay here a little while longer, but I also need to head on back home. Alice could sure use this full bag of coal. She'll be so happy when she sees this. And I know she'll be surprised to see you. I can't believe you found me, Dad. Wait until Alice sees you! She's going to be so happy."

"Art, there is so much you will learn about Heaven. I have a lot to explain to you. One of the first things you will learn is that it can be anything you what want it to be," his father replied.

"Don't you think we should be getting back home now? Let's go back now," Arthur suggested.

"We are home, Art. This is my home, and this is your real home," his father explained.

"Okay, sure, Dad, but isn't there a door close by somewhere? How do you get out of this place? You know how Alice is. She'll want me back at the apartment soon. I don't want to get her all worried"

"There's nothing to worry about here, Art. Alice will be just fine. Now, I want to show you something. Watch closely. I want to show you what I mean. Heaven can be what you want it to be, and it can be what I want it to be too. You can share your idea of Heaven with me like you just have with the pyramids of coal. And now I can also share mine with you. Just like this –"

His father swept his hand through the air, creating colored ribbons of light, which swirled and weaved magically around the valley of coal, turning it instantly into dazzling diamonds. There were bright clear ones, pinks ones, and yellow ones of every imaginable shape and cut. The chunk of coal in Arthur's hand was suddenly transparent and gleaming. It shot out beams of light in every direction.

"Holy-moly!" Arthur squealed. "How super keen!" He stared in amazement at the carpet of sparkling diamonds that stretched all the way to the end of the shimmering horizon. He looked down into his coal bag again, and saw that it was now filled with luminous diamonds. He tugged on the bag, and it still felt as light as cotton. Arthur lifted the weightless bag of gems, which started to spill over, releasing the diamonds freely into the air. They drifted and floated up into the azure sky like sparkling bubbles or fireflies, dancing high above the diamond pyramids.

"This is your true home, Art. You can create anything you want here—like I just did."

Arthur marveled at what was happening, and tried to understand his father's strange words. He wondered how he would suddenly appear again after being gone so long. And then he began thinking about his mother, remembering when she was sick in her bed, while he was playing beside Alice on the floor. And then one day, she was gone. His mind reached back, as far as he could remember. And he was there again. Arthur could see her melting brown eyes, and feel the gentle touch of her soft hands on his shoulders. As he dreamed, he could feel her close by. He gazed onto a yellow pasture that rolled out before him bursting with brilliant sunflowers. Row upon row, in perfect formation, the flowers swayed gently to the rhythm of a summer breeze. Arthur hadn't moved even one foot in any direction, and yet here he was in a whole new world. "What is this place?" he thought.

He felt like he was swimming in a sea of yellow petals, when the sunflowers suddenly parted, and a young woman stepped forward.

"Arthur? Arthur! Is that you?"

The female voice vibrated deep within him. He felt electric at the sound of her words. Arthur's whole body seemed to be buzzing gently. From below, the sunflowers parted again, and up jumped a golden puppy of light. The furry creature had a large brown nose and round saucer-shaped eyes that matched. Illuminated, she bounced up and down, running toward Arthur. The puppy looked like a cloud of light coming toward him. The playful dog landed powerfully in Arthur's arms, knocking him back onto the bed of flowers. She stood triumphantly on his chest, wildly licking at his face. Arthur's whole body jiggled with joy.

"She remembers you from when you were a young boy. You were too little to remember her, I think," the smiling woman said, emerging from the field.

Hearing the unmistakable sound of his mother's voice, Arthur looked up from the puppy. He leapt to his feet, shouting, "Mom? Is that really you? I can't believe you're here. I've missed you for so long. This is so amazing. It's really you!"

"Arthur, dear, it is me. I'm here with you at last."

His father stepped forward, adding, "You see, this is your

mother's Heaven. This is what she wants it to be."

The dog ran around Arthur's feet with its floppy ears bouncing in the warm sunlight. In response, he knelt down to pat the puppy, and exclaimed, "Hey, I think that I know this dog. Don't I?"

"Yes, you just might. This is your old friend, Cindy. She knew you when you were a baby. She was near the end of her lifetime when you were born. She was very old, and had some trouble getting around, but she spent her last days lying close to you, protecting you. She's very excited that you're here," his mother explained, watching the dog lick Arthur's face.

"Yes, I remember now. She would always growl at anyone who came near me who she didn't know. I remember feeling very safe by her side. But, if Cindy died when I was a baby, how can she be here now? I don't get it? Why is Cindy here?"

"Cindy is here because you want her to be. That's the way Heaven works. Heaven is always exactly the way you picture it to be. Heaven is what you think it is. It is always just what you imagine, but there will be plenty of time to talk about this later. I want you to come over here right now to give me a giant hug."

Arthur turned into the waiting arms of his mother, and quietly fell into her embrace. As they held each other, a perfect love ushered him down the familiar path to her soul. He felt like he was falling into a dream where he witnessed their ongoing connection through all of eternity. Time dissolved. Their energies merged together into a display of limitless love. He could feel the countless times they had spent together. Their soul energy was now joined again in the dance of creation. In that moment, Arthur knew they had lived many lives together. He could feel lifetimes when they were together as a parent and a child, and others when they were lovers, and others when they were friends. The agreement between them was made at the beginning of time. They would evolve together as they brought the lessons they needed to learn into each other's many lives. He could feel how their souls grew and expanded with each lifetime. Sometimes the lessons they learned together were gentle and painless like a great oak tree releasing its leaves before the cold winds of winter. Other times, the lessons learned seemed cruel and harsh. They rushed in upon them like a flood of pain, threatening to drown them in excruciating loss, and slicing their love in two. Yet always, there was the first agreement, which weaved together the tapestry of their lives with an unbreakable love. It was mysterious how these thoughts came over him in this magical place. It was something he just knew. Nobody had to tell him. And yet, he sensed there was so much more he would learn here too.

Arthur stood still, inhaling the images, musical poetry, and sweet scents of this unusual place. He started walking down a glimmering path toward the youthful figures of his parents, feeling a sense of completeness. This miraculous place was not quite what it appeared to be, he realized, as the path beneath his feet glowed with a colorful energy that seemed sturdy, yet was also strangely translucent like mist. He filled his lungs with sparkling air that rushed through him, filling every cell of his body with light. He was not just a visitor to this fantastic place, but rather he was slowly becoming part of it. He saw that he had been responding to this new environment just as he would the one he left behind. He was breathing air through his lungs, and he was walking on solid ground because that's what he believed he should do. Maybe he didn't need to breathe, and maybe he could float instead of walking – everything and anything seemed possible in this place. He remembered how his father told him, "Heaven is what you think it is," as the realization bubbled up inside him that he could change his environment by mere thought.

"Yes, that's the way it is here, Art. You can create anything you want. There is just one catch, though," his father cautioned.

"What's that, Dad?" Arthur asked as he watched Cindy

playfully run through the field, momentarily stopping on the path, encouraging them to follow her.

"The catch is that whatever you create here you must create for good. You see, Art, everything in Heaven, on Earth, and everywhere else, including you and me, are all part of God's creation. The surprise of creation is that God created everything from only one thing."

"What is that, Dad? What one thing?"

"It's love, God's love. Everything that has ever existed and everything that will ever be is made from love. If it isn't made from love, Art, it's not real," his father explained.

"So, the only thing that's real is love?"

"Yes, that's it. The only thing that truly exists is love. Anything else from the beginning to the end is an illusion. Nothing else is real. Just love, Art."

"What's an illusion? What are those made from?"

"Illusions are made from fear and fear is not real."

Arthur placed his fingers between his eyebrows looking puzzled and asked, "Does God create fear?"

"No, Art, God can only create from love. Fear is made by man and pretends to be real through the formation of false ideas or illusions. God is love, and love is the only thing that is real. Love is the only thing that exists. The stars, planets, you, me, and everything in creation are all made up from the same stuff. Love is the essence, the tiniest building block of creation, and God is the great builder."

He smiled knowingly at his father and nodded his head in agreement, "Sure, Dad, I knew that everything is made from love. Not a problem."

Arthur wasn't sure if he understood a word his father said as he quickly tried to change the subject.

"Look, Cindy wants us to follow her down the path."

Arthur pointed to Cindy barking musically as she leapt down the path toward a glimmering image emerging at the end of the valley.

"We'll have plenty of time to go over there soon, my son, but we must stay here for a little while until you understand better how things work here in Heaven," his father said.

Arthur watched Cindy disappeared out of sight. She ran down the translucent path toward the beautiful glowing city rising from the outer edge of the valley.

"I think we should follow Cindy. She's heading to that bright place in the distance and she might get lost."

"Don't worry, Art, Cindy knows her way around. She just wants to play. She'll find us later. Didn't I tell you earlier that there's never anything to worry about?"

"Yes, but I was just a little worried about Cindy. She's so far away now."

Arthur scanned the horizon again, saw no sign of the dog, and looked back at his father.

"Arthur, Heaven is always what you think it is, and there is never anything to worry about."

Arthur's father was trying to awaken him to the first rule of creation. Arthur stared up at him with a strained look of mild confusion and said, "Dad, I don't understand what you're trying to say."

"Well then, let's try this. There is certainly no better way to learn than by doing. Art, you say you are worried about Cindy being so far away, right? "

"Yes, but only a little bit."

"All right then, I want you to close your eyes and picture in your mind Cindy being safe and content. Picture her sitting right here by your side," his father instructed.

He thought of Cindy sitting next to him panting happily. Then, peering down at the shimmering ground, he said, "What happened? She's not here. Did I do something wrong?"

"No, you did nothing wrong. It just takes a little getting used to. It's important to believe. It is also essential not to worry. You can do it! Clear your mind of any negative or distracting thoughts, and try it again."

Arthur closed his eyes and tried to picture the peaceful field lit up with countless sunflowers that stretched out before him. He cleared his mind of worrisome thoughts about Cindy, and about not knowing exactly how to do any of this. He concentrated on how wonderful it was to be in such an amazing place and then, he pictured Cindy by his side. To his amazement, before he could finish that thought, he felt something warm rubbing against his right leg. Arthur opened one eye to peek down, and there was Cindy sitting right next to him, looking up trustingly with her shining eyes and big wet nose.

"Good girl! You're a good girl, Cindy," Arthur said as he patted the back of her neck feeling its perfect shape and soft curly hair.

"Nicely done, Art!" his father praised.

"Do you feel like you're beginning to understand how this works?" his mother asked.

"Well, I'm not sure how I did that, or why I could do it. I really don't get what's going on here," Arthur replied.

"You're in this place because your life on Earth has ended. You've been lifted beyond the physical plane to a place where you are also alive, but no longer in a physical body. Here you are free of pain and hardship. This is where you can fully awaken to the real purpose that has always been inside you. Every being is rejoicing at your return home. You have always been a child of the Creator. This is where you can claim the love that has always been yours. You are waking up to your true nature, and it's time to take your gift," his mother said.

"Mom, I guess I know I'm not really alive anymore. I mean, I'm not alive like I used to be and that's okay. I do like it here. I feel very happy, but what is this you're saying about a gift?" Arthur asked intrigued.

"Your gift, and the gift of all beings, is the ability to bring forth love from your heart. This is the sacred treasure passed down from the Creator to you and me. Inside each one of us a core of pure love was placed, at the dawn of time. Art, we all are nourished by the light of love, and grow from it. Like the seed of a great oak tree we take root and grow into the likeness of the one who formed us in love. And like the Creator, we were made to create from love. This gift is co-creation. It is our undeniable destiny to grow from the special seed of love inside us into full bloom and into the likeness of the Great One," his mother explained.

Arthur was dumbfounded. His mother was telling him that he was growing up to be some kind of partner, creating with God. "I can't even pass a fourth grade math test and she's telling me that I'm a co-creator," Arthur thought to himself, astounded.

"Yes! Arthur, that is exactly what I'm trying to tell you," his mother replied.

Arthur was stunned and somewhat disturbed by his mother's ability to read his mind, and said to her, "I didn't say that... That's not fair. I can't read your mind. How did you do that?"

She smiled broadly at his objections and stated, "Oh, but you can. You actually began doing this when you arrived here. Even on Earth, when you go to a new place it takes time to get used to new people and new ways of doing things. While you're adjusting, you are somewhere between your life before and the one now. What's different here is that there is no real need for speech, nor regular conversation as you knew it before. Your mind communicates through the intention of your heart. Each thought instantly moves into the mind of whomever and wherever it is directed."

"Yes, Art, that's right. Your abilities here are not limited like they seemed to be in your physical life. Here in Heaven, you can create anything you would like to through your thoughts. Your entire experience here follows your thoughts. That's why it is so important to think in good ways," his father added.

"You really mean I can make up whatever I want to just by thinking it? Anything at all?" Arthur asked.

His father nodded his head, and Arthur marveled that he could hear his father's words even though his lips were still. "Yes, you can. Your power to create is not limited here in Heaven, but your thoughts can be both limitless and limiting here. This is why it is very important to think correctly."

He felt a loving power quietly begin to grow inside, spreading gently through him along old familiar pathways, which led to the core of his soul. His body of light vibrated softly and oscillated with an energy that connected him to all things. He had a sense of peace and love that was complete as he slowly began to think about the one thing he wanted more then anything else in all of Heaven. It would be the most perfect thing he could create, and he set all of his thoughts and newly discovered power into creating it. Arthur wanted more then anything in the universe to see his sister, Alice, here beside him. He pictured her smiling right next to him, and he imagined the familiar feeling of her comforting embrace. He imagined her running up the path of light and jumping into his arms, thrilled to see him. Arthur applied the full force of his new skills to bring his thought-creation into being. His spirit soared with the antic-ipation of seeing his sister once more. He gazed outward, searching for her presence on the path of light. He stood very still, waiting. When she did not appear, he felt confused. Disappointment washed over him. Arthur thought he must have been doing something wrong.

He started all over again to set his mind to the task of thought creation, re-doubling his effort at intention when his mother interrupted by saying, "Arthur, Alice is someone you cannot bring here."

"Why not?"

"It isn't allowed. While you are here, your ability to create does not reach over into the material world. It is impossible for anyone here except for the Creator to bring anyone or anything here from the other side."

"I really want to bring Alice here, that's what I want more than anything. It would be so perfect. You're here, Dad's here, and Alice has missed you both so much. And now I really miss Alice too. I don't get it."

"I'm sorry, son, I had to learn the same thing when I first came here, and I wanted to bring you and all of my children here to this wonderful place with me. It isn't Alice's time yet. Your ability to create what you wish is limited to the world of the spirit. Sometimes you can petition for special permission, but this is only given if it is in harmony with Her divine will and timing."

"Why do you call God by different names? You used the name Creator, God, Father, and referred to Her divine timing. I don't understand."

"The Creator is everywhere and in everything, and has been since long before creation came into being and will be after its end. These names are attempts to define something that can't be defined or named, and such labels come only from those on Earth. We cannot possess the air we breathe. We cannot possess the wind or the sea. Even a star cannot possess its light. As you're discovering here in Heaven, words are limited. And names are limited. Men and women use names to define something they can not fully understand, and often these names are made out of fear," she said.

"God's names are made from fear?"

"Yes, in a way, that's right, Arthur. When human beings defined the Creator by name, they tried to possess God as their own. Then, selfishness and fear drove them to fight with each other for the sole ownership of the Creator. People have often tried to possess God to shut out the beliefs or spiritual under-standing of others. Afraid they'd lose God's love for themselves and power, they have tried to own the Creator by pushing others away. Countless wars have been fought to win one name for

God."

"Does God even care what name is used?" he asked even though he already knew what her answer would be.

"No, Arthur. God doesn't mind what name or gender is used, but does care deeply when a name is used to keep others away. We all belong to God. Each and every one of us matters. There is not one soul who is not chosen. It's not true that there is one way of thinking about God that others must go along with or they are lost. This is just not so. It makes human beings feel safe to believe this, but this comes from fear, not of love. The Creator cannot be owned by one group. Each of us is connected to the Creator. Love takes in everyone, Arthur. Love doesn't leave anybody out. We are all made of love," she said, motioning toward the path.

"Art, it's time. We need to leave here now. Let's walk down the path together toward that place off in the distance," his father said, pointing to an area off in the distance.

Arthur couldn't believe what he was seeing. At the end of the path, beyond the fields, was the most amazing city Arthur could have imagined. He felt drawn to its inviting glow just as he had been pulled toward the light earlier that first brought him to this spectacular place. The gentle pull encouraged him down the path toward an architectural display with dozens of prisms sending forth dazzling beams in all directions. Glimmering spires glowed with an energy that made them appear to be alive.

"Dad, what is that place?" Arthur asked.

"We are going to the great hall of light where you will meet old friends whom you haven't seen for a long while, but who were always by your side."

"Old friends? I have old friends here?"

"Yes, you have many friends here, Art, and they've all been waiting for your arrival. They are very anxious to see you again," his father replied.

"What's that?" Arthur asked, pointing to a large mysterious object off in the distance suspended high above the shimmering city.

"What you see there is God's diamond," Arthur's father replied.

"His diamond? Why does God have a diamond?"

Arthur looked up with great curiosity at a clear stone of pulsating energy covered by countless facets of brilliant, captivating light. The giant diamond pulsated and grew as new facets appeared on its surface. With each new facet a flash of beautiful, stunning light shot forth like lightening traveling all the way to the horizon. The diamond seemed to hum with a soft sound as it expanded, which filled Arthur with happiness as he listened. His father stepped forward, placing his hand on Arthur's shoulder and began to explain.

"Every time someone finds a brand new way back to the Creator, well then, God smiles and makes a new facet appear on the diamond. God is enormously pleased when we use His gift or the power to create to find new ways back to Him. The reason God gave human beings the inherent power to create was so that we could find our way back home again. During the very first instant of creation, God's love expanded to fill every corner of the universe. Everything that ever was and ever will be has love at its core. In life on Earth, the core of love often gets buried. We sense our core of love when we create, and we lose contact with our core of love when we destroy with hate or intolerance. Yet, God will wait for each of us with patience, compassion, and a love that knows no bounds. There is nothing for us to worry about no matter what happens to us on Earth because we will all return."

"Look, Art, we're almost there," his father said, pointing up toward the beautiful ornate buildings topped with towering spires that sparkled. Arthur's brown eyes opened widely with delight as he gazed upon a sight so beautiful that it made him suddenly stop and shout, "Jumping Jupiter! This is the most amazing place. It is so incredibly beautiful."

"Come on, Arthur, let's go in. Everyone's waiting for you," his father said.

He motioned to get Arthur and his mother to cross over the bridge leading to the city.

Halfway across, while admiring the perfect craftsmanship of the bridge, Arthur stopped. He ran his hand over the smooth stones that were inlaid with jewels of every brilliant color of a summer rainbow. Arthur looked back down at the field of sunflowers that were swaying in the warm breeze that swept across the valley. He watched Cindy race to catch up to them before they crossed the bridge and he thought, "I love this place. I really do love it here. I never want to leave."

Chapter 6

The Orbs

Arthur turned to follow his parents. He wanted to see what was inside the ornate structure just ahead. Searching his memory, Arthur could not remember ever seeing any place that was quite like this one. The closest thing he could recall that resembled what he saw was the fancy castle in the Christmas display in Boston, yet even that didn't do the amazing structure justice. Its walls of inlaid stone rose high into the deep blue sky. Halos formed around each of the breathtaking spires, which seemed to reach the very top of Heaven itself. They walked under a glowing arch made of pulsating pink quartz that seemed to transmit warm vibrations as they passed underneath. Arthur experienced a strange sensation as he continued to walk, almost like someone had their arms wrapped around him. It was like he had been stumbling alone and aimlessly through a desolate desert in search of his home for countless years, when out of nowhere, he finally reached his place of belonging. He knew he had reached a stopping point, where he felt calm and content. He was home.

The great hall ahead was alive with activity. Everywhere Arthur looked he saw radiant beings like himself while they were ushered about from one place to another. Some of them were moving about in a very studious way, while others were standing around reviewing some type of information with other beings who looked like teachers. Arthur thought that the hall had a familiar feeling to it, but he wasn't sure why. He couldn't quite figure it out.

"Is this place some kind of school?"

Arthur's voice made a slight echo that rang through the large room as if it were empty.

"Yes, Art, that's more or less what this place is," his father replied.

"What do they teach here?"

"It's not so much a place of teaching as it is a place of awakening," his father answered.

His father nodded in recognition to a tall distinguished-looking man who was quickly approaching them. He seemed to be almost gliding across the stone floor.

"Here he is now, Art. This is who we came to see. This is your old friend, George," Arthur's father said as he held out his hand to the regal presence now standing directly in front of them. George carefully surveyed Arthur, and then a wide smile came across his strong face that seemed more deeply etched from wisdom than age.

Arthur felt the center of his chest turn warm and expand. He instantly recognized his very old and best friend.

"Oh, hey there, George," Arthur declared with a smile that brightened the great hall, making it pulsate slightly with another subtle echo.

A soft blue light radiated out from his old friend, surrounding Arthur in a comforting embrace. Arthur was immersed in the familiar loving presence of his loyal guardian angel. A powerful silence connected them as he awakened to the realization that George had always stood steadfastly by his side. He had guided him through every moment of his life. Somehow he knew George had been there not just for the life he had just passed from to get to this place, but for every life he had lived before as well.

"I tried to warn you not to go near that train car ramp," George said, smiling as they left his parents behind and they moved together into a separate, smaller room ahead.

"I can see that now, George, but at the time it didn't really seem like a message from anyone," Arthur said with a mild shrug of his shoulders.

"I know, Arthur. I'm difficult to hear sometimes. I try to

message through feelings and intuition, but my messages to you and my other assignments often get lost in the jumble of ordinary everyday thoughts. Do you remember having the feeling that something bad was about to happen to you?" George asked as they walked ahead.

"Yes I do, and I almost turned around, but then Tommy called me a chicken," Arthur said, remembering his accident on the train tracks.

"Oh yes, chicken! I can't tell you how many times I have lost you to that one," George said with a roaring laugh. The next hall they approached was filled with the light of his laughter, and Arthur could hear the echo of George's deep belly laugh ring all the way back to the great hall.

"Sorry, George, I can never seem to get past a dare."

"That's okay, you're not alone. Most human beings have trouble hearing the voice of their spirit guides. Many don't even realize they have one, or that they have a natural ability to listen to us, but that's all about to change."

"What's going to change?"

"Well, Art, I'll tell you, it has to do with some big changes taking place on Earth right now. People are beginning to sense it, at least some of them. Every day now there are more human beings who are becoming aware of things beyond their own life. It's as if something inside them is waking up. All souls are standing in the doorway of a shift that will usher in a sense of love and purpose. This change that's beginning now is a leap forward that will awaken all people to their true nature," George explained.

"Is that what they mean about making good happen?" Arthur asked.

"I can tell that your earthly parents have prepared you, haven't they? Yes, Art, the great awakening that's coming is largely that, but the more immediate one will be the realization that we create our lives just by the way we think. Through our thoughts every aspect of our lives comes into being. Until people understand the role that our own thoughts play in creating our lives every day, the Great One knows they aren't ready to evolve to the next level of awareness," George explained.

"Everyone here tells me not to worry. Is that why it's so important to stop worrying?"

"Yes. Worrying is the most damaging form of fear. It eats away at God's love and makes it difficult for people to create anything real. Worrying is a wall to God's love that prohibits us from creating from love. It blocks good things from entering in. As a result, we end up creating most of the things in ours lives from our own fear. The reason why so many people feel their lives lack any purpose or direction is because they are driven by worry. As a result, they create an entire life that isn't real. Anything created from fear isn't real. Human beings spend way too much of their precious lives in habitual worry. If each person knew how incredibly powerful they truly are, they would never worry about anything at all, Art, ever again."

They passed in front of a side room with a peculiar rectangular table surrounded by silver with glimmering stones at its center. The stone table had a surface so clean and bright that Arthur had some difficulty looking directly toward it. He stood in the doorway, squinting toward its shimmering top.

"George, what's that thing for?"

"That is the table of knowledge. It helps those who are new here understand Heaven and helps with their awakening to the new way of being here," George answered.

"Can we go in the room and look at it?"

"No, not just yet, Art, there's someone I'd like you to visit with first. After that there may be time to go in there for a bit."

Arthur lingered behind by the entrance as George moved away. The table started to come to life. It glowed with a soothing yellow light, and hummed softly with a pleasant vibration that reminded Arthur of the sound made by God's diamond earlier.

He watched the table as an image of the planet Earth rose up out of the table's center. The green and blue globe floated in mid-air, spinning slowly as the bright yellow light of the sun marched steadily across its surface. Arthur thought how beautifully real the image looked, covered with white clouds and deep blue oceans. Looking up at the planet, he wondered if his family was all right, and if they ever felt sad that he had left them. His thoughts drifted back along the gentle stream of his memory to his sister Alice sitting at the old wooden table in her kitchen. He could see her watching him as he set up the cooking stove with coal, rubbing his hands, trying to ignore the chill of their apartment. George shouted from a distance, "Hurry, Art, we don't have much time."

Arthur resisted the pull of his voice, and closed his eyes for a moment to listen to the table's pleasing sounds—instead chaotic images began to appear. They rushed by in a cataclysmic swirl that picked him up, and flung him far out among countless tortured planets and stars. They were stretched out like fiery taffy that erupted into a violent stream made from an endless line of galaxies. Arthur's own body of glowing light was stretched out into a long ribbon that reached billons of miles toward a spinning blackness that seem to be devouring creation itself. Suddenly, Arthur's long thin presence began to twirl like the spinning tail of a flying kite as he moved up and away from the effects of the all-consuming blackness. He was safe.

"Come on, Art, we really need to move on now," George said as he approached.

Arthur opened his eyes, "What was that all about? It felt like I was a long string of spaghetti."

"The table revealed a possible end time to you, but things don't have to end that way. It's up to us how things end."

"It is? What's up to us? I don't understand."

"The Great One creates only with love. The end will come through fear. If time ends it will be by our hand, not the Great

One's. But even if everything you knew blew up into a giant ball of fire and steam, you would still exist. Nothing in God's creation can truly hurt you," George explained as he quickly moved down the hall.

"Hey, George, wait up. What's the big hurry? Who are we going to see that's so important?"

Looking ahead, Arthur realized for the first time how tall George was. He estimated that he must have been almost seven feet tall as he stood like a tower with flowing robes that made him appear to hover just inches off the floor.

Arthur gasped in fascination when he saw the glowing orbs of swirling colored light ahead as they approached another large circular room. Giant orbs floated in the air like shimmering hot air balloons hung in the night sky. Arthur left George's side, running into the center of the room. He looked up and circled around excitedly to get a closer look at the orbs. "George, what are these things?" he asked, reaching out to touch one.

"I wouldn't do that if I were you! You must make sure your thinking is correct before you engage a sacred orb," George warned.

"They're so neat! What do they do?"

"They are for life review. They help you awaken to the pattern of your past life experiences."

"Past lives? I don't remember having any past lives, George. Are you sure I had one?"

"Yes, you have had many."

Arthur gazed at the glowing orbs swaying slowly in the air with their warm, inviting light that beckoned him. The walls around them were purple velvet resembling the night sky. The orbs hovered like incandescent fireflies that enticed those passing by to share another place in time. They seemed to float along under a star-filled night sky. The mystery of the orbs enchanted Arthur, and he wondered if there were magical lifetimes they might be willing to reveal to him.

"George, can we stay here and try one?"

"Art, we really should be moving along now. If there's time we'll come back."

"Please, can I just try one? It won't take much time," Arthur pleaded.

"Only one, then we must move on. Why don't you step up in front of this one?" George encouraged.

"Okay," Arthur replied, positioning himself directly in front of the one George was guiding him toward.

"That's fine. Now clear your mind of all random thoughts. Try now to think only of God's love."

Arthur steadied himself as he stared directly into the swirling light. He thought of his mother standing in the beautiful valley. As this image drifted into his mind he felt a wave of love. Arthur felt completely calm as the swirling light began to oscillate. The orb's light shook vigorously for several seconds. All at once, Arthur found himself sitting next to a cool stream that ran through a cluster of sycamore trees. The air was warm and dry with the smell of burnt grass. Looking down, he noticed that one foot was bare, while the other was covered in the soft skin of a moccasin. Arthur wondered for a moment if he was putting the slippers on or taking them off. He turned to see the impressive figure of a man wearing an Indian headdress riding swiftly past him and over the top of the hill. Arthur could hear playful laughing off in the distance where the rider was heading. He realized that he was sitting at the edge of an Indian village. Somehow he was also dimly aware that his name was Bright Cloud, and that he was a 14 year-old Dakota Indian on the verge of manhood. Although young, he could feel his deep sense of pride. He could ride his pony as fast as any of the older warriors, and he could also shoot an arrow further than most. Adept at firing one of the rifles that an elder tribesman let him use, he was hopeful that he would soon receive his own rifle.

The late summer sun bathed his ancestral grasslands in a

golden hue as he watched a warrior ride into the village humming with activity. From the distance, he could see a crowd of men quickly gathering around the rider. Reaching down to pull on his other moccasin, he heard the familiar high-pitched shrill of the tribal war cry. Without hesitating, Bright Cloud jumped onto his pony to ride as fast as he could toward the crowd to find out what was happening. As he got closer, he could sense that something unusual had just happened. Woman and children were frantically running about gathering belongings, while men were readying themselves for battle. He could feel the blood pulse in his veins as he sensed the village was about to be attacked. He grabbed the arm of his cousin who had just emerged from behind the family's lodge.

"Slow Turtle, what is going on?" Bright Cloud demanded.

"They say all the buffalo have disappeared."

"The buffalo are not gone. I saw them myself. Under the full moon not more than one day's ride from here I saw them," Bright Cloud said.

"They say the white men have destroyed them all at the place of the iron horse,"

Slow Turtle replied.

"The buffalo are as many as the blades of grass in the great valley. It is impossible for anyone to destroy them. Not even the mighty Dakota could do that."

"Our warriors are preparing to attack those who are responsible. You should join them, Bright Cloud," Slow Turtle suggested.

"The white men are few, and they have no such power. I do not believe you, cousin. This must be a lie," Bright Cloud said as he turned to face a band of the Dakota warriors dressed in full war paint riding toward him.

The war party rode past him as they yipped and yelled and charged hard toward the east. Bright Cloud noticed his older brother, Long Eagle, along with his father Gray Wolf were riding among them. He yelled out as they passed, "Father, I wish to join you and my brother!"

His father turned his horse quickly, and said, "No, Bright Cloud, you must stay here to guard the village."

"Is it true about the buffalo?" he asked his father.

"Yes, it is true," he answered.

"Then you must let me ride with you to avenge the buffalo!"

"I say no to you. Stay and guard the village. Your time will come soon," his father   commanded, turning his horse to join the war party. Without another word, he rode off, leaving his son and nephew Slow Turtle behind.

Bright Cloud kicked the dry dirt hard with the tip of his moccasin, and yelled angrily into the air, "I am not a child! He still treats me as if I am still a child. Long Eagle is not yet 16 years and he rides. I can ride as fast and as long as he can."

"Your father says that guarding the village is an important task. He trusts that you will do that," Slow Turtle reminded him.

"Guarding the village is for old men and women," Bright Cloud complained.

"You must stay. Otherwise, you would dishonor your father."

"To stay dishonors me," he protested, jumping onto his pony and riding furiously toward the village.

The summer rains had not yet come. As Bright Cloud dismounted his pony and slowly marched through the blazing heat, puffs of dry dust stirred beneath his feet. The merciless midday sun cracked the parched ground. He felt angry that his father had left him behind. "How can I have honor if I am not allowed to fight with the others to avenge the death of the sacred buffalo? I am not a boy. I am a warrior."

He walked slowly, his head hung low, as he imagined all the reasons to disobey his father and follow the others into the battle. Just then, on the side of the trail, he noticed something dark protruding from behind a dry bush. As he moved closer, he saw that it was a water pouch, fat with water. Bending down to pick it up, he brushed his hand across the smooth, moist skin and measured its weight. He turned it over to see his father's symbol of a wolf etched into the leather. "My father's water pouch was dropped by accident when they were riding away," he thought. Looking up at the scorching sun, he reasoned, "My father will need this water. I will not be disobeying him if I bring this to him."

The hard-charging horses of his father's war party had chewed the dry ground into a ribbon of loose dirt that swirled and spun behind them. Bright Cloud followed their tracks to the east, stopping only once to let his tired pony drink a small amount of the water from his father's pouch. The sun beat down on his bare shoulders as he finally approached the ridge that overlooked the great valley. The iron trail of the white men ran all the way to this place, and he thought he would find the iron horse there. His pony struggled up the last few feet onto the ridge, and they reached the crescent. Bright Cloud stopped in shock. He looked out onto the most horrifying scene he had ever witnessed. Countless dead buffalo were strewn out before him. Endless, black waves of death made him gasp in horror. His pony reared up at the overwhelming stench, almost tossing Bright Cloud to the ground. Stunned tears of immeasurable loss blurred his vision. He began to shake. Blood-covered carcasses and flies surrounded him. Ravens swirled around overhead, chanting their ominous song of death. Bright Cloud fought back the childish sensation to run away. He thought again of his father and brother fighting bravely to avenge the Great Spirit of the buffalo.

"The buffalo have always come here to give my people life. Now they are gone. I must give my life for them," he murmured through tears that turned into anger, and then iron resolve.

"I will find my father, and fight with him," Bright Cloud shouted. He steadied his pony and began the torturous decent into the cradle of doom.

He made his way down the steep trail to the floor of the valley below. Off in the distance, wandering aimlessly among the dead buffalo, he saw the shattered remnants of his father's war party. His heart sank as he realized how few remaining warriors there were. He wondered if they were just mirages against the blood-red setting sun. Getting closer, he could see they were lost and disoriented, walking in circles.

"What happened, Standing Bear? Where are the rest?" Bright Cloud frantically asked.

"They are dead. Just like the buffalo," he answered.

Standing Bear looked dully ahead and staggered past him like someone possessed.

"Stop! Wait for the others. We must come together to fight again," Bright Cloud shouted.

"There is nothing to fight. We are the only ones who are left. The attack failed. We are finished."

Bright Cloud counted the remaining warriors wandering among the buffalo carcasses, and asked, "I count seven. Are there only seven left?"

"Yes, we are the only men left."

"But my father, and my brother?" Bright Cloud asked.

"They were among the bravest. They attacked the iron horse first. That's when we saw the white men had powerful new weapons that shoot bullets faster then a thousand warriors. They had a canon made of gold. One man stood behind it turning a handle, and out came more fire than all of the Dakotas have," Standing Bear moaned.

"My father and brother have died?"

He hung his head and replied, "Yes. They died, Bright Cloud. They died with great honor."

Bright Cloud stopped. He could not believe what he was hearing. He dropped down to his knees, stunned. He kept saying over and over again, "No, no. No, it can't be true."

Looking up at Standing Bear he stammered, "We were over

200 strong this morning. How can there be only seven?"

"The white man has a great power now."

"How can they be more powerful than all of the Dakotas?"

"You were not there to see our warriors fall like grass in a hail storm. We are defeated," Standing Bear said.

"What will become of us with the buffalo gone?" Bright Cloud asked.

"My thoughts are only of darkness. I think we have ridden to the last battle. I say we should do what we have always done before."

"And what is that?"

"Follow the buffalo. They have always led us to life. They lead us now to the hunting grounds of our ancestors. We are being asked to follow them," Standing Bear said, sweeping his arms around and pointing to the countless dead buffalo that surrounded them.

Bright Cloud understood now what his father had tried to tell him many times in the past. He was not ready to go on hunts or raiding parties with the tribal warriors. His life as a Dakota was disintegrating all around him, and he felt helpless to stop the onslaught. They sat down, and prayed among the dead buffalo while the crimson sun sank over the western hills. Bright Cloud slowly accepted his fate. He was a Dakota in life and also in spirit. He would be a Dakota in death. The spirits of his father and brother hunting with their ancestors seemed to call to him to embrace death.

"How will my own end come?" he thought.

The ground underneath them soaked up the blood of 10,000 dead buffalo. Something strange began to stir deep within him. It was a call from long ago, before memory, before thought; he could feel the vibrations of the spirits of his ancestors rippling like a breeze across the valley. Bright Cloud's mind and all his senses were alive with an ancient knowing that something profound was about to happen. Bright Cloud lifted his head toward the sky, and he felt such an immediate connection to the loving power within him that he stood up among the dead buffalo. He looked across the field of loss, and up into the vacant sky. His whole body began to shake as he gave into something he could feel, but not fully understand. Instead of collapsing in sobs, amazingly, Bright Cloud began very slowly at first, to move his feet rhythmically. He started to dance. Beginning as a soft whisper, he chanted the ageless prayers of his fathers. He began to dance faster and to chant more loudly trying to awaken the dead spirits of his ancestors. The dark sea of still buffalo surrounded him like great mounds of death. Bright Cloud's young voice broke the silence like light streaming into a dark room. It drove away the sound of death from the ravens above. He sang his people's ancient song of hope. He paused. The melody echoed across the wide valley. As the reverberations settled, he prayed out loud to his dead brother and to his father. Bright Cloud pleaded with all of the fallen warriors to get up and to join him.

Then something stranger happened. Standing Bear and the remaining band of warriors watched with awe as the fallen spirits of their ancestors mysteriously rose up. From among the dead buffalo, they joined them like shadows in the prayerful dance of hope. They swirled and danced together in the circle of life, chanting their ghostly prayers to the Great Spirit.

Standing Bear was the first to notice the great creatures return in the distance. He stopped dancing, and his eyes grew wide. He announced to the others, "Look! They have returned to us!"

In the distance, framed by the setting sun, the outline of a small group of buffalo was undeniable. Proud and defiant, they stood above the lifeless valley. The miraculous image of the buffalo on top of the hill brought cheers of joy and amazement from the band of dancing warriors.

"Look, the buffalo live! They are here to lead us again, not to death, but to life. We must come together as the buffalo have done. We must fight with them to live," Bright Cloud proclaimed.

"We must live to avenge their death," Standing Bear replied.

"No, we cannot avenge their death, but must rejoice with them in being alive. War will bring us nothing but our own death. We must live as the buffalo teach us to live. We must live in peace," Bright Cloud said.

"Your father was a great chief, and he died with honor. You are young, Bright Cloud. But you are also wise. You have brought the buffalo back. You are now a chief for us too, one with great power. We will live as you lead," Standing Bear proclaimed. The others nodded in agreement.

Bright Cloud looked at them silently for a longtime before saying, "I say the buffalo returned to tell us that our ways of fighting and war are wrong. We must live in peace with all things. As the buffalo live, we will live. Where the buffalo go, we will go. We must choose life as they have chosen life," Bright Cloud instructed.

Arthur fell back from the orb as if a sudden gust of wind had knocked him completely off balance. He landed hard on the floor, sliding to a stop right in front of George.

"Were you here with me the whole time? Did you see that?"

"Yes, Art, I was right here the whole time."

"I think I'd like to do that again," Arthur offered.

"Possibly, later if we have time," George answered.

"It all seemed so real to me. It felt like I was right there living it, the whole time."

"You were right there, Art. The laws of time and space, as you know them, have no bearing here whatsoever. Remember, you can create anything you want here just as long as it's for good."

"Did I really live back then, George? I mean, was it really like that?"

"Yes, that lifetime was exactly like what you just experienced.

It was one of your past lives that taught an important lesson."

"What kind of lesson?"

"Well, each one of our lifetimes has the potential to teach us everything we need to know to move onto the next level of our soul's learning, but it is uncommon for anyone to learn all that's needed in only one lifetime. We do, however, have a great deal of say as to what type of life we'll live. The bravest souls often choose a life that is very difficult because the opportunities to learn and progress further are greater. We are not victims of our own life. That is a common illusion. We choose our lives for the growth potential they offer our souls," George explained.

"Why did I choose that life? What was I supposed to learn?" Arthur asked.

"Well, let's see if we can figure this out together. Why don't you start by asking me a question?"

After several moments of silence, George prompted, "Just ask anything, Art. It doesn't have to be anything fancy. Whatever pops into your head."

"Let me think...Why did I want to be an Indian?"

"It wasn't that you chose to be a Native American as much as you chose a life that would teach your soul the lesson it was asking to learn."

"What did my soul want to learn that was so important?" Arthur asked.

"Your soul may have wanted to learn how to overcome fear. That's a good lesson for many of us," George replied.

"I was scared to death during that lifetime. I really don't think I learned anything."

"As Bright Cloud, you were given a lifetime when you were forced to face the possible end of your life, and even the extinction of your people. You did not give into that fear, but instead you drew on the lessons learned by your soul in earlier lifetimes. You chose the path of love and peace on purpose, and you rejected fear. This was a leap forward for your soul, Art. It's wonderful really. You faced your own destruction with love, and as a result, you learned that you are truly indestructible! You have done marvelously, Arthur."

"I have?" Arthur asked, scratching his head.

"Yes, you have."

"Then, why don't I feel like I know all of this?" he asked, puzzled.

"The understanding has happened at the soul level, and somehow you think you are separate from your soul," George said.

"I do?"

George hid the smile that was growing on his face, amused by his young friend's awkward attempt to understand.

"Yes, you do!" George said laughing, "Otherwise, you would not be asking these questions."

"Why are you laughing? What's so funny?" Arthur asked.

"I'm just having fun, Art, and I'm happy you're here, that's all. Have you thought of your next question yet?"

"Yes, where is my soul?" Arthur asked.

"Where are you?" George responded.

"I'm right here. You know that."

"That's where your soul is."

Arthur looked down around at his feet, and he stared into his hands, looking for some sign of his soul, and said, "I can't see it, George, are you sure I have one?

"Oh, I'm sure," George answered with a light-filled laugh. "Art?"

"Yes, George?"

"Your soul just answered me," George said.

"It did?"

"Art, look over there in the back of the room."

Arthur looked around and shrugged his shoulders.

"Your soul just looked toward the back of the room."

"George, are you trying to tell me that my soul and I – are the same thing?"

"Yes, thank you! That is exactly what I'm telling you."

"Is that why you tell me that I can create all of those fantastic things? Is it my soul that can create them?" Arthur asked.

"You are a child of God. You are a soul made from creation, however, on Earth, you are human. All those parts of you are one in the same. You can make all kinds of fabulous things happen because God gave you the gift to create from love."

"Okay. I think I understand now. It kind of makes you feel a little bit funny knowing you're so special doesn't it, George?"

"I guess it does, but you'll get used to it," he replied with a wink, and added, "The orb was trying to teach you that you must learn to trust the love that is always within you. The spark of love inside you is the greatest gift. It will always connect you to the Great Spirit whenever and wherever you are."

Arthur smiled, and nodded his head in agreement. He felt awestruck by George's wisdom and he was beginning to get a sense of what his old friend was attempting to pass on.

"Would it be alright if I tried another one?"

"No, I don't think so, Art. We really don't have much time to spare."

"Please, George, it won't take long. I'll pick a real fast one."

"Come on, let's go. We can't stay here any longer. We need to get going now," George said as he quickly moved toward the outer hall.

Arthur hesitated, and then stopped. Gazing into the mesmerizing light of the orbs he wondered what adventures the powerful orbs might bring to him now. Would he be pirate sailing the seas, or would he be an early explorer discovering new worlds in exotic places? With trembling anticipation, he stood in front of the orbs waiting for some hint as to which one he should choose. A small green one to his left caught his attention. When he gazed at it, the orb mysteriously responded by starting to pulsate and spin. It began to slowly expand in both size and intensity. As he stepped directly under the swirling orb, it illuminated a small corner of a lifetime that made him smile.

Cool sea foam splashed over Arthur's back as he happily rolled in the remnants of ocean waves. The rhythmic roar of the crashing waves filled his ears and the hot sun warmed his tiny body as he crawled like a sea crab along the wet sand. During his first experience at the ocean, he was discovering a new world of sun, sand, and shells. He felt happy and safe as he turned his head to watch his brothers and sister play in the shining dry sand only a few feet away. His mother and father sat nearby on old wooden chairs by the edge of the water, swooshing their feet through the warm shallow sea.

"How you doing there, Art?" his father asked with a broad smile, puffing on a fat cigar.

"I'm having fun, Papa!"

"That's good, Art, you have fun. Later on, I'll take you out into the waves. You will like that too."

"Archie, he's too young to go out in those waves. I don't want you to take him," his mother protested.

"It will be fine, don't worry. I'll have a hold on him the whole time. Nothing will happen."

"Oh, Arthur, look at this shell. It's perfect," his mother said, holding a blue-colored shell once home to a bay scallop. Arthur smiled broadly as he reached out to touch it. He stumbled backward, falling into the water, laughing.

"We're going to keep this one. We'll keep it on top of your dresser at home. How does that sound?" his mother said.

"Yeah – I want it to keep!" Arthur replied, rolling onto his pudgy stomach in the warm, wet sand.

Archie stood up, and he walked along the sand and through the scattered beach stones toward the concession stands. The oceanfront boardwalk was alive with the bells, clicks, and whistles of the distant penny arcade. His senses were filled with the smell of hot dogs grilling and cotton candy spinning. Spotting the man he had seen earlier who rented the small boats and floats to beach-goers, he walked straight toward him. For a dime, he rented two inner-tubes. One steadily under each arm, Archie was lured back by the call of crashing waves. He weaved in and around the Sunday afternoon bathers sprawled on blankets and towels soaking up the hot sun.

"Art, look here! See what I have for you," his father said as he approached.

Arthur squinted into the bright sunshine to see the unmistakable outline of his father as he tossed two large black objects up into the air one right after the other. Arthur watched, fascinated. The black circles spun through the air, and landed on the water with a giant splash. Startled by the sudden spray of cold water, he jumped up yelling, "Papa, no!" The inner tubes spun right toward Arthur in the shallow water; he reached out to touch the rubber with timid curiosity.

"Archie, I told you he's too young for that. I don't want you to scare him. I don't think he should go on those tubes. He can't even swim," his mother admonished.

"I can swim, Mama. Can I take one out?" young Alice asked.

"I suppose, but just a little way. Don't go out too far. Those waves are too big for you too. I don't think you should take Arthur out there, Archie, it will scare him."

"He'll be just fine. I'm only going to pull him around a little bit. Art, do you want to go for a ride?"

"Yes, Papa," Arthur said, climbing onto the side of the tube, tipping it into the air. He landed back into the shallow water with a splash.

"Hey, not that way!" his father said, laughing.

"Here, lay across the tube on your stomach, just like this–"

Arthur balanced himself on top of the floating tube, and became perfectly still as he looked down through the water at the sunlight dancing on the ocean floor below. An incoming wave made the tube rise swiftly up into the air, which startled him. He grabbed tightly onto the sides of the tube and yelled out, afraid of tumbling off into the white bubbling foam below.

"Let's head out a little further so we can have some fun," his father said.

He held on tightly to both sides of the tube nodding his head in agreement. His father grabbed the short rope attached to the tube, and pulled him slowly out into deeper water. Arthur watched as the ocean floor disappeared into the darkness. As they slipped away from shore, he braced himself like a wooden stick figure with both hands and feet clinging tightly to edges of the tube. He became more and more frightened with each step his father took. The incoming waves changed from gentle ripples to large rolling swells. His father saw Arthur's eyes widening with terror, and he stopped pulling the tube.

"Art, how are you doing there?"

Arthur was lying motionless across the tube, staring blindly into the ink black water below. He said nothing, but his bottom lip was trembling.

"Hey, Art, everything's okay. There's nothing to worry about."

"Papa, I don't like this. I want to go back. Take me back."

"Okay, Art, we can go back if you want, but there really is nothing to worry about.

I'm here, and I would never let anything happen to you."

"No, Papa, I don't like this. It's sc-scary," Arthur stuttered, and his eyes began to fill with tears.

"I know you can't swim, Art, but that's okay. I'm here. It's okay to be scared too. Everybody gets scared sometimes. It's what you do when you're scared that matters," his father answered.

Arthur rubbed his nose along the wet rubber as he turned his head to look at his father, and mumbled, "What, Papa?"

"You can't let fear win. You can never let being scared win, Art. If you do, it will run your life forever. It's when you do something that's scary, no matter how you feel, that's how you get courage."

With a mounting sense of dread, Arthur struggled to hear his father through the loud roar of the crashing waves.

"I don't like it, Papa. Take me back."

"Do you love me?" Papa asked.

"Yes," Arthur said, completely motionless on the tube.

"You know I would never let anything happen to you?"

"I know, Papa."

"Do you want to be afraid? And let the fear win?"

"Yes!" Arthur yelled back, his fingertips digging into the black rubber.

"Yes?" Papa laughed, and gently patted Arthur's arm.

Arthur looked up at his father to scold him. "Stop laughing, Papa. Stop it!"

"Okay, I'll stop, but you sure are a hot ticket, mister. I'll head in now if you want. Your mother is waiting on the beach for you with a towel."

Arthur looked up to see his big sister Alice, with a wide smile in her pink and white bathing suit, rush by riding a wave on the other inner tube.

"Hey, come on, Arthur, it's really fun!" she yelled out as she rumbled on by.

Arthur watched Alice ride the wave safely to shore, releasing her into a soft white blanket of sea foam, and onto the wet sand. Jumping up with delight, she started running back out into the waves again.

"Art, are you sure you want to go in?" his father asked.

Grappling with his fear, he looked over at Alice as she headed back out into the waves.

"No, Papa, take me for another ride."

His father grabbed the rope securely in his hand, and proudly pulled his son out into the roaring surf. Arthur could not believe the size of the waves as they crashed in front of him. They towered around his inner tube like raging mountains of blue, toppling over on top of themselves into torrents of white. Arthur was starting to think he had made a big mistake to go back out there, when his father stopped pulling the tube.

"Okay, Art, this is the place. Get ready!"

"No, Papa, wait! Did Alice go out this far?" Arthur asked.

"I don't know, but I know you're afraid. Trust me! Everything will be fine. There's nothing to worry about," he shouted over the roar of the crashing waves.

"Hold on, Art, here comes a good one."

Before Arthur could utter another word, the curling arm of a giant wave lifted his tube up, and he gripped the sides with steady determination. The wave swiftly propelled him toward shore on the churning mass of sea spray and white bubbles. Looking to the shore ahead, he saw his sister happily jumping up into the air, waving and smiling at him. The nervous excitement of trying something new made Arthur start to nervously giggle. As he laughed, almost without realizing it, Arthur began to feel like everything was going to be okay somehow. Seeing his father standing nearby gave him the confidence to brace himself steadily against the tube. He started to feel safe as he let go of what held him back seconds ago, and he was pulled into the thrill of the exhilarating adventure. He rode the wave with his chin held high, feeling like a champion, and knowing that he would make it to shore just like his sister had done.

The wave broke into a tumble of sand, broken shells, and sea foam that delivered him to the waiting feet of his mother. She picked him up off the tube, and asked, "Arthur, are you okay? My little baby boy, don't be frightened, I'm right here."

"Mama, I did it! I wasn't scared. It was fun!" he exclaimed.

"You weren't even scared a little bit?" his mother asked.

"Not really, maybe a tiny bit, but I did it anyway." Arthur said proudly.

"You sure did!" she said

"There's nothing to be scared of, Mom, it was fun!" Arthur added.

Arthur slowly stepped away from the orb. The outline of his silhouette shimmered with a greenish hue like a powerful aura lingering from the orb that then quickly faded. He lowered his head, blinking, and felt a strange sadness that he realized was a deep longing for his family. He stood motionless as he remembered the sound of the waves and the happiness of being a young boy playing at the beach. He missed his family. Tender thoughts of Alice and his two brothers rippled gently at the edge of his memory. Arthur looked over to see George standing nearby like a caring parent. He felt gratitude for everything his guardian angel had ever done for him. He knew by the look in George's eyes that he understood what Arthur was feeling.

"Art, are you all right?"

"Sure, George, I am. I just feel a little sad, that's all. Everyone is gone now."

"Don't worry, Art, no one is ever really gone. Besides, something tells me you'll be seeing everyone again."

Chapter 7

Joe Robinson's Garden

George moved swiftly toward the inner courtyard of the heavenly sanctuary, his robes sweeping behind him. The magnificent doors of the hall of review swung wide open as George approached them to reveal a spectacular courtyard ahead.

"Okay wait for me," Arthur yelled, chasing after him.

Arthur tried to keep up with George's quickening pace as he gazed into the courtyard floating high among the spires of light. There were waterfalls made of rainbows and tender white flowers that shimmered and smelled of jasmine. Arthur wanted to linger in the sweetness. He paused.

"Hey, George, what's the hurry? Can't we stop here for a while to just sit?"

"There's no time to waste right now. We must hurry," George replied.

"Can't we just stop to sit down for a minute? I like it here. Come on, will you just slow down? George, we're in Heaven. What's the big rush?"

"Arthur, everything will become clear to you soon enough," George explained.

"Where are we going?"

"We're going right here," George said as he turned to walk through an arbor gate leading to an elegant English garden.

"What's the rush all about, George? What's so important about this place here?" Arthur said.

Just past the walkways made of polished stone was a small, yet finer, garden. Swirling rows of tiny white flowers encircled spectacular pink roses that glowed with an indescribable vibrancy.

"Well, Mr. Arthur A. Chambers, could that be you?"

A vaguely familiar voice called out from behind a bush. Velvety leaves and tiny purple flowers seemed to wiggle and grow as Arthur gazed at them, wondering who had addressed him. A young man stepped out, smiling.

"Who's that?" Arthur asked.

"Don't you remember me?" the man asked.

Arthur guessed he was in his twenties or early thirties as he stood in front of him knocking some dirt off his garden gloves.

Arthur peered into his face, puzzled a bit, trying to place him, and slowly offered, "I think, I, hmm, yes, now I do remember you. Aren't you the man from the hospital? Are you Mr. Robinson? Joe Robinson, I think?"

"Yes, that's right, Arthur. I certainly am. I know we only met briefly, but I wanted to see you while you were still here."

"Sure, of course, nice to see you again. This is really a great garden you have here," Arthur offered.

"Thank you, Arthur. I'm happy you like it. I'm getting it ready for my dear Betty, he sighed, "She loves gardens. I thought it would make her happy if I could plant these flowers, especially the roses, for her before she arrives here."

"Who is she?" Arthur asked.

"Betty is my wife, and –"

George interrupted the conversation, saying "Art, there's something you need to know."

Arthur saw the serious look on George's face, and knew that he didn't have good news.

"What's the matter?"

"Art, I'm not sure how to say this to you, but you have to go back."

"I have to go back where, George?"

"You're being called back to your earthy life."

"I'm being called back to what?" Arthur asked.

"You are being asked to return to your life on Earth, your life with Alice and Charlie in Boston," George replied.

Arthur stood in stunned silence as he stared at George and Joe in disbelief. He shook his head, stepping back.

"But I don't want to go back there, George. I like it here! I won't go back!" Arthur declared.

"I'm afraid it's already been decided. You have to go back. I'm sorry, Art," George said, lightly touching his shoulder.

"Why?"

"Because you still have work to do, Art," George replied.

"Why can't I stay and do the work here?"

"I know it's hard to understand, Art. The real work you do is back there. Your heart knows what you need. And your soul has its path. Who you are deep down inside, meaning your soul, does not move forward in the most important ways while here in Heaven. Your soul can only grow and evolve while you are back on Earth. Trust what I'm saying, Art, your soul has work it must finish. This work requires that you return to your most recent earthly life."

"What work?" Arthur asked, crossing his arms.

"It's your work. It's the work of Art," George said softly smiling.

Arthur didn't want to hear any of this. He looked around at the garden admiring its perfect design, and he could feel Joe's deep love for Betty. He wondered why he felt such a connection to Joe. Maybe he knew him before the hospital. Maybe Joe would help convince George he could stay.

"Joe, please tell George that I want to stay here – in this place. Tell him not to make me go back."

Joe looked into Arthur's eyes. He could sense that Joe also felt a sense of connection to him too, but he knew there was nothing Joe could do to change the course of events.

"Arthur, before you go back I would like to ask you for a favor," Joe asked.

"Sure, Joe, anything you want. But I'm not going anywhere,"

Arthur said, looking intently at George. How could George send him back? This all seemed so unfair.

"I want you to say hello to Betty for me. Please tell her I love her, and that there's nothing for her to worry about. Tell her I said that you should be in 'the club'. Tell her this, please," Joe instructed.

"In the club? I don't understand. What club?"

"If Betty liked a person, well then, she would put them in her club of friends. After a while, everyone we knew moved away or died, and in the end it was just the two of us in the club. Tell her this, she'll understand. Oh, and one more thing – Tell her that I'm sorry I broke her green lamp, too, I didn't mean to upset her."

Chapter 8

The Return

Like pink sand slipping through his fingers grain by grain, Arthur's heavenly body began to dissolve. The tighter he tried to hold onto the grist of his soul, the faster it was swept up into the swirling light around him. As the magnificence of Heaven began to dim, Arthur sadly watched Joe and George fade and completely disappear from his view. With a great quake of his soul, the sharp, cold slap of earthly reality crashed in upon Arthur. He instantly found himself back in his physical body where he could not breathe and his heart could not beat. He lay on a metal table, imprisoned. In the operating room again, he felt the heavy force of gravity pressing down upon his cold body. He felt like his soul was trapped within a human coffin made of muscle and bone. Laying still in isolating darkness, he felt the divine life force tingle and awaken within him. Then, a numb feeling like sleep was quickly disturbed by lightening jolts of pain. He awoke to an annoying high-pitched buzzing sensation that raced down from the top of his head and shot like a razor right through to the tips of his toes. Arthur felt the rhythmic pounding in his ears as his heart began to beat. His lungs filled with gasps of cool, moist air.

"Doctor, I think he's coming back! His heart is beating and he's starting to breath," the nurse shouted.

"This is one for the books! I was just about ready to give up on him. Holy Mother of God! I cannot believe this. He's coming back!" Dr. Ingram exclaimed as he stopped massaging his heart.

"Let's close him up. He's going to have one hell of a headache when he wakes up. I should say if he wakes up. Nurse, monitor him closely while I finish positioning the metal plate in his skull," he instructed.

"Doctor, his blood pressure is rising 85/60, and pulse is 45 beats per minute," the nurse noted.

"Are you sure?"

"Yes, and it's still rising, doctor."

"Well, Mr. Chambers, you surely are an amazing young man. I guess it just wasn't your time to go. I really can't explain it any other way. He was gone for a full three minutes. You don't just come back in from that like nothing happened," Dr. Ingram said.

"Yes, doctor, I've never seen anything like it myself. Look at his face. He looks so peaceful," the nurse replied.

"I've seen some strange things, but this is beyond me."

Betty Robinson felt a quiet tug inside herself as she noticed the gold lettering on the glass panel of the door labeled "Hospital Records and Billing".

"I know this must have been what Joe had in mind when he asked me to help that young boy," she said out loud as her shoes struck the hard tile floor with a deliberate cadence.

"It's all I can think to do," she muttered.

She paused momentarily in front of the billing office. The doorknob felt oddly warm as she opened the door and walked into the hospital office.

"May I help you, ma'am?" a man asked from behind the office counter.

"Yes, my name is Mrs. Robinson and I would like to arrange for the payment of all hospital fees associated with the care and treatment of a young patient. His name is Arthur A. Chambers."

"Yes, Mrs. Robinson. Why does your name sound so familiar? I know why! I just had your file out in front of me as well. Yes, it's right here," the clerk said, reaching for the file.

"Yes, your husband Joseph Robinson was being treated here at the hospital and when all his treatment records come through the billing office, we will be sending a copy of the bill to 183

Grampian Way in Dorchester. Is that correct?" he asked.

"Yes, that is correct, but that's not why I'm here. I want to arrange to pay the hospital bills for Arthur A. Chambers, too."

"You want to pay the hospital bills for another patient?"

"Yes, that's correct. I would like all the hospital bills for Arthur Chambers to be sent to me at 183 Grampian Way, as well. I will be paying his hospital charges," Betty instructed.

"Arthur Chambers, let me see. Ah yes, the file is right here. He was admitted earlier this evening. Nothing has come through on him yet. Are you a family member?"

"No, I'm just a friend of the family. Is there a problem?" she asked.

"No, ma'am, not at all, it's just a little unusual and very generous, I must say. I'll have to prepare some paperwork for you to sign, but other than that, no, not a problem at all."

"That's good. Please send me the paperwork and I'll pay the bill promptly," she replied, and quickly left the office.

Dr. Ingram left the operating room thinking about the phone call he had received earlier that evening informing him that his youngest brother Bill had gotten into a car accident with his brand new car. He knew he shouldn't have let him borrow the car. He was too inexperienced a driver to be driving alone at night. The police officer reporting the accident told him that no one was hurt or injured except that a city telephone pole was knocked over when Bill clipped it with the car. Relieved that no one was hurt, the doctor was also upset with himself that he let his personal problems enter the operating room. He had let the news of the car accident distract him during the child's operation. "I almost lost that boy tonight. I need to be more disciplined," Dr. Ingram thought as he quickly made his way down the hospital corridor.

Over the years, he had learned not to question why one patient lived and another didn't, but he was glad to be able to tell the boy's family that their brother had survived the difficult operation. Alice and Charlie fidgeted nervously. Arthur had been in the operating room for over three hours, and they had watched as time slowly ticked by on the waiting room clock. Alice was the first to notice the doctor turn the corner into the waiting room, and she grabbed onto the sleeve of Charlie's coat anxiously.

"Charlie, it's the doctor!"

Dr. Ingram had the cautious look of someone who had just narrowly escaped the quick hand of fate, but said confidently, "I have positive news for you. Your brother has survived the initial operation and his vital signs are strong. It's going to be a wait-and- see game from here on. The next twenty-four hours are the most critical for him, but he's a very strong young boy, and I am cautiously optimistic that he is going to pull through for us."

"Charlie, that doesn't sound so good to me," Alice said as her grip on his arm tightened.

"Your brother has suffered a very serious head injury requiring extensive repair and reconstruction. A metal plate was grafted into his skull to replace a section that was lost through the injury," Dr. Ingram continued.

"Doctor, is Arthur going to be alright?" Alice asked.

"With head injuries of this severity you can never be certain how the recovery will go. For example, he may wake up soon with a very bad headache and require only a minimal amount of recuperation and rehabilitation. On the other hand, there could be brain damage to deal with," the doctor explained.

"What kind of damage do you mean?" Charlie asked.

"It could mean many different things, Mr. Chambers. Anything from a sore head and some degree of memory loss to a more severe situation."

"Like what?" Charlie asked.

"Perhaps a coma," Dr. Ingram responded.

"Do you mean a coma in that he doesn't wake up?"

"Yes, that is a worst case possibility, but I want to reassure you that I am optimistic that the outcome will be in Arthur's favor.

Like I said, he is a strong boy and he has already exhibited some amazing recuperative abilities," Dr. Ingram explained.

"When can we see him?" Alice asked.

"We should let him rest for awhile, and then I'll have the nurse come by, and she'll bring you to his room. You will only be able to visit for a short time. He'll be unconscious and won't be able to see or hear you. So please, don't become alarmed by that. It's a normal part of the recovery process. I'll keep you informed of any changes in his condition," Dr. Ingram said.

Charlie reached out to shake the doctor's hand to thank him.

"We'll do everything we can for him," the doctor replied.

Chapter 9

Betty's Ice Cream Palace

The taxi ride back from the hospital was mercifully short. The cab driver talked for the entire duration of the two-mile trip about his four beautiful children and how wonderfully special they all were. Betty was polite and pretended to listen, but she felt annoyed by his unfettered happiness and lively talk of all the people that filled his life. Still chattering, he pulled up to the driveway and exclaimed, "That's a long walk to the front door, lady."

"Yes, and it seems to get longer every year," she mumbled as she paid the cab fair.

As the taxi sped away, she stood alone on the sidewalk looking over a stately row of lilac bushes that had just shed their leaves. Like sentinels, they guarded the house against the onset of winter. The driveway curved up to a distinctive two-story house with elegant French windows and a graceful wrap-around porch. An arched greenhouse glowed eerily in the filtered moonlight in the adjacent yard. Betty slowly struggled up the steep grade of the walkway and paused, gazing up at the darkness of her empty home. The full moon cast its ghostly light through the branches of elm trees, creating an endless web of shadows over the house. For the first time, Betty felt her mournful longing give way to an unbearable loneliness that penetrated deep into her heart. Everything that happened at the hospital now seemed a blur as she was overcome with the sudden avalanche of emotions. Over the past few years, there had been times when only a whisper of what she now felt would call to her – making her tremble with fear. In bed at night, she used to stare at the ceiling with an unblinking gaze, afraid of how old both Joe and she were becoming, and she couldn't imagine what she would ever do without him next to her.

The porch stairs moaned in grief with each step she took, as her memories of their life together swirled around her. She remembered when they were first married, and they would walk by this house, and she'd say, "That's the house I want to live in, Joe. Just look at it. That house was made just for us." Joe would always smile back lovingly and say, "Maybe someday, Betty, maybe someday." Then one day, Joe came home from work, and never said a word about it being Betty's birthday. Instead he said, "Let's go for a walk along the beach and go get some ice cream." When they walked by the house on the way to the beach, Betty looked up ahead to see the sign hanging on the driveway gate with "Betty's Ice Cream Palace," scribbled in pencil and a big arrow pointing up to the house. Betty looked at Joe in total disbelief as he announced with a broad grin, "Happy Birthday, Betty!" She had adored the house with its bright sunny rooms, and windows that reached all the way from the floor to the ceiling. Later, she would make candlelight dinners for Joe each night because he had once read a line of a poem to her that said, "On the gentle glow of candlelight her beauty came to me." She thought of the many joyful hours she spent in her beloved garden on the hill by the side of the house. She used to sit on the front porch in the afternoon feeling the crisp ocean breeze cool the baking heat from a long summer day.

The hinges creaked on the oak door as it swung open into the darkness of a Victorian foyer that led down a hallway lined with memories of her life with Joe. The rooms beyond seemed to echo with the emptiness of a future without him. The cold house radiated a dark loneliness that made Betty search for the comfort of her overstuffed Victorian chair by the fireplace. She sank deep into the soft tapestry feeling the security of its tall, straight back and the protection of its padded wings. Buried in sadness, Betty sat directly across from Joe's empty chair with the worn footrest.

What began as a subtle trembling became molten fear that surged up from deep within her and cascaded back down upon a bottomless mountain of grief. Betty got up to light a single candle, and placed it next to Joe's picture on the mantel with tears in her sad brown eyes. The flame meant to comfort her couldn't chase the terrible grief from her heart. She was heartbroken. The love of her life was gone. She knew that nothing could change this hard fact as she swooned with waves of panic.

In the weeks ahead, the lethal combination of fear and grief growing within her would escalate to such a degree that a knock on the door or a ring on her phone would send bolts of terror through her body. She would avoid the discomfort of looking at her melancholy image in the mirror. Her grief would come to devour her. She would wander aimlessly through the empty house in search of Joe in the days ahead. Betty would feel she was disappearing into a mere wisp of the woman she had once been. The last thread of her sanity would be pulled from her by a terrible force destined to turn the rest of her life into nothing but fleeting images and shadows of her sad nightmares.

Chapter 10

A Short Visit

The nurse appeared out of nowhere, standing in front of them like a starched-white angel wearing a winged hat. She looked like an apparition to Charlie who opened his tired eyes widely when she announced, "Hello, I'm Nurse Flynn. Dr. Ingram has instructed me to bring the three of you in to see Arthur for a short visit. You'll only be able to stay for a minute or two. Dr. Ingram feels it's important for you to see him now so Arthur can start to receive some familiar external stimuli."

"Excuse me, nurse, but I'm not sure we understand what you mean," Charlie said.

"The doctor would like you to talk to your brother even though he can't hear or respond to you," the nurse replied.

"You mean if we talk to him maybe that will help him wake up?" Alice asked.

"Yes, that's right, miss. It may help him to sense familiar people around him," the nurse responded.

"Okay, if everyone is ready, I'll take all of you over to intensive care where Arthur is recovering," she continued.

"Yes, we're all ready, thank you. Let's go," Charlie nervously replied, getting out of his chair.

Alice whispered into Charlie's ear, "Is intensive care a bad place?"

"No, I don't think so. I'm pretty sure it's where everyone goes after they have an operation."

Alice silently nodded her head in understanding as they entered the area of the hospital where Arthur was recuperating. Alice squinted from the incandescent lights of the room, anxiously looking for her brother. The ward was a jumble of frantic activity as doctors and nurses busily attended to an emergency situation near the back of the room. Alice's heart sank to the tiled floor as she watched the nurse lead them in the direction of the medical crisis. Her eyes frantically scanned each of the rows of hospital beds with tall white railings looking for her brother. Dread grew within her as she walked past each of the beds. She did not let her gaze rest upon the ill strangers she passed, knowing somehow that it was wrong of her to look directly at them. She felt relieved when the nurse turned around and told them, "Arthur is right over here behind this column."

Alice peered around the wide column as tears welled up in her eyes. Arthur had two black eyes surrounded by a red swollen face, and his head was twice its normal size. Charlie and Tommy stared in dead silence while Alice gasped in horror.

The thick bandage wrapped around his head made him look like some kind of exaggerated cartoon caricature out of the funny papers. Charlie made a dim attempt at humor, "Looks like he won't be wearing his old scaly cap for a while."

"Yeah, I don't think they make one big enough to fit on that head," Tommy said with a nervous laugh.

"Stop it, both of you! Can't you see that he's badly hurt? I don't think you two should be making fun of him," Alice reprimanded.

A chill ran down the back of her neck when she touched Arthur's cool hand. Alice's mind floated back to the snowy track as her brother lay dying in her arms hours before. She had promised him that everything would be all right. As she had listened to his shallow breathing and felt the coldness of his hands, she feared the worst. She had been petrified that her young brother wouldn't make it.

"Nurse Flynn, I think he needs the doctor. He feels cold," Alice said, trembling.

"All his life signs are stable right now, dear. The doctor will be by on his rounds in a few minutes. I think it would be a good idea if all of you would try to talk to Arthur as the doctor suggested," she requested.

"Hi, Art, how you doing?" Tommy blurted out.

"Tommy, that was stupid. Can't you think of anything else to say?" Alice said.

"Art, this is your brother Charlie, here. We're all here, Alice and Tommy too. It's going to be okay. You got hit on the head pretty good there, but the doc fixed you up. You won't be here long, Art. We'll bring you home soon," Charlie said.

Alice stood next to Arthur trying to warm his hands between hers and said softly, "We love you, Arthur, and we want you to come back to us. Everything is going to be just fine. You wait and see. Charlie says the new apartment has a kerosene heater on the kitchen stove that you put quarters in to turn it on. Won't that be nice, Arthur? You won't have to look for coal after school anymore."

With tears gathering in her eyes, she searched Arthur's face for a slight quiver or some other sign of consciousness, but he lay completely expressionless on the pillow between the iron sidebars of his hospital bed.

"I promise you everything will be okay. Just please try to get better. All I ask is that you try. Please try, Arthur," Alice begged.

"Okay, I think we should leave and let him rest now. That was just what the doctor wanted. I think all of you did just great. You know it's very possible that he may just be able to hear all of you," the nurse added.

Alice noticed Arthur's bottom lip began to move, "Hey, his lips just moved. He's trying to say something."

"That's probably just an involuntary movement," Nurse Flynn replied.

Alice lowered her ear closer to Arthur and said, "No, I think he's trying to say something."

"Alice, what is it?" Charlie asked.

Alice lifted her head up with a puzzling look and said, "I think he said 'the Club'. Huh? That's weird."

"Why would he say that?" Tommy asked.

"I don't know. Maybe he thinks he got hit in the head with a club?" Charlie wondered.

"He said it as clear as day. He said 'the club'! I know he did," Alice offered.

The nurse motioned with her arms to usher them from the intensive care ward as she said, "Well, whatever he meant, it is an excellent sign, but I really must insist that we all leave now. I think you should head home and get some rest. You all have had a long night here. Arthur will be sleeping for the rest of the night, and I think you all should too."

Chapter 11

The Fantastic Story

Alice quietly placed her dolls to bed in a row, carefully instructing all of them to pray for Arthur's safe return. The house was completely still and the ticking hands on the wind-up clock by her bedside read 2:30am. She had never been up this late before and the silence of the early morning sent shivers down her neck. Their cold-water apartment had a kitchen, living room, and only one bedroom. When they first moved there, Alice had painted the kitchen blue and yellow with cans of half-used paint she had found in the barn at the back of the house. A simple oval table stood next to what was most important to Arthur, the coal stove.

She felt special and also guilty that as the sole girl in the family, she was the only one with a real bedroom to herself. The archway above the door was filled with colored glass. The room just barely fit her wrought-iron bed and the rickety pine table next to it. She had placed a narrow clay vase with a single yellow dandelion on the table to brighten up her room. The closet had a built-in dresser with roomy drawers that led her to imagine a time long ago when the house was stately and elegant, filled with all kinds of fancy things. Alice often sat alone in her room on the late afternoons, watching as the sun moved slowly through the panes of blue, green, and yellow glass painting dancing rainbows on the walls. Watching the colors swirl and give way to shadows, she hoped one of her brothers might bring something home to cook that evening.

The three boys slept in what should have been the living room if they had more space. Two old leaky windows in the room often shook violently in the wind like someone was trying to pull them out by their frames. A small fireplace burned coal to chase the winter frost from the air. It was so cold on most nights that they frequently slept in thick sweaters and even wore woolen hats to keep warm. Arthur would spend a few minutes on the coldest mornings chipping away the ice that built up on the inside of the windows. Ed and Arthur shared the heavy double bed that had belonged to their mother, while Charlie slept on the floor on a pile of blankets until he managed to find a single frame and mattress. They all could have managed to sleep together in the large bed, but Charlie said it gave him bad dreams. No one would ask why, but Arthur knew it was because their mother had died in it.

An hour earlier, upon returning from the hospital Charlie and Alice had found their younger brother Ed fast asleep at the kitchen table waiting for their return. Ed had no knowledge of Arthur's accident, and had no idea why everyone was gone. He was furious when Charlie woke him up from his restless sleep.

"Where has everyone been? I've been worried sick all night," Ed demanded, rubbing the sleep from his eyes.

"We've all been at City Hospital. Art had an accident down on the train tracks and he needed an operation," Charlie replied.

"What kind of operation? Is he all right?" Ed asked.

"The doctor isn't sure yet, but he thinks he's going to pull through okay."

"Pull through okay, what do you mean 'pull through okay'? What happened? Will you please tell me now," Ed asked.

"I'm sorry, Ed. It's been a really long night and I'm tired. He was playing on one of the train cars down on the tracks behind the Sears building. A train ramp came loose and hit him in the head. He was hurt really bad. They had to operate and put a metal plate in his head," Charlie explained.

"Can I go up and see him now?" Ed asked.

"No, it's too late. I think Alice and you should go up to see him after school tomorrow and I'll come by after work. We can all visit with him for a while and then walk home together," Charlie answered.

"I guess there's nothing we can do now, but I wish you had sent someone back here to let me know. I was worried sick."

"It's been a bad night, Ed. Let's try to get some sleep. I think we're all going to have a long day tomorrow."

"Charlie, who found him and how did he get to the hospital?" Ed asked.

"Come on, let's go to bed. I'll tell you before we go to sleep," Charlie promised.

The early light of day slowly crept through Alice's bedroom window as the smell of strong coffee drifted in from the kitchen. Alice was lying awake with her eyes aimlessly following a crack in her bedroom wall that ran from floor to ceiling. It traveled through the old dusty pink Victorian wallpaper like a river winding its way through the elaborate floral pattern that had once looked regal. She often imagined what elegant lady had once slept in this room before the house was broken up into apartments. The sound of dishes clanging in the kitchen alerted her that Charlie was already getting ready for work. She forced her bare feet onto the cold floor, squinting into the harsh light of the kitchen.

"Good morning, Charlie," Alice said, wrapping her kitchen apron around her nightgown.

"What's so good about it?" he replied.

"I don't know? We're going to get to see Arthur today. That's good, Charlie."

"Yes, that is good. I'm just so exhausted from last night."

"How much sleep did we get?" she asked.

"Not much. I stayed awake thinking about Art most of the night."

"Well, no mater how terrible we feel right now, it's not as bad as Arthur feels," Alice added.

"You're right. Thank God Art pulled through," he replied.

"Do you want something to eat?"

"No thanks, Alice, I have to get to work. I'll see you and Ed after work at the hospital," Charlie replied.

"You have to eat something, Charlie. You'll starve to death," she protested.

Charlie smiled, lifting the flap of his wool coat pocket to reveal a blue and white checkered napkin wrapped around a fossilized chunk of French bread.

"Come on, will you? You can't eat just that for breakfast. Let me make you some oatmeal."

"Sorry, I have to get to work. I'll see you at the hospital," Charlie said as he slammed the door and ran down the stairs."

Alice sat down at the kitchen table basking in the warmth that radiated from the coal stove. "Charlie does so many things that go unnoticed," she thought as her eyes roamed through the kitchen. Her eyes rested upon the purple vase on a white painted shelf made from roughly-cut pine. Alice admired the elegant curve of the vase with its luminous glass that flowed up to the round delicate lip. She watched as the morning sun drifted through the kitchen carrying weightless specs of dust on currents of warm air that seemed to dance and drift around the vase. It had belonged to her mother and was now Alice's most cherished possession. The sole decoration in her kitchen, the purple vase seemed to vibrate against the backdrop of the pale yellow wall. Memories of her beloved mother swirled along with the currents of light and dust, and then flashed off the perfect curve of the glass. It comforted her to look at the vase, thinking about her mother. She often felt so lost and helpless. Alice was too young to be so well-versed in the language of loss. She longed for her mother's embrace and the sound of her voice when she would call her name. Her dream-like state was interrupted by her brother Ed as he entered the kitchen with heavy steps.

"Good morning, Sis. Is there anything to eat?"

"The only thing you ever think about is food," Alice replied.

"That's because I'm always hungry."

"I was going to make some oatmeal. Do you want some?"

"Sure thing, that sounds perfect. How did Art seem when you saw him last night?" Ed asked.

"He wasn't really awake when we were there. The nurse said that he couldn't hear or see us, but I think he tried to say something to me just before we left," Alice explained.

"What did he say?"

"It was kind of weird. I don't know what it meant. He said, 'the club.' Does that make any sense to you?" Alice asked.

"The club? Art's not in any clubs. I don't know what that could mean. You said he got hit in the head pretty good. Maybe he's just goofy."

"Maybe," Alice replied.

"It's getting late. We need to get going to school," Ed said.

"Finish your oatmeal first," she instructed, smoothing out her apron.

Ed gulped down the remainder of the thick oatmeal, saying, "Let's meet outside the front door right after school at 2:10pm and we'll walk down to the hospital together."

"Okay, that sounds good. I'll meet you then."

The school day seemed to drag on forever. The classroom clock slowly moved toward two o'clock. Alice's last class of the day was ending and she wondered if feeling unsettled about returning to the hospital to visit Arthur made her a bad person. She didn't like the hospital with all its sick people and bad smells, and she didn't want to go back there again. She had been thinking the worst all day, and she was worried that something bad had happened to Arthur while she was gone. Alice's breath quickened and her palms began to sweat at the thought of being told bad news by the doctor. The nightmarish scene had been playing out in her mind all day long. She imagined herself standing alone in the intensive care ward looking at Arthur's empty bed, and a doctor coming by to ask, "Can I help you, young lady?"

"That's my brother's bed. He's supposed to be here."

"Are your parents here with you?" he would ask.

"No, I don't have any," she would answer.

"Oh, I see. Please follow me," the doctor would say, leading her down a long, dark hallway that never ended.

Alice felt she knew that something bad had happened to Arthur. And now, she couldn't shake her growing sense of impending doom. She opened the front door of South Boston High School. Her brother was leaning up against the flagpole underneath the American flag unfurling gently in the wind beneath a gray sky.

"Hey there, Sis, you're right on time!" Ed said.

He looked down at his watch that was several sizes too big for his wrist.

"Hi," Alice said looking down.

Ed believed himself to be the paramount expert on his sister Alice's variable moods, and he could sense something was amiss.

"What's wrong, Alice? You look a little pale. Are you sick?"

"I don't want to go anymore."

"You don't want to go where?"

"To the hospital!" Alice answered.

"Why?"

"Because I know something bad is going to happen and I don't want to go," she explained.

"Alice, we promised Charlie that we would go. He'll be really mad when he gets there and sees that we didn't show up," Ed warned.

"I know."

"Plus, Art's been in that stupid hospital all night and day without anyone to talk to."

"Yeah, I know, Ed."

"Well then, why are we stalling? Art is waiting. Let's go!" Ed said, motioning Alice to walk alongside him.

Alice ran up the endless steps of the hospital with her leather shoes slapping against the hard granite stone. She was trying to outdistance the haunting feeling that something terrible had happened to Arthur. She placed the entire weight of her slight frame against the massive hospital doors as she struggled to get into the lobby. Ed followed her from behind and together they pushed into the frenzied entryway of the City Hospital. Alice quickly remembered the way to the intensive care ward, and she instructed Ed to follow her. She turned the corridor into the ward, marching right past the nurse's station to find her way to what should have been Arthur's bed. Stunned, her heart began to pound while her mind raced in horrifying disbelief. She quickly looked around the ward in a panicked search for Arthur. Sleeping in his bed was a sick old woman.

"Excuse me, ma'am!" Alice said trying to wake up the elderly lady.

"Alice, she's sleeping. Don't wake her!" Ed admonished.

"Ma'am, do you know what happened to my brother, Arthur?" Alice asked as she tugged on her blankets.

"Where's Art?" Ed asked, confused by his sister's behavior.

"He's supposed to be right here by this pole. This is where he was last night when we left him. Why isn't he here?"

"They probably just moved him," Ed said.

"Why would they do that?"

"I don't know. Maybe they moved him so he could look out a window? Calm down, why don't you," Ed said.

"I knew this was going to happen, I just knew it," Alice said as she started to cry.

"I'm sure he's just someplace else in the hospital and he's just fine, Alice. Please don't cry. We'll find him."

Waves of panic surged through her as she visualized what might have happened. Holding onto Ed's arm she tried to catch her breath when from behind a nurse interrupted, "What is the matter here?"

"I came to see my brother and he's not here. He's gone," Alice cried.

"Your brother? What is his name?" the nurse asked.

"Arthur. Arthur Chambers."

"Okay, calm down, young lady, and let me see here," she said, reaching for a clipboard.

"Yes, he's right here, Arthur Chambers. We moved him into a private room this morning. He's in room number 1064 just down the hall. If you'll wait just a minute, I can take you to him myself," she offered.

"Oh, thank you so much. That is very kind of you," Ed said in his most polite manner.

"You're welcome, young man. Just wait here for just a second."

"See, Alice, I told you they just moved him," Ed said as he patted her on the shoulder.

"I know," Alice replied.

Blood rushed back into her cheeks.

Upon entering Room 1064, both Ed and Alice stopped in the doorway stunned by what they saw. Arthur was sitting up in bed with a bandage wrapped around his head, eagerly eating a bowl of green Jell-O.

"Arthur! Oh my God, Arthur! Are you okay?" Alice squealed with uncontrollable glee as she raced to Arthur's side.

"Yeah, I'm okay. I feel fine," he replied.

"I was so scared last night that you wouldn't make it," Alice said as she straightened his blankets and kissed him softly on the cheek.

"Alice, I'm fine, really. The doctor told me I have a metal plate in my head. Isn't that neat, Alice?" Arthur asked, smiling.

"Yeah, that's neat Art, but I think you should try to rest now," Alice said.

She glanced with concern over to the nurse standing behind them.

"Nurse, should he be up like this? I mean, shouldn't he be resting or something?" Alice asked.

"He doesn't seem to want to and let me assure you, we've tried. I must say that he really has the most impressive recuperative powers and he is quite the storyteller," the nurse said with a quick wink and smile at Arthur.

"What do you mean? What kind of stories is he telling now?" Ed asked.

"He's been talking about being able to fly and a seven-foot friend made from light that goes by the name of George. Yes, your brother is a fantastic storyteller. I'll for sure give him that much," she said rolling her eyes.

"I could fly! George is seven feet tall and he is made of light. You're made of light too, but you just don't know it," Arthur said to the nurse standing across the room.

"Oh, I am, am I?" the nurse responded as she continued to laugh.

"Why is he talking like this? What's the matter with him?" Alice whispered to the nurse.

"Yes, don't worry. It's not uncommon for patients that have had a serious head trauma like Arthur has had to find some difficulty adjusting emotionally during recovery. It may be best to just go along with him for a while to let him adjust on his own. It is a little bit unusual though for someone to seemingly have no physical side effects from such a serious head injury, but we can't find anything wrong with him. Quite frankly, I have never seen anything quite like it in my 20 years on the job," the nurse replied.

"I don't care if no one believes me. I know where I was and what I saw," Arthur protested.

"What are you talking about?" Alice asked him.

"Nothing, you won't believe me anyway."

"No, Art, I will, what did you see?"

"You won't laugh?"

"No, of course not, Arthur, tell me. I want to know," Alice pleaded.

"Okay, but this really happened. It really did."

"I know, tell me," she softly encouraged him.

Arthur's eyes brightened as he considered telling Alice and Ed his fantastic story of his visit to Heaven. He took a deep breath, looked at Alice, and began.

"It first started to happen on the railroad tracks after I got hit in the head. It was really weird because I saw myself on the ground, hurt bad, but there was another part of me that kind of bounced out and up into the air. That's the part of me that could fly. I could fly anywhere I wanted just by thinking. For a while, I just floated around the train looking and waiting for Tommy to come fly with me, but he never came out. After that, I wondered what you were doing, Alice, so I flew to the kitchen just like that," Arthur said, snapping his fingers. The hairs on the back of Alice's neck began to tingle as she recalled standing at her kitchen sink worrying about Arthur when she had the premonition that something bad had happened to him.

"I remember trying to touch you, Alice. I must have scared you pretty good because you dropped that big bowl into the sink. I'm sorry I scared you, Alice. I didn't mean to."

"How do you know about that?" Alice asked as she quickly scanned her memory, concluding that no one else knew about the bowl breaking except for her.

Arthur shrugged his shoulders, and replied, "Because I saw it happen, Alice. I was there."

"You weren't there, Arthur, you couldn't be. You were down on those tracks. This is just crazy talk," she said, looking around the room for the nurse.

"I told you that you wouldn't believe me. There's no sense talking about it if no one believes me," Arthur protested.

"I'll be right back," Alice said as she noticed the nurse walk by in the hall.

"Nurse, can I see you for a minute?"

"Yes, miss, what's wrong?" the nurse asked.

"It's Arthur. He's talking really crazy and I don't like it. I'm worried. Are you sure there is nothing wrong with him?"

"What is he saying?"

"He's talking about flying and these weird things he saw," Alice continued.

"He's been talking about that all morning. Just humor him and listen. Let him work through this on his own," the nurse suggested.

"You don't think he has brain damage or something like that, do you?" Alice asked.

"No, we don't think so, but we'll keep a very close eye on him to make sure. Dr. Ingram will be coming by to visit in a little while. You can talk with him about it if you like."

As Alice walked back into the room, Arthur continued, "I met Cindy."

"You met who?" Alice asked.

"Cindy, our old dog. Don't you remember she used to live with us?"

Ed joined the conversation, shrugged his shoulders, and replied, "The only Cindy I ever knew was Dad's dog. Her name was Cindy."

"Well, that can't be who he means. I don't even remember that dog. I was even too young to remember that," Alice added.

Ed rolled his eyes, turned toward Alice, and whispered, "I remember what she looked like. I'll get him on this one."

"Okay, Art, I remember Cindy. She was a big black Labrador retriever, right?" Ed asked, winking at Alice.

"No, she wasn't. She was a pretty dog. She had golden hair with long floppy ears and big brown eyes with these long curved eyelashes that made her look like a person. And she had a wet brown nose," Arthur answered.

"Oh my God, that is exactly what Cindy looked like," Ed said out loud.

"Not exactly the same," Arthur added.

"What do you mean, Art?" Alice asked.

"She was made from light."

"Made from light?" Alice said, puzzled.

"Yes, everything is made from light in Heaven, Alice."

"Oh, so you met Cindy in Heaven?" Alice asked, remembering the nurse's advice to just go along and humor him.

"Yes, when I saw her she was with Mom in a valley of flowers. Dad was there too and they talked to me."

Alice felt the goose bumps on her arms tingle as she listened to Arthur describe his heavenly encounters. She knew that these visions of Arthur's had to be imaginary, yet she found that his stories stirred something within her. She felt thirsty to hear more, even though all of it seemed like pure nonsense.

"What did they say to you?" Alice asked.

"They told me about how things work in Heaven. About how there is never anything for anyone to ever worry about down here," Arthur replied.

"Really?" she responded as she sensed a presence behind her in the room.

"Hello, Alice, and who is your friend?" Dr. Ingram asked as he entered the room.

"He's my brother Ed," Arthur quickly responded.

"I'm pleased to meet you, Ed. I'm Dr. Ingram," he said, laughing at Arthur's rapid response.

"So how is my remarkable patient doing today?" the doctor asked.

"I feel great!"

"That's good, Arthur. I am going to look you over a little bit, and we're going to do some tests to see how great you're doing. Okay, Arthur?"

"Yeah sure, doc, anything you want," Arthur replied.

Chapter 12

A Private Room

Charlie caught the 2:35 p.m. bus from his latest public works job, which was to build stone retaining walls along the Charles River in Cambridge. Just a short bus ride down Massachusetts Avenue to Boston City Hospital, Charlie thought he could easily make it there by 3:00 p.m. He fell back into the hard leather seat at the back of the bus. Exhaust fumes drifted in through the rattling windows, making him feel nauseous, as thoughts of his late mother haunted him. He had promised his mother several days before she had died that he would take care of Arthur if something ever happened to her. Images of her looking up at him from her sickbed flashed through his mind as the bus rumbled down Massachusetts Avenue past rows of Victorian brownstones huddled together like they were trying to keep each other warm against the cold winds of winter. The hospital had felt ominous to Charlie. The building had a heaviness that felt like a prison with cells that many walked into, but few ever left. He felt overmatched by the gloomy circumstances of his life. Approaching the front desk of the hospital, he was worried sick that he would not be able to fulfill the solemn promise made to his dying mother.

"Can I help you?" the desk attendant asked.

"I'm looking for my brother who was admitted last night," Charlie replied.

"The patient's name, please?"

"Arthur A. Chambers."

"Let me see here. Yes, he was moved this morning. He's now in a private room. That's room number 1064," the attendant said as he picked up a ringing phone. Charlie waited impatiently for him to hang up and asked, "A private room? I think there's been a mistake, sir. I didn't ask for a private room."

"He was moved into a private room at the authorization of the person paying the bill," the attendant informed.

"Well, I am the person paying the bill and I did not authorize this. I can't afford a private room," Charlie replied.

"I can tell you right now you're not the person paying Mr. Chambers' hospital bill," the attendant answered with slight smirk.

"And how's that?" Charlie asked.

"Because it's a woman."

"That's not possible. It's a mistake. There is no woman who would pay his bill."

"May I ask what relation you are to the patient?" the attendant asked.

"I'm his oldest brother and legal guardian. My name is Charles Chambers."

"I don't mean to sound impolite, but do you have any proof of that?" the attendant asked.

"Yes, I do," Charlie said as he retrieved the official paper work granting him guardianship of Arthur from his back pocket.

"This is most unusual. Do you know Mrs. Betty Robinson? She, in fact, is the one paying the hospital bill."

"No, I have never heard that name before in my life. That doesn't make any sense at all. Can I see the paper work?" Charlie asked, writing down the mystery woman's name and address.

"Well, I don't know what's going on. I hope someone has an explanation for all this," he continued.

He walked away from the front desk to go find Arthur's new and likely alarmingly expensive private room. He felt the familiar rumble of hunger rise up from his empty stomach as he reached Room 1064. The soft rays of the afternoon sun drifted in through the dusty window casting long shadows across the walls. In stark contrast, the room was filled with the bright sound of laughter as he entered. The sight of Arthur sitting, smiling on his bed chased away the rumbling hunger from his bones. Charlie stood back wide-eyed and astonished to see his happy, energized-looking little brother.

"Well, I'll be a monkey's uncle! Art, you look like a million bucks," Charlie exclaimed.

"I do?" Arthur asked.

"Yes, you do. Just like a million bucks, all green and shiny," Charlie said, laughing.

"Art, I can't believe you're doing so good. Last night you looked like a goner. How's he doing, Dr. Ingram? I mean is he really doing as good as he looks?"

"Yes, Mr. Chambers. As of right now, he is doing quite well. I'm very happy with his progress so far. Everything is going much better than we could expect at this juncture. He's done extraordinarily well on the limited motor and cognitive testing we've been able to do. He appears to be a bright young boy."

"Dr. Ingram, how's your car doing?" Arthur asked.

"What do you mean, Arthur?" Dr. Ingram said, moving closer to the bed.

"I mean your new car that got cracked up. How bad was it?" Arthur asked.

"How do you know? Who told you about my car?" Dr. Ingram inquired.

"No one told me."

"You must have overheard the nurses talking about it, then?" Dr. Ingram said as he saw the nurse shake her head back and forth.

"I didn't hear anyone talk about your car. Just before I went into that tunnel I knew you were upset about it," Arthur responded.

"What tunnel?" Dr. Ingram asked.

"The tunnel of light in the operating room. You were also really upset that I had died," Arthur told him.

Dr. Ingram stood next to Arthur's bed in quiet amazement. He wasn't sure quite what to do or say when he thought to ask, "Arthur, who was it that got into the accident with my car?"

"Oh, your brother."

"And why did I think that you died?" Dr. Ingram asked.

"My heart stopped."

"These are all things that he could conceivably guess at. Like I said, he is a very bright boy," Dr. Ingram explained.

"Yeah, Art, stop talking crazy or they'll never let you out of here," Ed warned, standing behind the doctor.

Arthur fidgeted in his bed and frowned. He was annoyed that no one believed anything he said, when the doctor asked one last question.

"Arthur, is there anything else you remember from the operating room?"

"Yes. You were very upset that you let your personal problems enter the operating room and distract you," Arthur replied.

Dr. Ingram felt his clipboard slip from his fingers as its corner struck the hardwood floor with a sharp clap. The startling sound rattled through the room as the clipboard wobbled to a stop on the hard, varnished floorboards.

"Doctor, he's been talking crazy like this ever since we got here. Is he all right?" Alice asked, as she bent down to retrieve the clipboard for Dr. Ingram.

"Physically, he appears to be doing very well, but I would like to conduct a few more psychological tests just to make sure," Dr. Ingram answered, trying to regain his composure.

"See, Art? You had better learn to keep your mouth shut, or they're going to lock you up," Ed warned.

"No one is going to lock anyone up. Arthur, you just behave yourself and do what the doctor asks," Charlie instructed.

"Sure, Charlie. Anything you say. What do you want to know, doc?" Arthur asked.

"What I have heard of your story is quite fascinating, and I do want you to tell me all about it. However, first I would like to see if a colleague of mine is available to join us tomorrow morning for a little chat. Would that be all right with you, Arthur?" Dr. Ingram asked.

"Sure, doc, is your friend a head doctor like you?

"Yes, in a way he is."

"Mr. Chambers, could I please see you out in the hall for just one moment, please," Dr. Ingram said, motioning to Charlie.

"Is Arthur going to be alright? I mean he's talking kind of crazy right now. Is he okay in the head?" Charlie asked as they entered the hall.

"Right now, Mr. Chambers, your brother is obviously suffering from some delusions, but I do think in good time he will recover fully. The sticky part of this is that we just don't know when that will be. He may snap out of this very soon or it could take some time," Dr. Ingram replied.

"How long is some time?" Charlie asked.

"Well, often it's many months, Mr. Chambers. There really isn't any way to predict the course of his recovery. I'm going to ask the Chief of Psychiatry at the hospital, Dr. Phelps, if he could evaluate Arthur tomorrow. After that, I think we may have a better idea about what we're dealing with."

"Sure, doctor, whatever you suggest."

"There is one other matter that I hope you would be kind enough to help me with," Dr. Ingram added.

Charlie's throat suddenly felt dry as he swallowed fearfully at Dr. Ingram's coming inquisition. The "other matter" could only mean one thing. Grim images of debtor's prison raced through his mind. He thought that the man at the front desk had made a huge mistake. Arthur's hospital bill could not have been paid for by some mysterious woman. He wondered how foolish he must be to think some stranger would be willing to pay Arthur's hospital bills.

"What's that?" Charlie replied in a muffled, raspy voice.

"It's about Arthur's room," Dr. Ingram replied.

"Dr. Ingram, I didn't ask for that private room and I can't afford it. Can we just move Arthur to a cheaper one? I really don't think it's fair to make me pay for a private room that I didn't ask for."

"Mr. Chambers, that's not it at all. From what I understand, the room is completely paid for, including all of Arthur's other hospital charges. I want to ask you if you would be kind enough to allow a young boy named Billy Brown to share the room with Arthur. He is a hospital hardship case with a failing heart, and I thought that he may benefit from staying with Arthur in a quiet room," the doctor explained.

"Oh, yes! Bring him in. We'd be very happy to share the room," Charlie replied, sighing with relief.

Chapter 13

Chief of Psychiatry

"Good morning, Arthur. Boy, it sure is warm in here this morning. Would you like me to open the window a bit so you can get some fresh air in here?" the nurse asked.

"Sure, that sounds good," Arthur answered as he eyed the breakfast cart rolling down the hall past his door.

Arthur looked out the window as the cool air covered everything with shimmering dew that reflected the red glow of the morning sun. Everything outside seemed tinted pinkish-red as Arthur watched an old workhorse pull a rickety rag-cart down the street. He shut his eyes as he listened to the hypnotic sound of the horse's hoofs rhythmically striking the cobblestones. The sights and sounds of the morning drifted through the window, filling Arthur with restless anticipation. He was ravenous as the breakfast cart rolled into his room. When the tray landed in front of him, he hungrily ate the cream of wheat, fresh fruit, and bran muffin. He practically inhaled his breakfast while two hospital attendants finished setting up another bed in the opposite corner of his room.

"Are they bringing someone else in here?" Arthur asked the workers.

"They must be, kid, but I can't say for sure. I just set them up," one of them answered before leaving the room.

An empty wheelchair made an appearance at the threshold to his room pausing momentarily before rolling in.

"Hi, Art, looks like you're traveling in style today," Nurse Flynn said as she pushed the wooden wheelchair next to Arthur's bed.

"Where am I going?" Arthur asked.

"Up to see a real big shot. Yes indeed, Dr. Peter Phelps, Chief of Psychiatry. You must be a very special young man to get to see him so early in the morning. They say he's the most brilliant doctor in the hospital. And the nicest doctor too. Maybe he'll even show you the special telescope he has in the corner of his office. He loves to talk about the solar system with all the patients who go see him," Nurse Flynn replied.

"I don't need that chair. I can walk on my own to see him."

"Sorry, you must comply with hospital rules, Arthur. All patients must ride in a wheelchair. You wouldn't want to get me in trouble, would you?" she asked.

"No, I wouldn't want to do that. It's okay, I can ride."

"That's great. Let me help you into the chair and we'll get going."

"I don't need help. I'm all set," Arthur said dangling his feet off the side of the bed ready to jump.

"Hold your horses, mister. We'll have none of that. Hospital rules say I have to help you into the chair."

"Gee whiz, there sure are a lot of rules around here."

"I can't argue with you on that," Nurse Flynn replied.

The two wooden wheelchairs almost collided in the doorway when Arthur was pushed out into the hallway.

"Hey, watch out!" Arthur shouted as they just barely avoided a head-on collision.

"I'm so sorry. It's my fault. I should look where I'm going," the young nurse's aide said, pushing the wheelchair off to the side.

"That's okay. No damage done," Nurse Flynn interjected.

Sitting in the wheelchair across from him was a boy a couple years younger wrapped up to his neck in olive green hospital blankets. He had jet black hair surrounding the palest face Arthur had ever seen. The boy peered out over the top of the green blankets just staring blankly ahead.

"Is this my new roommate?" Arthur asked.

"Yes, it is. This is Billy Brown and he'll be staying with you for awhile," the nurse's aide said.

"Hi, I'm Art Chambers," Arthur said with a short wave of his hand.

"Thanks for sharing your room with me," Billy weakly whispered over the top of the blanket.

"No problem. It was getting kind of lonely in there. I'll be back later. I have to go to meet with the chief of the hospital now."

Arthur rolled up to the massive oak door with its frosted glass panel bearing the name of Dr. Peter W. Phelps, Chief Psychiatrist, Boston City Hospital in gold block letters.

"Is this the place?" Arthur asked.

"We're here!" Nurse Flynn replied.

Arthur pushed the office door open and said, "Wow! This place is sure a lot bigger than Iron Finger's office."

"Iron Finger? Who's Iron Finger?" the nurse asked.

"He's the principal at my school."

"That's an odd name. Why do you call him that?"

"It's a long story. I'll have to tell you later."

The door to Dr. Phelps' office swung wide open. Standing framed by the doorway stood a tall man with thinning brown hair, kind blue eyes, wearing a charcoal gray tweed jacket and a olive paisley bowtie that made him look like he should be working behind the ivy walls of academia rather than an inner-city hospital.

"Well, Mr. Chambers, do please come right in. Thank you, nurse, for bringing him up. My secretary will call you when Arthur is ready to return to his room. I know you are already good friends with Dr. Ingram here. May I call you Arthur, young man?" Dr. Phelps asked.

"Sure, that's okay. So – is that your telescope by the window?" Arthur asked.

"Yes it is. Have you ever looked through a telescope before?"

"I've heard about them, but I've never actually seen one up

close before. What can you see with it?"

"Well, at night, you can see planets and stars."

"Can you see as far as Heaven with it?" Arthur asked.

"I don't think I have ever been able to see quite that far, Arthur," Dr. Phelps replied.

"How far away is Heaven?" Arthur asked.

Dr. Phelps peered over his narrow reading glasses, and said, "That's a most interesting question. And, tell me, why do you want to know about this?"

"Because when I was there, it didn't really seem that far away. I just wondered if you could see it with your telescope, that's all," Arthur replied.

"When were you in Heaven, Arthur?"

"You want to see if I'm crazy, don't you?"

"Why do you say that, Arthur?" Dr. Phelps asked.

"Because no one believes what happened to me. Everybody I tell this to doesn't believe me and thinks I'm just nuts," Arthur explained.

"Well, I assure you, Arthur, neither Dr. Ingram nor I think you're crazy or nuts, or anything like that at all. In fact, Dr. Ingram tells me that you are a very bright young man and that something truly interesting has happened to you. I've invited you here to ask you some more about your experience. I'd be fascinated to hear more about this from you. Would you be willing to tell me what happened?" Dr. Phelps asked.

"No, I really don't think so," Arthur said, staring out the office window.

"Can you tell me why, Arthur?" Dr. Phelps asked.

"Because after I tell you, you won't believe me just like the others. So why should I say anything? You're just going to laugh."

"Arthur, no one here is going to laugh at you. I promise," Dr. Ingram said.

"Plus, what good is it to have such an amazing story with no one to tell it to? I think the limits of possibility for human experience are as endless as the galaxies I can see through my telescope," Dr. Phelps added.

"It really did happen, you know."

"We believe you, Arthur. It's safe to tell us," Dr. Ingram promised.

Arthur bowed his bandaged head, taking a long, deep breath through his pursed lips that made a swooshing sound like a hollow whistle. He exhaled back out loudly like he was trying to force the mistrust out from himself.

"Okay. I'll tell you if you want, but only if you promise me you won't laugh," Arthur requested.

"Arthur, the last thing we would ever do is laugh at you," Dr. Phelps assured.

"Well, what do you want to know?"

"Start at the beginning and tell us everything that happened," Dr. Phelps said.

Arthur settled back into the deepness of the oxblood leather chair and began to tell the doctors the incredible story of his near-death experience on the railroad track leading up to his visit to Heaven. He told them how he could fly anywhere he wanted just by thinking. He told them about being transported inside Buffalo Bill's train car, and about visiting his sister in her kitchen. Arthur spoke of his joyful reunion with his mother and father in the beautiful valley of sunflowers, and about seeing Cindy, the puppy of light. He described with awe God's giant diamond in the sky, and how God would smile every time someone would create a new way back home to him. He described how his seven-foot guardian angel named George brought him to the table of knowledge and the orbs of review, but both doctors were amazed when Arthur revealed to them that he had been given an important message from Heaven.

"Arthur, excuse me. I don't mean to interrupt, but you said something rather intriguing. Did you just say you were given an important message?" Dr. Phelps asked.

"Yes," Arthur replied.

"What sort of message? What did they say?" Dr. Phelps asked.

"To stop worrying."

"Stop worrying? You believe that you have been asked by Heaven to tell people to stop worrying?" Dr. Phelps asked raising one of his bushy eyebrows.

Arthur folded his arms across his chest and sunk deeper into the chair, lowering his head. He was silent for several moments.

"See – I told you. You don't believe me either, do you?" Arthur huffed.

"No, no, Arthur. I do believe you. I'm finding your story truly amazing. I'm sorry if I gave you that impression. Please tell us more," Dr. Phelps encouraged.

"Well, you see, everyone I met in Heaven said the same thing," Arthur continued.

"And that was? What did they say?"

"They said that everyone down here, I mean everyone on Earth, spends way too much time worrying about stuff that they don't have to worry about," Arthur said.

"Why do you think they do that?" Dr. Phelps asked.

"Because they don't know who they really are, and they don't know they're not supposed to worry about anything,"

"Now you said that they don't know who they are. Who are they?" Dr. Phelps asked.

"Everyone. You and me – it's everyone!" Arthur said.

"And what is everyone supposed to know?"

"That they create their own lives. It's just that mostly everyone doesn't know this yet," Arthur informed.

"You said *mostly* everyone? Who do you think the people are who know about this message?"

"Well – now you, me, and Dr. Ingram, too."

"I mean besides the people in this room, who else knows?" Dr. Phelps asked.

"I'm not really sure, but don't you think it would be pretty silly if we were the only people on Earth who knew about this?" Arthur exclaimed.

A soft tapping on the office door interrupted Dr. Phelps' concentration. Just then, a secretary walked in carrying a tray of coffee.

"Excuse me. Here's your coffee, doctor, and your nine o'clock appointment is already in the waiting room," she said.

"Oh, I see. Would you please apologize for me, and tell them that something has come up? Try to reschedule the patient if you can. If they can't come back, I should be through here in about 30 minutes," Dr. Phelps instructed.

"Yes, doctor."

"I'm sorry, Arthur. Now, where were we? Yes, this thing you're saying about creating our lives, this is also part of the message?" Dr. Phelps asked.

"Yes, that's right."

"What exactly would you say this is?"

"It's our gift from the Creator," Arthur informed.

"Arthur, would you please explain to Dr. Ingram and me what you think your gift from the Creator is exactly?"

"Sure, I'll try. It's a present from God. He gave it to us because we're just like him. We are his children. God made everything, everywhere, in the snap of his finger, but he made us all different. He put a divine seed in us. All we have to do is know that it's there and let it grow inside us."

"Why do you think you were chosen to carry this message?"

Arthur paused, shrugged his shoulder, and said very slowly, "I think someone probably made a mistake."

"A mistake? Why do you think that?"

"Because I'm too young. No one will ever believe me. The message was sent to help people. How can I do that? I'm only ten," Arthur explained.

"So you believe the message was meant for someone else to

bring?" Dr. Phelps asked.

"Yeah, I think it had to be, don't you think so?"

"I couldn't really say," Dr. Ingram interjected.

"I think it was meant for someone older and more important. Maybe it was meant for someone like you, Dr. Phelps. Could I just tell you and then you could tell everyone else?"

"Well, that's a novel idea. I think we should talk some more about it before we decide anything. What do you say to that?" Dr. Phelps asked.

"Sure, that sounds good to me," Arthur answered.

Chapter 14

The Wheelchair Race

Arthur thought Billy looked like a wounded soldier he had once seen in a faded photograph, stretched out on a gurney in a Confederate field hospital after the Battle of Bull Run. He was lying in his bed with the linens pulled up over his chin, motionless. His face was tilted slightly while he gazed expressionlessly at the wall ahead. It seemed to Arthur like he was trying to hide a great sadness beneath the blankets, and Billy's dim presence seemed to be fading right before Arthur's eyes.

"Hey, Billy, how are you feeling over there?" Arthur asked, sitting in his bed.

"I've been better," Billy replied with a muffled voice.

"Would you like some of my green Jell-O? It's really good," Arthur asked as he felt the sweet, cool emulsion slide down his throat.

"No, thanks. I'm all set. What did you say your name was again?" Billy asked.

"Arthur Chambers. My friends call me Art. You can call me Art if you want to."

"Okay, Art, thanks."

"What's wrong with you? I mean what are you in here for?" Arthur asked.

"A weak heart," Billy answered.

"Oh."

"Thanks again for letting me share the room with you."

"That's okay, but it's not my room. The hospital can put anyone they want in here."

"My mother told me this is an expensive private room just for you, and that you were good enough to share it with me. The

131

doctors thought it would be easier on my heart to be in a quiet room," Billy explained.

"I don't have any money. I don't even have any parents. I don't know why they would put me in this special room."

"What happened to your parents?" Billy whispered.

"They died."

"Both of them?" Billy asked as his eyes grew wide.

"Yes, it's just my older brothers, Charlie, Ed, and my sister Alice now."

"Boy, that's tough!" Billy exclaimed.

"Yeah, but everything will be all right. There's nothing to worry about, you know," Arthur offered.

"Boy, I wish I could say that."

"You can!" Arthur answered.

"I don't think so. The doctor says my heart is too weak. I overheard him talking with my mother. He said there wasn't much time left for me," Billy answered.

"They think you're going to die?"

"Yes, and it really scares me," Billy said with trembling lips.

"Well, it shouldn't!" Arthur replied.

"How can you say that?"

"Because I died once before, and it really wasn't that big of a deal."

"You don't know that! If you had really died, you wouldn't be here. I'm not stupid," Billy replied.

"I did so! You can ask my doctor if you want. I thought it was really kind of neat. I didn't want to come back," Arthur explained.

"You didn't? Why?" Billy asked, intrigued.

"Because it was so beautiful there. You could make things like you wanted them to be just by thinking. Heaven is just what you want it to be."

"Did it hurt when you died?"

"Not really. It was like standing next to a cold pond on a hot summer day. You're standing there looking into the water while you're feeling really, really hot, but you're afraid to jump in because you know how cold the water is. Then, you do it anyway because once you're in the water, you know it will make you feel cool and refreshed. You can dive to the bottom of the pond or float on your back in the warm sun. You're free to swim just the way you want. That's what dying is like. It's like jumping into cool water on a hot summer day," Arthur explained.

"That doesn't sound scary at all. That sounds like fun," Billy exclaimed.

"It is, but instead of swimming in water, you can fly through the air."

"Wow! You can fly like a bird?" Billy asked.

"Sort of like a bird, but it's more like you can fly just by thinking. All you have to do is think about a place, or a person, and then you're there. Just like that," Arthur answered snapping his fingers.

"That's sounds great. What else was it like?" Billy asked as he sat up in his bed and lowered the blankets down to his lap.

"Billy, are you sure you don't want some of this Jell-O? It's delicious. I have two right here."

"Okay, I think I will. I'm starting to feel a little hungry," Billy replied with a smile.

"Don't worry, Billy, everything will turn out just fine. There's never anything to worry about. I promise."

"I want to believe you. Why do I feel so scared?" Billy asked.

"Because you don't know who you are."

"I don't? Who am I?"

"You're one of the greatest things God ever made and you can have anything you want," Arthur replied.

"I can?"

"Yes, if you knew how great you really are, Billy, you would never worry about anything ever again."

"I would like to not be so scared. I always feel weak, and I'm always worried about what's going to happen to me," Billy replied.

"Remember how I told you that when you're in Heaven you can make things happen the way you want them to just by thinking about them?" Arthur asked.

"Yes."

"Well, would you believe me if I told you, you can do the same thing down here?" Arthur said.

"What do you mean?"

"I mean, what if you could change everything in your life just by changing how you think? Would you do it?"

"Sure, I would!" Billy replied.

"What would you change?" Arthur asked.

"I would change being sick."

Thoughts are the most powerful thing God ever made. That's how he made everything you know, by thinking about it. That's what no one understands," Arthur explained.

"What's that?" Billy asked.

"That we all make up our lives by our thinking. That's why it's important to think the right way. You can do exactly the same thing. You just have to learn to think right to make your life the way you want," Arthur answered.

Billy settled back into his fluffy white pillows, pondering the amazing story of Arthur's adventure to Heaven. He thought that it all sounded more than crazy. How could he believe a kid who talked about visiting Heaven who sported a giant white bandage wrapped around his head? His mind told him that he couldn't but something else deep inside him told him to believe what Arthur had said. It felt like a quiet knowing that resonated as true and simple in an instinctive way like knowing the difference between what's right and what's wrong. Billy began to feel like a window had opened into his life that blew in fresh air to chase away the sadness.

"Art, would you show me how you do that? I think I would

like to know," Billy asked.

Arthur looked over at the two wheelchairs sitting empty in the corner of the room. He was silent for a couple of minutes, and then a smile spread across his face. He turned over toward Billy, and whispered, "Hey, Billy, what do you say we go for a ride in our wheelchairs after you finish your Jell-O?"

"I don't think that would be such a good idea," Billy said as he eagerly captured the last sliver of the elusive green Jell-O on his spoon and slurped it into his mouth.

"Why not?"

"Because the doctor said I needed peace and quiet. I'm too weak. I'm supposed to have rest," Billy explained.

"Oh yeah, I forgot," Arthur softly replied.

"That's okay," Billy answered.

"How are you feeling?" Arthur asked.

"Right now I feel great. What's in that Jell-O?" Billy asked.

"I don't know, but I wish my sister Alice could make that."

"That had to be the best Jell-O I ever tasted."

"Good enough to want to go for a nice, easy ride down the hall in the wheelchairs?" Arthur asked winking at Billy.

"I guess it wouldn't be so bad if we went real slow, and just down the hall a bit."

"Now you're talking, Billy. Let's go and have some fun."

Billy quietly followed Arthur's slow pace as they wheeled their chairs cautiously out into the empty hallway. Arthur noticed the open door across the hall and rolled over to take a peek. Inside there were two boys about the same age, sitting on their beds talking.

"Hey there, we're going for a ride down the hall to see what's there. Do you want to come?" Arthur whispered into their room.

"Sure, anything's better then being stuck in here," one of the boys replied.

"I'm with you!" said the other.

"What are your names?" Arthur asked.

"I'm Fitzy and this is Jack."

Fitzy was shorter than Jack, with bright red curly hair and a wide impish grin that made Arthur like him instantly. Under a Red Sox cap, Jack seemed to regularly cast a weary eye towards his friend.

"You're not coming unless you give me back the dime I lent you this morning," Jack said.

"I'd rather owe it to you than cheat you out of it," Fitzy replied laughing.

"What are you guys here in the hospital for?" Arthur asked.

"The doctors say we both have cancer," Jack replied.

"I'm getting a second opinion," Fitzy added.

"What about you two?" Jack asked.

"This is Billy. The doctors say he has a weak heart. And I'm Art."

"What do they got you for?" Fitzy asked.

"I got hit in the head. I have a metal plate there now," Arthur said.

"Really, can you see it?" Jack asked.

"I don't know. I've had this bandage on my head the whole time," Arthur answered.

"That would be neat if you could see it," Jack replied.

"You're a big goof. They should put a metal plate in your head!" Fitzy said to Jack poking him in the side.

"Do you guys know each other?" Arthur asked.

"Yeah, we're friends. We met about six months ago during treatment. They always try to put us in the same room now," Jack responded.

"I'm his friend. He's not mine," Fitzy said grinning.

"Come on, let's go," Arthur instructed as he quietly rolled down the hall.

The line of boys in wheelchairs quietly crept down the hall, pausing momentarily when Arthur thought he heard the sound of someone approaching. He whispered, "All clear!" down the rest of the line when he sensed the danger had passed. Fitzy and Jack were holding down the rear of the line when they noticed the open door of a supply closet across the way. Arthur became annoyed when he heard a clattering noise as he turned to see Fitzy handing Jack neatly folded white bath towels and two brightly polished metal bedpans.

"Hey, what do you think you're doing back there?" Arthur whispered angrily.

"You'll see!" they replied.

Arthur watched Fitzy and Jack tuck the long towels into the back collar of their hospital pajamas and place the shiny bedpans on top of their heads.

"You two are just going to get us in trouble," Billy warned.

"We're flying tanks now!" Fitzy shouted.

Fitzy rolled his wheelchair faster and faster toward Arthur and Billy, shouting, "Jack, first one to the end of the hall wins everyone's dessert tonight."

Jack sprang into motion. Both of his arms exploded like pistons firing down onto the wheels of his chair, propelling him forward in pursuit of his buddy. With their flying white capes and their gleaming helmets, they charged down the hall past Arthur. They headed toward an imaginary finish line.

"Let's go! We can't let them win," Arthur shouted over to Billy as his wheelchair lurched forward to join the race. Billy's bone-thin hands gripped the edges of the wheels of his chair, joining in the chase. The distance between them grew as Arthur watched the back of Fitzy and Jack's wheelchairs moving further and further down the hall. Jack's more powerful arms helped him to inch past Fitzy into the lead.

"Not so fast, you big goof!" Fitzy yelled as they flew right past the nurses' station.

"Hey! You boys stop those wheelchairs right now!" the nurses' supervisor yelled from behind the office counter as she slammed down her clipboard, and leapt up out of her chair.

Arthur and Billy followed a split second later as the nurse screamed, "Oh my God, that's Billy Brown in that wheelchair! Call Dr. Ingram immediately to tell him there's a bad situation going on right now in the Children's Ward. Tell him Billy Brown is right in the middle of – oh heavens – a wheelchair race," she instructed, glaring at her assistant before she ran down the hall after the runaway wheelchair racers.

Fitzy sensed that Jack was about to gain the upper hand in the race so he lurched his wheelchair to the left, striking the back edge of Jack's wheel with his own. The wheelchairs careened off to the side and crashed into the wall, leaving them in a jumble of bedpans and towels with both boys sprawled out on the floor. Arthur, following closely behind the two fallen leaders, slammed the brakes on his chair to avoid tumbling along with them into the crash scene ahead. Billy, who had been racing down the right side of the hallway, took his opening for victory, sailing past the wreck of scattered towels and clanging bedpans. Billy steered his wheelchair as close to the right wall as he possibly could, and he glided past all of them to finish first at the end of the hall.

Billy was so excited by this unexpected win that he stood up from his chair, and began to jump and cheer.

"Yahoo! I won! I won!" he yelled dancing around his prized wheelchair at the end of the hall. He saw Fitzy and Jack sprawled about the hallway floor, and started to laugh hysterically.

Arthur was the first to notice the nurse running down the hallway in frantic pursuit of the boys as she yelled, "Mother of God! Billy Brown, are you all right?"

Arthur quickly rolled the wheelchair up next to Billy and whispered under his breath, "We're in for it now, Billy!"

Billy was so enthralled by winning the wheelchair race that he didn't quite hear Arthur's warning. He continued to shout and dance joyously around his wheelchair.

"Billy, calm down. Sit back in your chair," the nurse sternly instructed.

"I won! I won!" Billy shouted, jumping in the air.

"Please, Billy, stop this right now. You can't get this excited. Your heart, Billy. You're going to make yourself sick if you don't stop," the nurse pleaded.

"I'm not sick, nurse. I feel great!"

"Get into that chair and do it now, mister," she loudly commanded, pointing to his vacant wheelchair.

The sheer force of her booming voice made everyone in the hall stop and look, including Dr. Ingram who was just turning the corner at that moment in response to the call for help.

"What the devil is going on here?" Dr. Ingram demanded.

"These crazy boys were having a wheelchair race right down the middle of this hallway," the nurse yelled back.

"They were? Which one of you is responsible for starting this ruckus?" Dr. Ingram asked.

"It's him. It's Arthur Chambers. He started it," a muffled squeal pronounced from beneath the towels.

"Did you, Arthur?" the doctor asked.

"Yes, but I didn't mean for this to happen. Really, I didn't, sir," Arthur said.

"Well, I don't have time for this right now. We'll deal with this later," Dr. Ingram retorted.

"Mr. Brown, would you please sit down in your wheelchair right now," Dr. Ingram firmly said and asked, "How are you feeling, Billy?"

"I feel great. Never better. I beat everyone. I won the race," Billy said beaming.

"That's wonderful, Billy, but you must calm down right now," he instructed reaching for Billy's wrist to check his pulse.

"Doctor, I'm sorry, but they just came out of nowhere. I couldn't stop them," the nurse said.

"Yes, I imagine you couldn't, but we need to get everyone back into their beds right now," Dr. Ingram said.

"Do you feel any dizziness, Billy?" Dr. Ingram asked.

"Nope!" Billy replied.

"How does your breathing feel?"

"I feel like I could breathe forever," he said taking in a long deep breath.

Dr. Ingram looked at his wristwatch as he timed Billy's heartbeat. A puzzled look grew across his face. It was beating with such a slow and steady pace that Dr. Ingram doubted his own assessment. He shook his head baffled.

"Nurse, would you come over here for a minute?"

"Yes, doctor. What is it?" she asked.

"Would you please check Billy's pulse for me – tell me what you get?"

"Certainly, doctor. Right away."

"I get 65 and strong," the nurse reported.

"This is impossible. His heart can't do that," Dr. Ingram mumbled.

"His chart says that less than an hour ago his heart rate was normal, I mean normal for him resting. One 120 and beating weak," the nurse replied.

"Let me listen to your heart for a minute, Billy," Dr. Ingram said, shaking his head.

After listening a few moments he removed the stethoscope from his ears, blew gently into its end, and tapped it against the palm of his hand like he was trying to dislodge the charred remains from a smoking pipe. He carefully repositioned the earpieces snugly into both of his ears, and placed the scope directly over Billy's heart. He lowered his head, closed his eyes, and scrunched his brow as if he was listening for some hidden message buried deep within Billy's chest.

After some time, Dr. Ingram lifted his head again and proclaimed, "Nurse, I cannot believe this. This is truly amazing. Miraculous, really. I can't explain it. His heart appears to be functioning normally. Billy, would you describe to me again how you are feeling?"

"Actually, doctor, I'm starving," Billy replied.

"Well that's something I think this hospital can actually help you with. What do you feel like eating?" Dr. Ingram asked.

"A big, fat juicy steak," Billy answered, smiling.

"We'll see what we can do about that, Billy. Nurse, after you take Billy back to his room would you please call Dr. Weir in Cardiology and ask him to contact me," Dr. Ingram instructed.

"Yes, certainly, doctor. Right away."

Chapter 15

Miraculous Recoveries

Alice sat alone sipping her breakfast tea at her wooden table that was a hand-me-down given to her mother before she was born. She ran her hand along the smooth surface as she tried to picture the different families who had sat around it, eating meals and telling stories. Their lost voices had faded away into the past leaving a haunting emptiness. Her thoughts turned to Arthur. The house felt hollow without Arthur. Sound and light seemed to move through the apartment differently without him there, casting unfamiliar shadows and releasing peculiar sounds from behind the plaster walls. All she wanted now was to have Arthur back home with her where she could take care of him. Charlie and Ed easily cared for themselves, but she would always tend to Arthur. She wanted her beloved little brother safely home.

The dark heaviness that seemed to hang over everything had lifted when the doctor told her that he expected Arthur to make a full recovery. She had informed Charlie that he would have to give up his single bed to Arthur and sleep in the large bed with Ed until Arthur got better. She cleaned up the boys' bedroom as best she could. She placed all her dolls on a chair in a corner of the bedroom facing the door so they could look in to watch as Arthur came home. Alice sat quietly in the silence of her kitchen sipping the last drops from her teacup before heading off to school. She hoped that the school day would go by quickly so they could get back to the hospital to see Arthur.

The bell mercifully rang, signaling the end of the school day so Alice made her way to the front of the building.

"Hey, Ed, over here!" Alice shouted.

"You're early," Ed said, running down the front stairs of the school.

"I know. I didn't bother going down to my locker after the last class," Alice explained.

"Well, let's get going to see how Arthur's doing today."

"I'm worried. How do you think he is? I mean with all his crazy talk, do you think he's going to be okay?" Alice asked, struggling to keep up with her brother along the uneven cobble-stones. They quickly passed by row after row of pale sandstone front steps that led to the tall and narrow Boston brownstone tenements.

"Sure, he's going to be fine. Don't worry, he just got a good bump on the head. He'll settle down after a few days."

"Ed, how do you think Arthur knew what Dad's dog Cindy looked like?

"I don't know, but he sure hit the nail on the head when he described her. Maybe getting that knock in the head made him remember things from when he was a baby. Anyway, he'll be fine soon enough. He's just goofy from getting banged on the head."

"I hope you're right."

"But, I didn't tell anyone about that bowl," Alice added.

"What bowl? What are you talking about?'

"The glass bowl I broke in the sink just before I went to look for Arthur outside. Ed, Arthur told me about that," she explained.

"What do you mean?"

"Arthur told me he saw me break the bowl. That's not possible."

"Why?" Ed asked.

"Ed, you're not listening to me! No one was in the kitchen with me when I broke that bowl. I threw it out and didn't tell anyone. Arthur was knocked out on those railroad tracks when that happened. How could he know about that?"

"How would I know? What did Art say?"

"He said he knew about it because he was there," she replied.

"That's just crazy! He can't be in two places at once," Ed responded.

"That's what I've been trying to tell you! I'm not so sure Arthur would agree because he says he was there."

"What are you saying, Alice?"

"I'm saying that he's telling us he was in Heaven. Why wouldn't he think he could be in two places at once?"

"Good point. I see what you mean."

"It's all starting to scare me a little bit. I don't like it," she added.

"It's just talk, Alice. Don't let it scare you."

"I know, but it's starting to sound real to me."

"What is?" he asked.

"Seeing Mom and Dad and Cindy. Even his big friend made from light. It's all starting to sound spooky to me, like it really happened. That's what's scaring me."

"Don't you go goofy on me too," her brother replied.

"Look Alice. We're almost there. See – Charlie's already waiting for us out front. Hey there, Charlie!" Ed said as he crossed the street.

"You're late. Where have you two been?"

"I was talking a lot and I slowed him up. Sorry," Alice offered.

"Yeah, Alice is getting scared about Arthur and his wild stories," Ed added.

"No, I'm not, Ed. Stop fooling!" Alice countered.

"Well, Alice, I wouldn't blame you if it did. It's got me a little worried too. I've been thinking about it all day," Charlie replied.

"How do you think he knew all that stuff, Charlie?" she asked.

"Tell him about the bowl, Alice," Ed instructed.

"What bowl?" Charlie said.

"I got this feeling when I was washing a glass bowl in the kitchen sink. The bowl slipped out of my hand and shattered into pieces in the sink the afternoon of the accident," Alice explained.

"So, what's the big deal about that?" Charlie said.

"Arthur knew all about it. He said he was there in the kitchen with me and saw me drop it," Alice explained.

"Maybe he..."

"Charlie, no one knew about that bowl breaking except me. I've thought about this a million times. There's no way he could have known. There's just no way!"

"Alice, what did he say about it?" Charlie asked.

"That after he got hit on the head, he could fly. He said he flew into the kitchen and that he tried to touch me, and when he did that's when I dropped the bowl. He said he was sorry for scaring me. Charlie, how do you think he knew all that? It's giving me the creeps."

"I'll be damned if I know," Charlie replied.

"Do you think someone can go to Heaven and then come back?" Alice asked.

"I'm not sure why someone would want to – come back I mean – but who knows?" Charlie replied, shrugging his shoulders.

The three of them walked silently down the hospital corridor. Charlie could smell it wafting down the hall before he turned the corner toward Arthur's room. It was the distinct greasy aroma of pan-fried steak. He had only tasted steak twice in his life, but that was before his mother had died. He had always told his brothers and sister, "it was just as easy to fill up on bread as it was on steak", but just then he had to admit he felt a little envious of patients who were enjoying the good fortune of steak for dinner. Charlie's mouth began to water at the captivating smell as they walked into Arthur's room.

"Hey there, Charlie, wanna bite?" Arthur asked as he held up a forkful of the thick juicy meat with one hand, waving a steak knife in the other.

Charlie couldn't believe his eyes as he beheld Arthur and Billy dining in their hospital beds on a meal he could barely even dream about having.

"Who's paying for all this?" Charlie demanded with alarm.

"I don't know, but it sure tastes great," Arthur said with a shrug.

"First a private room. And now this! What the heck's going on?" Charlie scolded.

"Billy won the wheelchair race so they said he could have a steak," Arthur added, winking over at Billy in the next bed.

"Billy won what?" Charlie asked.

"He won the wheelchair race. Came in first place. Beat everyone," Arthur announced loudly. Billy chuckled in the next bed and then began coughing on a mouthful of the tender beef.

"I thought Billy had a bad heart condition. What the heck was he doing racing a wheelchair?" Charlie asked.

Dr. Ingram appeared in the doorway saying, "Yes, he did have a heart condition when he was admitted, to answer your first question. Your second question is a little easier to explain. Arthur and two young cancer patients from across the hall somehow convinced Billy to join them in a raucous wheelchair race through the hallways of the hospital."

"They did, did they?" Charlie said, casting a weary eye over toward Arthur.

"Yes, they had all the nurses of the floor in quite an uproar over it. With such serious medical conditions, nobody including me expected them to have the ability to get out of bed, never mind racing wheelchairs down the hall," Dr. Ingram explained.

"If they were so bad, why are you letting them have steak?" Alice asked.

"Billy here wanted a steak. After spending the good part of the day in the cardiology department getting every test Dr. Weir could possibly think of, I thought Billy deserved it," Dr. Ingram replied.

"If Arthur caused all that trouble I don't think you should have let him have a steak too," Alice said, looking sternly at her remorseless brother who was chomping happily on his meal.

"Well, I see your point, but no one likes to eat alone so we gave Arthur a steak too. I really hope you don't mind," Dr. Ingram explained.

"I don't know. It doesn't seem fair to me after Arthur caused all that trouble here," she answered.

"Doctor, it sure doesn't look to me like there's anyone sick in this room. How are these two hooligans actually doing?" Charlie inquired.

"They're both doing remarkably well. After testing Billy, we can't find anything wrong with his heart. It's like there was never anything wrong with him. According to every test administered by Dr. Weir, his heart now seems completely normal. Along the same lines, Arthur has a head injury that is healing at a rate that is really quite astounding. His injury has healed to a point now that would have normally taken at least several weeks. I don't have any explanations for how all of this could have happened. I have heard of miraculous recoveries before, but to have two of them in the same room is, well frankly, amazing."

"If Arthur is doing so well can we take him home soon?" Alice asked.

"We don't want to rush anything, miss, but if your brother keeps up this remarkable recovery, I don't see why he couldn't be discharged home in a few days. I know that Dr. Phelps would like to see Arthur again for some routine IQ and psychological testing. So, let's see how everything is in a few days, okay?" Dr. Ingram said.

"Oh, that would be just fine, doctor," Alice answered, and turned to Arthur. Shaking her finger at him, she commanded, "And you, mister, better be good in here. No more crazy races if you want to go home! Do you hear me?"

Chapter 16

House on the Hill

The black and white taxicab drove past the endless rows of triple-decker tenements on the way back from Boston City Hospital to Dorchester. Charlie rode shotgun with his window rolled down to enjoy the unexpected warmth of the early December afternoon. He turned around to glance at the others in the back seat. The ruffles on Alice's blue gingham dress flapped in the wind, and her black leather shoes were securely placed together, hanging over the edge of the seat. Charlie imagined that she looked just like one of her treasured dolls in her bedroom with stiff legs that wouldn't bend at the knees. Alongside Alice, Arthur peacefully looked out the window with his bandaged head, watching the cramped tenements go by. The taxi came to a slow rolling stop in front the shabby green house at 11 Maryland Street.

Arthur let out a sigh of relief, exclaiming, "It sure feels good to be home."

"Now let Charlie and Ed help you up the stairs, Arthur. You have to take it easy for awhile," Alice said.

"No, sis, I'm fine. I can make it up by myself," Arthur proclaimed as he started to swing the taxi door open.

"You just wait there one minute, mister," Charlie said as he handed the taxi driver one dollar for the ride.

"That's right, there's not going to be any wheelchair races around here," Ed teased.

"I feel fine, honest. I don't want any help," Arthur protested.

"Dr. Ingram said we could take you home with us if you followed his orders, but if you didn't, he told us to bring you right back," Charlie warned.

Arthur smiled as he entered his room to see his bed pushed up against the back wall with several crisp pillows neatly lining the headboard. His mother's prized patchwork quilt was folded back inviting him into the bed. The afternoon sun tumbled through the window, cascading softly onto the array of bright colors on the quilt. Just under the window on top of the nightstand next to a water pitcher, was a bag of marbles and several colored drawing pencils. He looked over at Alice's dolls sitting together on an old wooden kitchen chair by the door. He imagined she must have placed them there to witness his return into the room. Arthur wondered how his tiny sister could have such a big heart filled with so much love as he crawled into the inviting bed.

"Okay, Arthur, I want you to take a nap while I make you some supper," Alice chirped at him, smoothing the covers carefully over his shoulders.

"It sure is good to be back here, back home again," Arthur said as he let his bandaged head drift back into the softness of his pillows.

"There's no fancy steak here like there is at that hospital," Alice answered.

"That's okay. Anything you make sounds good to me."

"We're having Irish spaghetti and bread. Well, that's if Charlie can find some day-old at the bakery."

Arthur always liked the plain cooked pasta with butter and salt. Charlie called it Irish spaghetti because it was cheap and easy to make, with no tomato sauce.

"Where are the bag of marbles and colored pencils from?" Arthur asked.

"Those are 'coming home' presents for you. I wanted to get you something better, but you know how it is."

"Sure, I think they're great. I love them," he replied.

"I thought you could draw some pictures for us, and the marbles just looked pretty to me. Maybe when you're feeling better, you can play with them outside. And I got you these two books from the library to read, *Ride Like an Indian* and *Ten*

Thousand Leagues Under The Sea. They looked like good ones," Alice said as she handed him the used books with flimsy bindings.

"Now, you try to get some rest while I make supper."

"Okay," Arthur replied.

He closed his eyes and drifted off into a dream. In a few minutes, Alice could hear his heavy breathing, followed by gentle snoring from the kitchen. She walked to the doorway to look in upon her younger brother sleeping peacefully. Her eyes started to well up again at the dreadful thought of almost losing him.

Arthur fell into a late afternoon dream that brought him back once more to the edge of the valley of sunflowers. He stood at the base of mountains that stretched up into the sky. As he looked up, he felt oddly aware that he was there to meet someone, but he wasn't sure who it might be. From out of the glimmering forest at the base of the mountain, his father walked up to him.

"Hey there, Art! It's such a beautiful day. And a perfect one for a hike if you ask me."

"Hey, Dad, what are you doing here?"

"Don't you want to see me?"

"I guess so, but…"

"What do you say we go for a hike?" his father interrupted.

"A hike? Huh? Where would we go?"

"Up there."

Arthur looked up at the dizzying peak his father was pointing toward and asked, "Can't we just *think* about going there instead of actually climbing up? It would be a whole lot faster."

"But this isn't Heaven. You're not in Heaven anymore."

"I'm not? Where am I? This place looks like Heaven," Arthur said.

"It's the place 'in between'. It's where Heaven and Earth meet. It's the place of your dreams. And you can't create things in your dreams like you can when you're in Heaven," his father explained.

"Why are we here?" Arthur asked.

"There's something I want you to see."

"There is? Where is it?" Arthur asked.

"Up there," his father said, pointing toward the top of the mountain.

"What's up there that I should see?"

"You'll know when you see it. Let's get going as we don't have much time to waste."

Arthur walked behind his father, following him up the steep mountain trail. The trail was rough, and Arthur had trouble keeping pace with his father's rapid ascent up the steep path. He couldn't understand the urgency, or why his father was so far ahead of him.

"Hey, Dad, wait up. I can't go as fast as you," Arthur shouted up the trail toward the blurry image ahead.

"Climbing a mountain is just like life, Art."

He heard his father's last statement echo loudly three times off the surrounding mountains, and he marveled at what that was supposed to mean.

Completely out of breath, he was forced to stop to regain his bearing. Panting loudly, he looked up to see his father far off in the distance. He bent over, breathing heavily and clasping his knees. He looked up at the trail ahead again. Strangely, he now found himself face-to-face with his father who was standing only few feet away. Arthur felt dizzy. If this wasn't Heaven, how could his father move back and forth like that?

His father spoke, "Sometimes the climb up is so tough that you just want to give up, but the most experienced hikers know when the climb up is the hardest, you are near the top, and shouldn't give up."

"Are we near the top yet?" Arthur asked.

"It's not too much further now."

The steepness of the rocky grade made it difficult for Arthur to keep his footing. He slipped, and then stumbled forward, tripping on a tree root, which landed him in the dirt and loose rocks.

"Can we stop for a little while, Dad? I'm getting really tired," Arthur yelled ahead as he picked himself up with his hands and knees.

"Too many people stop their life climb just before they get to the summit. If they knew how close they were to the top, they would keep going," his father replied, glancing behind him down the steep trail.

"Why do we have to get there so fast?"

"There's not much time left. We must get to the top," his father warned.

Arthur realized the trail was leveling off as his labored breathing brought him closer to the mountain summit. The peak itself was dark, obscured by ominous clouds. Thick clouds swept past his father who beckoned Arthur toward an old house that mysteriously appeared from behind the thinning clouds.

"What is this place?" Arthur asked.

"There is something here you need to see."

Arthur felt unnerved by the gloomy sight of the decrepit house and said, "Okay, I've seen it. Can we go back down now?"

"I have not brought you here to show you the summit of your own life, Art."

"That's good. Whose summit is it then?"

"Someone who needs your help," his father replied.

"Why would anyone want the summit of their life to look like this?" Arthur asked.

"They don't necessarily want it to look this way. They just don't know what *you* know."

"What's that?"

"You can create the trails, the mountains, and even the summit of your life. The terrain can be smooth and easy, or challenging and difficult to pass. The mountains can be tall and majestic, or dense and dark. The summit can be bright and glimmering, or dark and foreboding. And this all comes about by the way you think," his father replied.

"I know, but you told me we could only do that in Heaven, Dad. I thought you said this isn't Heaven."

"Your thoughts create your life no matter where you are."

After pausing a moment to absorb his words, Arthur nodded his head in agreement.

As they stood together, suddenly the wind started to blow hard and a tremendous mist began to envelope them. Arthur could hear still his father's voice, but it grew dimmer as he faded away into the rolling fog.

"Dad, are you there?"

"Son, I'll always be with you. Always!"

When the fog cleared slightly, Arthur walked up toward the Victorian porch that wrapped around the house like the arm of a mythical giant holding on to a fading dream. He walked up the stairs toward the French windows, and wiped clean a spot on a dusty pane with his hand. Peering into a grand room with high ceilings, he imagined that someone wealthy must have lived there long ago. Ornate chairs were evenly placed around a dark mahogany table set with fine china covered in a layer of dust. Arthur surveyed the area when he suddenly saw an inner door quickly slam shut. He shook his head, thinking he must have imagined it, yet the cobwebs hanging from the chandelier inside still quivered from the sudden vibration. Perhaps he had not imagined it after all, he thought. He knocked on the rattling window to get someone's attention inside. The window was unlocked so he pushed the frame open. It creaked. He stuck his head inside, and hollered, "Hey! Is anyone home?"

Silence returned. Arthur crawled through the window to take a better look. Before his feet hit the dusty floor beneath him, Arthur sensed there was something odd about this crumbling mansion. He felt it radiating off every object in the room like swirling, dark energy. He wanted to run, but felt drawn in at the same time. The feeling of unfathomable loneliness swept down from the high ceilings above, clung to the dusty portraits and mirrors, and seeped out from behind the dark wallpaper. The table had place settings for only two. The fine china with tarnished silverware was uniformly displayed next to the finest crystal glasses Arthur had ever seen. It felt like a mystical, yet sad, memorial to a cherished time. It seemed to him as though a part of someone was unwillingly lost in this strange place, someone who was impossible to forget. Arthur didn't know why these odd thoughts were coming to him like someone was whispering into his ear. The heaviness of the room weighed upon him. He felt empty and alone. He struggled to move his feet to leave the room. It took all the power of his will to push away from that spot to reach the door. Arthur staggered out into the darkened hallway. As soon as he entered, he saw the flash of a full-length dress swoosh across the floor as it passed through another door at the opposite end of the hall.

"Excuse me, ma'am! Can I talk to you?" Arthur shouted down the long hallway. The door slammed shut.

Arthur ran in pursuit of the elusive woman, shouting, "Ma'am! Ma'am! I just want to talk to you. Don't run away."

When he opened the door a floor lamp was casting a green hue onto an armchair, while the corners of the room remained in thick darkness. He felt the floor tremble slightly, and he sensed the woman's presence lurking at the edge of the room. Once again, dark energy engulfed him. Arthur felt a sadness that slid out from the shadows like a ground fog that swirled about his feet. It rose up from his shoes, covering him with a blanket of joyless mist that chased the lightness from his soul. The intricate weavings on the oriental rug beneath his feet began to spin in a kaleidoscope of moving patterns that transformed the rug into a pool of sinking sadness. Arthur felt like he was drowning in sorrow.

Then from the shadows a tormented voice wept, "Go away!

You're not supposed to be here."

Startled, Arthur opened his eyes wide, and softly replied, "I want to help you."

"I don't need help," the untrusting voice screeched.

"Why do you say that? We all need help, sometimes," he responded.

"Not me! And that lamp you've been staring at—my Joe broke that lamp, and he never came back to fix it. That was my favorite lamp. I'm angry with him. Joe did this to me."

The base of the lamp looked like the trunk of a tree swirling up into a Tiffany shade covered with leaves and exotic birds. Arthur noticed a crack running down the side of the stained-glass shade, slicing the birds in two. Pointing at the lamp, she inched out ever so slowly from the shadows. He began to make out the outline of her hunched shoulders.

"I'm sure he didn't mean to," Arthur reassured.

"Did you hear that?" she snapped, turning her head as she strained to hear in the dark silence.

"I didn't hear anything," Arthur replied.

"That sounds like him! Excuse me, but I have to go find Joe now," she said as she moved further out of the shadows.

Arthur saw her for only an instant. Her gray hair looked like it hadn't been combed for weeks, and her penetrating eyes betrayed an unimaginable grief. She seemed to glide along the lifeless landscape of the parlor as if she was pushed along by a lost wind. As she passed into the adjoining room, he sensed how her once regal nature had collapsed into a fragile wisp of a woman.

Arthur followed her moaning voice into a large room at the center of the house where hunting trophies hung eerily on paneled walls. The fieldstone fireplace still smelled of stale smoke, and radiated chilly foreboding out into the rest of the house. Each trophy head stared frightfully ahead into the cold darkness. His heart pounded and he couldn't breathe. Arthur could feel the cold panic in his bones as he watched the crazed woman pacing back and forth along the back wall, mumbling and wringing her hands together.

"Joe, where are you? Where have you gone? Why won't you come home to me?"

Arthur mustered the courage to step forward and asked, "Ma'am, excuse me, can I talk too you please?"

"Oh, no, it's you again? I told you to leave! Go away," she growled.

"I have something to tell you," Arthur replied.

"I'm not interested. Now, will you get out of here?"

"I'll leave if you let me tell you something."

"You are infuriating. Just get it over with. Tell me if you insist, but only if you leave right away."

"I will but, Joe asked me to say something to you," Arthur offered.

She stepped forward, and fearfully looked at him for a moment before asking, "What? He did? Why would he talk to you? Where is he?" and then she hissed, "You're lying."

"No, it's the truth. He told me to tell you that he loves you very much, and that he misses you."

"Why won't he come home?" she wept loudly.

"It's because he can't, ma'am. He just can't."

"What's he doing that's so important?" she demanded.

"He's making you a garden," Arthur answered.

"He is? Where?" she asked, softening slightly.

"In Heaven – ma'am. Joe's in Heaven and he's making you a garden there."

"Why's he doing that? Where is my Joe?"

"It's supposed to be a secret, a surprise; the garden is a present. He knows how much you love a beautiful garden. I saw him planting roses for you, lots of them, and bright pink ones."

"Really? My Joe? Joe was always so kind to me," she said as tears streamed down her face.

"He told me something else too. He told me to tell you to stop worrying."

"You don't know anything. I'm scared without him," she answered, quivering.

"There's nothing to worry about. Nothing at all," Arthur replied.

"How would you know that? You're just a boy," she said.

"I know because Joe told me so. He wants you to stop worrying."

"That's easy for him to say. He's in Heaven."

"Joe knows it's not easy to stop worrying, but he wants you to try," Arthur insisted.

"That's not possible. There's no way I can stop unless he comes back to me."

"I have an idea," Arthur offered, "Let's try to do it together. I can show you how to stop worrying."

"I don't know. I wish you would leave me alone in peace. I don't understand why you are here. You are telling me that Joe sent you? I wish you would leave me alone, but if you get it over with, and promise to leave right away."

"Come here for just a minute. It's okay. Here, hold my hand and close your eyes," Arthur said reaching for her hands timidly.

The woman reluctantly held out her trembling hands as Arthur said, "Now think of the most peaceful and beautiful thing you can possibly imagine. Think of your Joe's love. Think of God's love."

"What? I don't know if I believe in God or his love. God took my Joe away. Didn't he?"

Arthur squeezed her hands gently. In his mind, he steadily held the image of his smiling mother walking toward him through the field of flowers. He repeated to himself, "I'm a child of the Creator and made from love." Arthur repeated the simple mantra "fear is not real" silently to himself over and over again, while he firmly grasped her soft, wrinkled hands. A subtle glowing light began to appear around them. It grew in intensity, chasing away the dark fear. Even the corners of the room seemed to brighten. The woman's eyes opened with awe as she looked upon Arthur's glowing presence.

"Oh my, you look just like my Joe did when I saw him in the hospital hallway. Who are you?" she stepped back again, gazing wide-eyed upon Arthur who was surrounded by the warm, tantalizing light.

"See! This is how you do it, ma'am. It's easy once you know how," Arthur replied.

"Why did Joe want you to show me how to do this?" she asked.

"He wants you to be happy like he is. He wants you to know that there is nothing to worry about. Nothing at all," Arthur said as he was pulled away by a familiar voice echoing off in the distance calling, his name.

"Arthur! Arthur! Wake up, dinner's ready," Alice announced as she walked toward the bedroom from the kitchen. Arthur opened his sleepy eyes to see his sister standing in the bedroom doorway wearing their mother's white kitchen apron that was dragging behind her on the floor. She had a bright smile that made him glad to be back home.

"Arthur, did you get some sleep?"

"Yes, and I had this really strange dream too."

"You did? That sounds interesting. You can tell everyone about it at dinner."

"Charlie, Ed, bring the folding table right in here and put it next to Arthur's bed," Alice instructed from the doorway.

"Sis, what are you doing?" Arthur asked.

"I don't think it's a good idea for you to be getting out of bed just yet, so we're all going to have dinner with you in here on the folding table," Alice said as she pushed the table Ed delivered snugly up against the bed.

"That's nice, Alice, but I feel fine. Really, I do. I can eat at the big table with everyone."

"Shush!" she said, spreading a white tablecloth out neatly across the folding table.

"We're all having dinner in here with you and that's that."

Arthur looked over from his bed at the table being set for four with a large yellow mixing bowl in the center overflowing with plain boiled spaghetti. A glass dish filled with fresh butter sat next to it.

"Look what I found, Art. It's a nice loaf of day-old Italian bread. It was just sitting in the bakery window waiting for me to take it home," Charlie said, placing the crusty loaf on the table.

"Wow! This looks like a meal fit for a king," Ed said, pulling back a chair.

"Charlie, put some butter on that spaghetti before it cools down," Alice instructed.

Ed started to hungrily dig his fork into the heap of buttered pasta when Alice interrupted, "Wait a minute, Ed. Someone should say grace first before we eat. After all, this is Arthur's first night home."

"I think Charlie wants to say it tonight." Ed replied.

"No, Ed, you go ahead. It's your turn anyway," Charlie answered.

"I'll say it then, if you're going to argue about it. The food's getting cold. You'd think that someone was trying to torture you two by asking you to say grace," Alice said as she bowed her head slightly to pray.

"Heavenly Father, Jesus, and all the angels in Heaven, thank you for protecting our brother Arthur, and sending him back to us. We all promise to be good. Please keep us safe and sound in Jesus' name. Amen."

"Is it okay to eat now?" Ed asked.

"Yes it is," Alice replied, whispering beneath her breath, "Jesus, please forgive him."

"Art, how are you feeling tonight?" Charlie asked.

159

"Great!" Arthur said as he shoved a mound of buttered spaghetti into his mouth.

"No headaches or anything like that?" Charlie inquired.

"Nope, I feel good Charlie."

"Arthur just had a nice nap before dinner, and he told me he had an interesting dream," Alice added.

"A dream? What kind of a dream did you have?" Charlie asked.

"It was just a dream. I don't want to tell," Arthur replied.

"Why not, Art? Tell us. We want to hear about it," Charlie said.

"No. You'll just laugh," Arthur replied.

"No, we won't. Come on, tell us. Please?" Ed pleaded.

"Okay," Arthur said while placing his half-eaten plate down on the table.

"Well, at first I thought that I was back in Heaven. It seemed like Heaven to me, but Dad told me it wasn't. He told me that it was the place where Heaven and Earth meet," Arthur started to explain as Charlie began to nervously squirm about in his chair looking agitated.

"Dad wanted me to climb the purple mountain of light with him. He said there was…"

"Arthur, please stop!" Charlie said with alarm.

"Why, what's wrong?" Arthur asked.

"Charlie, let him finish. You said you wanted to hear his dream," Alice protested.

"We have to stop pretending that everything is just fine here. It's just not. Art, I want you to stop talking about all this crazy stuff. You didn't see Ma and Dad in Heaven. You don't have a seven-foot friend, and you didn't climb a purple mountain made of light," Charlie said tersely.

"I did so! How do you know, anyway? You weren't there with me."

"Charlie, it was just a dream he had and it doesn't mean

anything," Alice added.

"You're saying these things really did happen, aren't you, Art?" Charlie asked.

"I'm not saying anything anymore to anyone. No one believes me anyway so why should I talk about it? Everyone just gets upset if I do," Arthur replied, crossing his arms across his chest and pushing away his plate of spaghetti.

"Art, I want you to try to think this through. Heaven is a place you go to after you die. People don't go to Heaven and then come back," Charlie said.

"Most of the time they don't," Arthur responded.

"So, Art, what you're telling me is that you think you died, went to Heaven, and then you came back?" Charlie declared.

"I'm not talking about it," Arthur snapped.

"Why not?" Charlie insisted.

"Because you told me not to," Arthur answered.

"Okay, Art, have it your way. I just don't want to hear anymore talk about Heaven or any place else you think you went. Do you understand me?" Charlie commanded.

"Sure, Charlie, I understand you. No more screwy talk," Arthur replied.

"Come on now. Let's forget about the whole thing. I think I'll go out for a walk by the water for some fresh air," Charlie said.

"Good luck! There's not much fresh air down there," Ed said with a laugh.

"Thanks for dinner, Alice. That tasted good," Charlie said, grabbing his hat as he walked out the door.

"Whatever you want to do, Charlie. Close the door. You're letting the draft in," Alice said.

Alice turned to Arthur and said, "I'm sorry. If I knew Charlie was going to be like that I wouldn't have mentioned your dream at all. He's so bossy sometimes."

"That's okay, sis, you didn't do anything wrong. It's just that no one understands."

"I want to understand, but it's just that your stories sound so real, they give me the heebie-jeebies," she explained.

"Do you think I'm crazy, Alice?"

"No, I don't think you're crazy at all."

"Do you want to know what I think?" Arthur asked.

"Sure I do. What, Art?"

"I think this is all happening for a reason. I mean, I think I'm supposed to do something important, but I don't know what it is," he explained.

"Ma told me once that we are all here for a reason and that's to do God's work," Alice replied gently.

"Alice, I want to be the way I used to be. I don't want all this stuff in my head that no one wants to hear."

"It will be all right, Arthur. Don't worry. It's just going to take some time. Let me clean up here and you lie back down there and go to sleep if you like."

"Okay, but if I have a dream, I'm not telling," Arthur whispered.

Charlie slowly walked among the broken seashells scattered along the hard sand of the dark empty beach. A biting wind pushed against his back, forcing his shoulders up into a scrunch as he watched the cold moon rise over Dorchester Bay. It started as a sliver of flame that rose out of the eastern night sky. Charlie stopped to watch the growing circle of orange light paint the far edge of the bay with a haunting glow. The psychological report from Dr. Phelps that he carried in the side pocket of his coat detailing Arthur's psychotic symptoms seemed too heavy a weight to bear as he turned around for home into the bitter night wind. Charlie felt frightened for his little brother, and by the burden of his responsibility as his guardian. As he walked, the light from the rising moon behind him cast a long shadow onto the hard sand, which followed him home like an eerie companion. The warm rush of air seemed to soften his tense face as he opened the back door. Charlie sat down in the warmth of the empty kitchen and listened to the peaceful silence of sleep in the apartment. He took out the white report from his coat pocket and read it in the low light of the kitchen.

It read, "Arthur A. Chambers' psychotic symptoms include acute and persistent features of delusion that are accompanied by vivid hallucinations and illogical thinking that resembles a schizophrenia-like psychosis."

Charlie folded the report and placed it back into his coat pocket, grateful for the brief reprieve of his sleeping family. "I'll tell everyone tomorrow," Charlie muttered to himself as he headed off to bed.

Chapter 17

Green Marbles

Tommy climbed the flight of narrow stairs that led up to his best friend's apartment. He had always taken this back way up to Arthur's place because using the front hall was strictly forbidden by the Irish landlord. The back hall had no windows, which made it dingy even on the brightest of days. The only light came by a single low-watt light bulb that hung high from the ceiling on a chain, but Tommy knew from experience that the chances were slim that it would be on. The stairs were completely dark except for a band of sunlight that crept through the cracks of the exterior door just barely illuminating the bottom of the stairwell. In the darkness, Tommy groped his way up the stairs with his hands extended outward, hoping that he would not come into contact with something unfamiliar. His slow, deliberate climb through the musty darkness brought him safely to the top landing of the hallway stairs at the back door to Arthur's apartment. Tommy could barely see the outline of the wooden box that Arthur used to store his coal. Tommy knocked on the door.

"Who is it?" a muffled response came from the other side.

"It's Tommy! Art, school just got out so I came by to see how you're doing."

"Come on in. The door's open," Arthur shouted.

Tommy opened the door and quickly passed through the empty kitchen, noticing the breakfast dishes that were washed and neatly stacked alongside the gray soapstone sink. As he entered the room, a single piece of paper slipped from Arthur's hand and landed among a dozen or so colorful drawings strewn about on the bedroom floor.

"Hey there, Art! How are you doing?" Tommy asked.

"Hey, Tommy, where have you been?"

"I got grounded pretty good after the accident at the tracks. They wouldn't let me go out except to go to school. This is the first chance I've got to come up to see you."

"That's okay, Tommy. I know you would have if you could. I mean, you saved my life and everything. Alice told me all about it. Thanks for that, Tommy," Arthur said, shaking his friend's hand.

"Don't mention it. You'd do the same for me, right?" Tommy replied.

"You bet, Tommy. Any time."

"Hey, where did you get that shiner?" Arthur asked, pointing to a deep purple bruise under Tommy's left eye.

"I just ran into a door."

"No you didn't. What happened? Did someone jump you?" Arthur asked.

"No, it wasn't anyone."

"Who did it? Tell me!" Arthur demanded.

"Hey, what's up with all these drawings? Are you turning into an artist or something?" Tommy asked, picking up one of the drawings to change the subject.

"No, they're nothing. Give that back to me, Tommy. I don't want anyone to see it."

"Why not? What is it?" Tommy said, backing away from Arthur to get a better look.

"It's really nothing. Alice gave me some colored pencils and paper to pass the time. I was just drawing some goofy stuff, that's all."

"It doesn't look that goofy, Art. It actually looks pretty good. It looks like some kind of floating giant. What is it?"

"You won't understand. It's too complicated."

"Try me! Art, I think this looks really keen," Tommy offered.

"You do?"

"Yes! What are these colored balls floating around the giant for?"

"He's not a giant. His name is George, and they're not colored balls, they are orbs of review," Arthur explained.

"Oh! What's the heck's an orb?" Tommy asked.

"An orb is like a globe. It's something round," Arthur tried to explain.

"Like a ball? Why not just call it a ball then?"

"Yeah, but they're not balls, they're different."

"Where did you see this?" Tommy asked.

"I can't tell you."

"What, is it too complicated for me?" Tommy asked.

"No, Charlie told me not to talk about it any more, that's all."

"He doesn't want you to talk about what?"

"What happened to me after I got hit in the head," Arthur replied.

"Charlie doesn't want you to talk about going to the hospital?" Tommy asked.

"No, that's not it."

"Then, what is it, Art? Tell me."

"Do you promise not to tell anyone?" Arthur asked slowly.

"Sure, Art."

"Cross your heart?"

"See!" Tommy said crossing his heart.

"Okay, remember when that train ramp fell down and hit us?" Arthur asked.

"Yeah, how could I forget that?" Tommy replied.

"Well do you remember anything that happened to you after the ramp hit us?"

"I remember waking up and finding you hurt."

"Do you remember anything before that, I mean?" Arthur asked.

"No, I was knocked out on the ground."

"Well, I do remember what happened to me. I remember everything," Arthur explained.

"How could you? You were knocked out worse then me. You were out cold, Art."

"I wasn't knocked out. It was a lot worse than that."

"What are you saying, Art?"

"When that train ramp hit me, I was dead before I hit the ground," Arthur said.

"Get out of here! Yeah, that's a good one, you look real dead to me," Tommy replied.

"Tommy, I'm not lying. That's what happened," Arthur said crossing himself.

"How do you know you died? What happened?" Tommy asked.

"I hit the ground real hard, but I didn't really feel anything. That's when I popped out of my body and floated around the track. I was trying to get you to pop out too, but you wouldn't come out. It was the greatest thing, Tommy. I could fly up into the clouds or just float through walls. I could do anything or go anywhere just by thinking."

"This sounds like a dream to me. Maybe it was just a dream you had," Tommy offered.

"It wasn't a dream. If it was a dream, how would I know that the train ramp ripped the buttons right off your coat and then sliced right through the belt of your pants?"

"I don't know, but that doesn't mean you were dead," Tommy argued.

"Answer me this, how do I know that you were praying to God not to take me when you were running for help, and then, you thought to yourself that you felt like you were running in slow motion?" Arthur asked.

Tommy thought for a minute trying to remember the chaotic scene on the tracks and said, "There's no way you could know that, no one knows that. Art, you're really starting to give me goosebumps. Did you really die?"

"Yes, Tommy, I'm telling you I did, honest to God, I did,"

Arthur replied.

"Wow! What was it like, Art? Tell me!"

"It would take me a million years to tell you everything."

"Are all these pictures you drew about what happened?" Tommy asked.

"Yeah, but they are not very good drawings."

"They look okay to me. Hey, why don't you tell me about them? They're really good, I mean it. I didn't know you could draw like that," Tommy said as he gathered up the drawings from the floor.

"I didn't know I could either. It's a new thing for me."

"Okay, I'll tell you what. Here give them to me. I'll put them in order," Arthur instructed as he sat on his bed. He took the pictures, and meticulously placed them according to the proper sequence of events. Then he turned toward Tommy and said, "See the first picture. This is me and you on the tracks right after the ramp came down."

"Wow, Art, this looks like a real picture. I bet you could make money doing this," Tommy replied.

"Look. That's you on the ground and that's me flying over you."

"Who's the other guy on the ground?" Tommy asked.

"That's me too. I know this sounds crazy, but when I died, I came out of my body just like it is here in the picture."

"Were you a ghost?" Tommy stammered.

"I don't know. I guess I kind of was. I remember looking down, and I didn't have any feet," Arthur replied.

"Did you have wings?"

"No, I didn't have wings. You big goof," Arthur said, laughing.

"How could you fly if you didn't have wings?"

"I flew by thinking. I thought about being some place, and then I was there. Like this," Arthur answered, snapping his fingers.

"Huh? Where did you go?" Tommy asked.

"I went up into the clouds. I went to visit Alice in the kitchen. And I went into Buffalo Bill's train car."

"You got to go into the train car? I can't believe it! You are so lucky, Art. What was in there?"

"I was only in there for a second, but I saw a pearl-handled six-shooter with a silver handle, and a carved leather holster hanging on the wall," Arthur explained.

"Do you think it might have been Buffalo Bill's?" Tommy asked wide-eyed.

"Maybe, but I don't know for sure."

"Art, what's this big light by your head?" Tommy asked, pointing to the picture.

"That's what you go through to get to Heaven."

"To Heaven? You went to Heaven?"

"Sure did, and when I got there I met a lot of people."

"Like who?" Tommy asked.

"I met my mother, father, my guardian angel George, and a guy named Joe."

"You met a guy named Joe in Heaven? This sounds to me like you were down at the corner store, not in Heaven," Tommy said chuckling.

"I met Joe at the hospital. He was in the bed next to me. He told me there's nothing to worry about just before he went to Heaven," Arthur explained.

"What did he look like when you saw him in heaven?" Tommy asked.

"He looked young and happy. Everyone is young and happy in Heaven. That's the way it is there."

"How bad do you have to be not to get to go?"

"I don't know, but look, I made it and I was pretty bad," Arthur said laughing.

"Good point, Art. I guess it can't be that hard to get in," Tommy said, with a smirk.

"But, Tommy, it was so great there. I didn't want to come back. I remember I wanted to stay there forever."

"Why did you come back then?"

"Because I had to. They said I couldn't stay anymore," Arthur said.

"Why?"

"I'm not really sure, but I think I'm supposed to do something."

"Like what?"

"I don't know. I think maybe it has to do with the secret they told me," Arthur offered.

"What secret? You were told a secret? What was it?" Tommy asked.

"That there's nothing to worry about."

"That doesn't sound like much of a secret to me," Tommy replied.

"Oh yeah, then why doesn't anyone know they're supposed to stop worrying?"

"I don't know, Art, but come on, that can't be the big secret."

"That's not all of what they told me, there's more," Arthur injected.

"Like what?"

"Like we don't know who we are. We're the most powerful things in the entire universe, and we don't even know it," Arthur replied.

"I think if I was the most powerful thing in the universe, I'd know it," Tommy argued.

"Well, you don't."

"Tell me a special power I have that I don't know about," Tommy asked.

"You have the power to do anything you want."

"Name one," Tommy challenged.

"You have the power to stop your father from beating you," Arthur said.

Tommy stood in stunned silence staring at Arthur for a moment before saying,

"I didn't say my father beat me."

"You could stop him from beating you if you knew the other secret. But it doesn't really work if you don't believe in it. You have to believe." Arthur offered.

"How did you know he beat me?"

"I just knew," Arthur answered with a shrug.

"Is that how the power works?"

"Tommy, the power is inside you. It's inside everyone, but hardly anyone knows it."

"How do you turn it on? I mean, how do you make it work?"

"By believing that it's there, and by believing that you have permission to use it," Arthur explained.

"Who gives permission?"

"You do!" Arthur answered.

"Art, I'm really confused now."

"Okay, this is how it goes. God made everything, right, Tommy?"

"Yeah."

"Do you know that God made everything out of the same stuff?"

"What do you mean?" Tommy asked.

"God made everything out of just one thing," Arthur explained.

"What's that?"

"Love. God made everything from his love. This glass of water, this bed, the stars in the sky, everything, but He made us just a little different," Arthur replied.

"How's that?"

"We can change things. That's the way He made us different," Arthur explained.

"Like what?"

"Like the way we think. We can change things by the way we

think."

"I'm lost!" Tommy said.

"It's really not that hard to get, Tommy. A long time ago, before anyone can even remember, God gave us the power to change things, but most people thought it was just the power to change things on the outside. There weren't many people around who knew the power was really meant to change things on the inside," Arthur explained.

"Inside where?"

"Inside here!" Arthur said pointing to his heart, "And inside here," he added, pointing to his head.

"This is where God wants us to change. He wants everyone to wake up to who they really are – and to change," Arthur continued.

"Why?"

"Because it's time to, and if we don't, we can't do what He wants."

"What does He want?" Tommy asked.

"He wants us to live and create things every day with love," Arthur replied.

"I don't get it," Tommy said completely frustrated.

Arthur grabbed the bag of marbles on his bedside table that Alice had given to him and removed one single green marble.

He said, "See this marble, Tommy? It was made from God's love, just like you and me. It has enough love in it to change everyone in the whole world. If God put that much love into a little marble, just think how much love He must have put into you. You have all the power you need to stop your father from beating you or to do anything else you want to do. You just have to believe you do."

"How do I do that, Art? I'm so afraid of him. I really hate him," Tommy declared.

"You do it by filling yourself up with love so that there is no room for the hate and fear. Your father beats you, Tommy, and you are filled with fear. If you were filled with love, he wouldn't be able to beat you," Arthur advised.

"That sounds just crazy. I could fill myself up with anything I want, but if my father wants to knock me across the room that's what he'll do."

"Well, Tommy, you have nothing to lose then, do you?" Arthur said as he tossed Tommy the little green marble. He caught it and opened his hand and stared down at the bright green marble.

"Tommy, I want you to keep this marble in your pocket all the time. The next time your father tries to beat you, I want you to hold onto it in your hand, and imagine that your whole body is filled with love. If you'll do that, I bet he won't beat you."

"You're nuts!" Tommy said as he shoved the green marble deep into his pants pocket.

"Well, get in line. You're not the only one who thinks that," Arthur replied.

Chapter 18

The Conspiracy

Later the next day, Alice and Ed sat together at the kitchen table sipping hot black tea waiting for the family meeting to start. Alice disliked drinking tea without milk and sugar, but there was no money for milk and she had used the last of the sugar days ago. Charlie had called for a meeting to discuss what he ominously said was good news and bad news.

"What do you think the good news is that Charlie wants to talk to us about?" Alice asked, gently putting down her tea cup.

"I don't know, but I'm more worried about what the bad news is. I don't think I can stand much more of that," Ed replied.

"That's the back door. Charlie's coming!" Alice said as she listened to the distinctive heavy steps of her oldest brother climbing up the stairs.

"Hey there. How ya doing?" Charlie asked with a wide smile as he opened the door.

"What do you have in those grocery bags?" Alice asked.

"Oh, not too much. Just a few things that I picked up at the store."

"Like what? It's not payday, Charlie. Where did you get the money?" she asked as she looked into the two brown paper bags overstuffed with groceries.

"I hit the number," Charlie said proudly.

"How could you hit the number? You never play it," Ed asked.

"Well, I played it today, and boy, did it hit good," Charlie boasted.

"Charlie, I can't believe you bought a smoked shoulder. They're so expensive. Milk, bread, and sugar, too!" Alice said.

"Charlie, what made you play the number?" Ed asked.

"I had a dream about Arthur last night," he replied.

"What's the number?" Alice asked.

"That's a complicated question," Charlie replied.

"It's like winning at church bingo," Ed explained.

"Oh, did Arthur give you the number in your dream?" Alice asked.

"No, but I was looking for him in the dream. I kept finding this envelope over and over again with a clue hidden inside. Every time I opened the envelope I saw the same thing," Charlie explained.

"What was it?" she asked.

"Arthur's birth date, 12/15," Charlie answered.

"You played 1215? That never comes out! That must have paid off big," Ed offered.

"That's saying something," Charlie replied.

"How much did you play?" Ed asked.

"I was walking to the train this morning thinking about that dream when I ran right into Tony the bookie. I had some small change burning a hole in my pocket so I put it on Art's birthday. And what do ya know, it hit!"

"How much did you put on the number?" Ed asked again.

"A quarter."

"You spent a whole quarter on the number? That's a lot of money," Alice admonished.

"How much did it pay?" Ed asked.

"50 dollars," Charlie replied.

"50? 50 dollars!" Alice shouted.

"That's more money then you make in a whole week," she added.

"A lot more," Charlie replied.

"Do you think maybe you should play it again tomorrow?" she asked.

"No, I don't think so," Charlie laughed.

"That's how people end up with a problem. They win and

175

don't know when to stop," Ed offered.

"That's right, Ed, let's thank our lucky stars and not get greedy," Charlie replied.

"This must be the good news you wanted to tell us about?" Alice asked.

"No, actually it's not. If you can believe it I even have better news," Charlie replied.

"What is it? Tell me!" she said.

"I met the landlord this morning and he asked me about Art. He said he thinks Art's a good kid and he didn't want to make us move while Art was still sick. So we don't have to move. That's the good news."

"I can't believe this. That's so wonderful. Thank you, Charlie, you're just the best." Alice said as she sweetly kissed him on the cheek.

"So, what's the bad news?" Ed asked.

"The bad news is right here," Charlie said, as he reaching into his coat pocket to retrieve Arthur's psychiatric report.

"What's that, Charlie?" Alice asked.

"It's a report from one of Arthur's doctors."

"If it's bad, I really don't want to hear about it," she warned.

"We have to talk about this. It's important," Charlie replied.

"Are you going to tell us he's going to die?"

"No it's nothing like that. This is his psychiatric report," Charlie said, spreading the report out onto the kitchen table.

"What's a psy-chi-at-ric report?" Alice asked.

"It's something that says he's nuts, right?" Ed joined in.

"No, he's not nuts. Come on. Will you both just stop it?" Charlie said.

"Sorry, what does it say?" Ed asked.

"It says that Art is suffering from delusions, hallucinations, and irrational thinking. It's like something called schizophrenia."

"That sounds nuts to me," Ed offered.

"Let me see that," Alice said, grabbing the report.

"What's this thing here? What's a 186 IQ?" Alice asked.

"That's how smart you are. I just took an IQ test in school," Ed offered.

"What was your score?" Charlie asked.

"They wouldn't tell us. It's some kind of big secret," Ed explained.

"Why?" Alice asked.

"I don't know, I guess they just don't want you to know how smart you are," Ed replied.

"Mr. Kennedy, my gym teacher, says mine is probably the same as my waist size," Ed added.

"What's that?" Charlie asked.

"It's about 28," Alice said chuckling.

"Well, it look's like Arthur has you beat by a fair bit here," Charlie said.

"He just can't be that smart. He hardly makes it through school," Ed retorted.

"That doesn't matter. What matters is that we get him to stop talking about all his crazy talk. Who knows what the doctors will do if he doesn't stop?" Charlie added.

"It's a free country, Charlie. I think he can say what he wants," Ed proclaimed.

"It's not that simple, Ed. If the doctors say he has that schizophrenia and he's not getting better, they could lock him up," Charlie warned.

"The doctors are not going to send Arthur to jail, Charlie. That's stupid." Alice protested.

"Not to jail, Alice. Maybe to a state mental institution. I'm afraid if he doesn't shape up, they'll send him to a mental hospital," Charlie stated.

"Art is not going to any nuthouse if I have anything to say about it," Ed said angrily.

"I'm with you on that, but we have to stick together on this one and get him to stop talking so crazy. We have to get him to act normal," Charlie said.

"Shush! I think Arthur can hear us," Alice warned.

"His bedroom door is closed tight. Isn't he sleeping?" Charlie asked.

"He was, but I have an odd feeling that he might be listening," Alice answered.

"This is great! Charlie hits the number from a dream, Art went to Heaven, and now Alice can hear through doors. I think they're going to lock us all up if we don't watch out," Ed said.

"Did I just hear someone at the back door?" Charlie asked.

"Let me check," Alice replied.

"It's Tommy. Why are you so out of breath?" Alice asked.

"I ran all the way from my house and up your stairs."

"What's the matter?" Alice asked.

"Nothing, I just want to know if I could see Arthur, that's all," Tommy replied.

"I don't know, Tommy. I think he's sleeping."

"Ask him to come in, Alice. I think it may do Art good to see an old friend," Charlie said.

Arthur had been quietly lying in the darkness of his bedroom straining to listen to the disturbing conversation that was unfolding out in the kitchen. He had only heard bits and pieces of his brothers and sister's conversation, but like a good code breaker he listened carefully enough to pull together the general meaning of the muffled words and phrases. Arthur's body grew stiff as he thought, "If I don't stop talking about my trip to Heaven they're going to send me away. They're going to put me in a nuthouse, and Charlie wants them all to pull together to make it happen."

Arthur was stunned by the betrayal. He lay motionless in his bed, staring at the dingy cracked ceiling, wondering how they could do this to him. He could understand his older brother, Charlie, wanting to do him in because he thought him an annoyance, but his sister joining in the mutiny was just beyond belief. His legs began to shake as he thought he was about to scream out in tortured betrayal when suddenly, there was a knock on his bedroom door.

"Arthur, are you awake?" Alice softly asked.

"What?" Arthur said pretending to be stirred from his sleep. His mind quickly raced to how he might escape and run away. He imagined packing up a few belongings in his coal bag.

"Tommy Laucka is here to see you. Do you feel like company?" Alice asked from outside his door.

"What? Oh. Sure, Tommy can come on in," Arthur stammered, feeling like he wanted to faint or scream.

"Arthur, I need another one," Tommy said right away as he entered the room.

"Close the door fast and help me pick up all these Heaven pictures," Arthur ordered.

"What's the matter?"

"They want to send me to the nuthouse."

"Who does?"

"All of them! Ed, Charlie, and Alice. Can you believe that? Alice is in with them!"

"I don't think they're out to get you. Why would they do that? It's just your imagination. Hey, remember there's nothing to worry about, right, Art?" Tommy said.

"Tommy, I just heard them talking in the kitchen. They want to put me in a state mental place if I keep talking about what happened to me. I need to hide these pictures somewhere!" Arthur said as he shoved the pictures underneath his mattress.

"Well, that's kind of why I'm here, Art," Tommy offered.

"What? Are you in on it too?"

"No, I need another marble. Remember how you told me to hold onto the marble and to fill myself up with love the next time my father went to beat me?"

"Yes, of course, I remember," Arthur replied.

"It worked, Art! It worked like a charm."

"Really? That's great Tommy. Tell me about it."

"I did just what you said. I didn't run. I just stood right in front of him and held onto that marble as hard as I could. I tried to fill myself up with good happy thoughts, and when I opened my eyes again he was gone. I wasn't afraid of him anymore," Tommy described in awe.

"It sounds like you did it just right, Tommy. Nothing can harm you when you know who you truly are."

"So can I have another marble?" Tommy asked.

"For what?" Arthur asked.

"It's for my little sister, Amy. I want to give one to her so she doesn't have to get beaten either."

"Sure, Tommy, you can have another one," Arthur said as he retrieved the bag of marbles from his bed table.

"Can I have a green one?"

"I don't think it really matters what color the marble is."

"You gave me a green one last time. I think the green ones are the best."

"Okay, if there's a green one in here it's yours," Arthur said as he poured out the bag of marbles onto his bed.

"There's one, right there in the middle," Tommy spied.

"Looks like you're in luck," Arthur said, handing the green marble to Tommy.

"Hey thanks, Art! I have to get home now to get this to my sister."

"Sure, Tommy, I'll see you around," Arthur replied.

"Art, can I borrow your coal bag for a while?" Tommy asked, noticing the bag hanging off a nail in the back of the room.

"I don't think so, Tommy. I think I might need that before too long."

"Art, I was down by the track yesterday and there's tons of coal down there now. I thought I could walk through there to get you a couple of bags. Your coal box must be empty by now, isn't it?" Tommy offered.

Arthur's eyes widened at the thought of the train track covered with shiny black coal and answered, "Okay, but you better bring my bag back right away. I have a feeling I'm going to need it."

Arthur gathered up the multicolored marbles scattered about his bed and placed them one by one back into their ivory flannel sack, leaving one solitary green marble sitting on the edge of his bedspread. He dropped the bright green marble into the shirt pocket of his pajamas, and held his hand over it momentarily. The delightful aroma of boiled potatoes and smoked shoulder drifting in from the kitchen made Arthur start to feel sleepy again. His eyelids slowly closed, and he began to fall asleep wondering if the special dinner being prepared was a "send off" dinner. He drifted into a dream.

"Bright Cloud, there is no other way," his father Gray Wolf said as they stood on the high hilltop overlooking the black death that covered the valley floor.

"There must be another way," Bright Cloud proposed.

"Our people must see what the buffalo have sacrificed so that we can continue to live. There is no other way," Gray Wolf replied.

"I can take them to the west by the Great Valley. They will not understand this, Father. They will have no hope, and they will fail to reach the new land where the buffalo wait," Bright Cloud warned.

"Our people must travel through this valley of death to reach were the buffalo live. There is no other way, my son. We must walk into our fear and stand with it. We must breathe the fear into our lungs and feel it pound in our hearts until it passes through our spirits, falling still and quiet. We must know how the great buffalo sacrificed their lives so that we may live without fear. Here we will learn the great lesson of peace. It is not only peace with our enemies we seek, but also the sacred calm deep within ourselves. Fear is our only true enemy. Fear is the great illusion. The sacred buffalo have given their lives so that we may know this truth."

"Arthur, Arthur, it's time to wake up! Dinner's ready. Look what I've made for you," Alice beckoned.

Arthur opened his eyes and paused for an instant before answering her so his thoughts had time to adjust from the dream. He laid still in the quiet darkness of his room.

"Okay, Alice, I'll be right there."

"No, Arthur, you stay in bed. Charlie will come in to help you out into the kitchen. I don't want you walking around on your own just yet," she yelled back.

Arthur thought of declining the help for a moment, but had second thoughts, quickly surmising that the path of cooperation best suited his present predicament.

"Okay, Alice, thank you!" Arthur replied.

Arthur was silent as Charlie escorted him to the kitchen table.

"Arthur, sit down and dig in," Charlie instructed.

"Wow! Where did you get all this food?" Arthur said.

"Charlie came into some extra money today and brought all this home for dinner. Isn't that great, Arthur?" Alice asked.

"It sure is! Thanks, Charlie," Arthur responded.

"You're welcome, Art. Now sit down and enjoy," Charlie replied, smiling.

Arthur looked down at the giant mound of steaming food. Lined up in a row, like a fanciful dream in front of him, were bowls of boiled potatoes and carrots topped with heaps of melting butter. He pressed his finger into the fresh white bread from the bakery and it was still warm to the touch. There was even a bottle of cold milk, but the most spectacular sight of all was the giant smoked shoulder towering over the rest of the meal.

"What's the special occasion? Did something good happen? We never eat like this," Arthur said as he looked suspiciously at his brothers and Alice.

"No, not really, but Charlie did find out that we don't have to move," Alice answered.

"I didn't know that we were moving again," Arthur said in a startled voice.

"There was just some talk about it. Nothing's going to happen," she explained.

"Could you pass me the carrots please, Art?" she asked.

"Gladly!" he replied with a wide smile, and added, "Was everyone going to get to move to the new place?"

"That's a funny question. Why do you ask?" Charlie said.

"Art, would you like some potatoes?" Ed asked.

"Yes, thank you, Ed, I would. That is very kind of you," Arthur responded with an overly bright smile.

"Art, are you feeling all right?" Ed asked, sending a worried glance in Charlie's direction.

"I feel great! Thank you for asking," Arthur replied, still smiling broadly.

"Art, what's going on? You're acting awfully strange. Are you sure you feel okay?" Charlie asked.

"Here, Arthur, have a nice big piece of this smoked shoulder. It will just melt in your mouth," Alice said, placing the steaming meat on Art's plate.

"Thank you, Alice! Have I ever told you how much I love living here with you?" Arthur asked.

"Okay, what's up?" Charlie demanded, putting down his knife and fork.

"Nothing, Charlie. Nothing's up."

"Why were you asking if everyone would get to move to the new place?" Charlie insisted.

"Where is the new place?" Arthur asked.

"There is no new place, Art. We're not moving. We told you that. Now tell me what the heck is going on with you," Charlie demanded.

"Nothing. You wouldn't understand. It's too complicated," Arthur answered.

"Okay, you think so? Try me!" Charlie said.

"Alice, would you please pass those delicious carrots. Have I ever told you what a great cook you are? I am so lucky you're my sister. I love being here with you," Arthur politely stated.

"That's it! Art, either you tell me what you're trying to get at, or I'm going to bring all this food back to the market," Charlie warned.

"That might be a little hard to do, don't ya think? Everything is cooked and half eaten," Ed chuckled.

"Art, have you been having any of those dreams?" Charlie asked.

"No, I haven't had one, not one," Arthur stated flatly.

"What about Heaven? Do you still think you went to Heaven?" Charlie continued.

Arthur took the green marble from his shirt pocket and firmly clutched it in his hand. He thought of George his guardian angel made of light, his mother and father, and Joe Robinson making the garden for his wife, Betty, and said silently to himself, "I'm sorry everyone. I'm sorry I can't do it. No one believes me." Then, he answered, "I didn't go to Heaven. That was just a dumb dream."

"That's good, Art! So let's not have any more of that heaven talk, okay?" Charlie asked.

Arthur held the green marble tightly in his hand, thinking about his mother in the valley of sunflowers and asked, "Will we all stay together here if there's no more talk?"

"Yes, Art, of course. We'll always stay together. That's what we promised," Charlie answered.

"Okay, Charlie, it's a deal," Arthur said as he rubbed the green marble between his fingers and slowly put it back into the shirt pocket of his pajamas.

Chapter 19

Back to School

The deep snowdrift had completely disappeared in the alley next to Arthur's house. The snow bank had almost reached right up to the bottom of Arthur's bedroom window the day after the big winter storm. Alice had caught Arthur that afternoon opening the window in his bedroom in a playful but dangerous attempt to jump out into the steep mountain of snow. She was horrified at his reckless behavior, but she knew she couldn't keep him locked up in his room forever. Arthur was becoming a little stir-crazy being in the house for so long and Alice promised him that when the snow melted he could go back to school.

Tommy walked alone down the cobblestone street toward Arthur's apartment. The crisp morning air held a hint of spring that seemed to lighten the weight of the coal bag that pressed down onto his shoulder. He had faithfully walked the railroad track every day after school through the long winter searching for coal. He had managed to keep the coal box that belonged to Arthur's family on their stairs full of coal. Walking the tracks and gathering coal made Tommy feel connected to his best friend. He also considered his service as payment to Arthur for helping to make his little sister Amy's and his own life better. The regular nightly beatings administered by their father had miraculously stopped ever since Arthur had told him the secret. He felt grateful to his friend as he fiddled with the green marble in his pants pocket while climbing the dark narrow stairs. He unloaded his last delivery of coal into the wooden coal box. The back door to Arthur's apartment opened suddenly before Tommy even had a chance to knock.

"Hey there, Tommy!" Arthur said loudly with a wide smile.

"Hey, Art, are you ready for school?"

"You bet I am!"

Arthur added, "And I never thought I'd ever say that."

"It does sound kind of goofy, Art. Who wants to go to school?"

"It's better then being cooped up in my room forever."

"Yeah, I guess so. Are you bringing the marbles with you?" Tommy asked.

"I told you last week I don't have anymore. I gave you the last one weeks ago."

Arthur paused, looking at Tommy, and asked, "What are you doing with them anyway?"

"I'm giving them out."

"To who?"

"Kids around the neighborhood."

"Why?"

"To help them- - just like you helped me," Tommy answered.

"How many have you given out?"

"14."

"14! Wow, I didn't know I gave you that many," Arthur said.

"That's nothing, Art, look at this," Tommy said as he reached into his shirt pocket pulling out a folded sheet of white lined paper.

"What are all those names for?"

"That's the waiting list for marbles. Everyone wants one now."

"What have you been telling them?" Arthur asked suspiciously.

"The same thing you told me – that they're magic marbles that can make their lives better. I told everyone to fill themselves up with love and not to run," Tommy replied.

"That's not exactly what I said."

"It is too!" Tommy protested, "You said you brought them back from Heaven."

"I didn't tell you anything about those marbles being magic or coming from Heaven, Tommy," Arthur declared.

"And what are you telling them not to run from?" Arthur inquired further.

"Whatever they're afraid of, that's what. I told them to hold onto the marble, to fill themselves up with love, and not to run away from what they're afraid of."

"That sounds okay, I guess, but there's no power in those marbles, Tommy. The power's in you," Arthur stated.

"Maybe, Art, but everyone likes the marbles and they seem to be working."

"Well, I guess it's okay to say it that way as long as it helps."

"Hey, Art, I almost forgot. Here's your coal bag back," Tommy said as they crossed the old wooden bridge leading to their school.

"Oh good, yeah, I'll need that now. That was really something the way you got all that coal for us," Arthur said gratefully.

"Don't mention it. I was glad to do it."

Arthur felt oddly anxious as he walked up the granite steps of the John L. Motley Elementary School on his first day back since the accident. As he climbed the stone steps, he grimly recalled the unpleasantness of his last day there when he received a whipping for himself and his runaway friend.

Arthur and Tommy had been 25 minutes late for school that day, and upon arrival, they were immediately sent to the principal's office. He recalled how they both sat outside Mr. Adams' office on the wooden bench reserved for students who broke school rules awaiting their punishment. It was rumored that Principal Adams had been an army captain during the last war who had been captured and tortured by the Germans. He was a short, oversized man with stubby fingers. Arthur and the other boys always called him "Iron Finger" because when he was angry and trying to make a point, he would shove his right index finger into a student's shoulder like a pounding exclamation point. Iron Finger had been bored and disgusted at the sight of the two habitual offenders. They knew it was better to agree with Iron Finger and go along with the inescapable punishment than to argue about why they were late for good reason.

Iron Finger had walked into his office, turned around to stare back at them as they fidgeted on the bench. He had opened the narrow door to the office broom closet to reveal three long bamboo rods in a simple glass vase filled to the brim with cider vinegar. Arthur and Tommy could smell the vinegar and each other's fear as they sat trembling. They watched as Iron Finger deliberately slid one of the forty-inch bamboo rods from its glass holster. They had heard that he frayed the edges with a razor-blade to make it more lethal. He lifted it high above his head, displaying it like the "Staff of Moses" and then, let it fall with one powerful smooth motion. He whipped the slender rod down through the air, making a crisp snapping sound. His tool of doom rested with an abrupt crack on the lacquered floor below. Raw fear had engulfed the boys as they watched Iron Finger disapprovingly assess the performance of his bamboo weapon. He had closely inspected the frayed end of the rod that dripped with stinging vinegar, and determined for reasons known to him alone that the rod was somehow imperfect, not worthy of his punitive ritual. The boys had watched apprehensively as Iron Finger gently returned the bamboo rod to its glass holder and delicately retrieved yet another. He softly slid out the next one to closely inspect its perfectly frayed ends. He snapped the rod quickly in the air, deeming it acceptable with a menacing smile. The scene came back to Arthur with crystal clarity as if it had happened only yesterday.

Principal Adams had turned to face his two delinquent students and bellowed, "I expect both of you to take this like men!"

Just then Tommy had looked wildly at Arthur, and proclaimed the most ridiculous and wonderfully outrageous words Arthur had ever heard.

With a crazed look, Tommy yelled right at Principal Adams, "Not this bird, not today, anyway!"

Tommy had shot up from the wooden bench, and bolted as fast as his powerful legs would propel him out the front doors of the school and down Savin Hill Avenue to freedom. Arthur had been sitting gleefully stunned as Iron Finger chased Tommy in vain down the stairs, out into the street, waving his bamboo stick as he yelled, "Get back here, you upstart! Return here at once!"

Arthur hadn't moved one inch during Tommy's miraculous escape. He sat statuesquely motionless as he watched Principal Adam's labored ascent up the two flights of stairs back into the school. Red-faced and out of breath, Principal Adams stood sternly in front of Arthur. He rhythmically tapped his right pant leg with the stick, seemingly lost in an internal dialog.

"Well, Mr. Chambers. I'm certainly relieved that you had the good sense not to run like your foolish partner in crime. You will, of course, have to take the punishment intended for Mr. Laucka, as well as your own, but through the goodness of my heart, I will spare you the more serious punishment that awaits your accomplice, Mr. Laucka, once he returns. He may very well wish he had kept right on running once his parents receive my notice that their adoring son has been permanently expelled from elementary school. What a noteworthy achievement at such a young age. Don't you agree, Mr. Chambers?"

He could still feel the hot sting of the stick, and he hoped there would be no more days like that one. Now as he swung open the doors to the school, he was immediately struck by the distinct smell of old textbooks and sour milk. He stiffened at seeing his academic nemesis, Principal Adams, standing right in the middle of the corridor, watching with a disapproving eye as a second grade class filed by. Each child seemed to walk a tad faster as they passed him. Arthur held tightly onto the green marble in his pocket as he pretended to walk invisibly behind the throng of students, right past Iron Finger Adams. Arthur imagined the fear being squeezed out of his body like soapy water from a sponge as he repeated silently to himself, "My fear is not real. I'm made of love."

"Mr. Chambers! There you are. Well now, I am pleased to see you're back in school," Principal Adams said loudly over the crowd of students as he ever so slowly managed a rarely seen half-smile.

"You are?" Arthur replied suspiciously, lowering his eyes.

"Yes. The whole school has been waiting for your return. We heard you received a pretty nasty bump on the head. How are you feeling today?"

"I feel fine, sir."

"Well that's good to hear. Now run on to class, Mr. Chambers. I wouldn't want you to be late on your first day back."

"Yes, Principal Adams," Arthur replied, quickly marching down the hall. When he was well past Iron Finger and out of his sight, he pulled the green marble from his pocket and gazed at it in the palm of his hand as he thought, "I can see why Tommy wants more of these marbles. They do work pretty good!" Pleased by the way he handled his brief encounter with Principal Adams, Arthur tossed the marble up into the air and caught it with a snap of his wrist. He reached the open door to Miss O'Brien's classroom.

"Class, Arthur's here!" Miss O'Brien declared.

"Class, let's all welcome Arthur back to school."

"Welcome back, Arthur!" the class sounded out in unison.

"Class, now please pass forward your homework assignment from last night," she said.

Arthur watched as row after row of students passed forward handwritten cards welcoming him back to school.

"Here, Arthur, these cards are all for you. Your classmates and I wanted to let you know how very happy we are that you're back with us in school today, safe and sound. You can look at them later on," Miss O'Brien said as she handed Arthur a paper bag stuffed with cards.

Arthur stood in silence, slightly embarrassed by all the attention. As he looked at the smiling faces of his fourth grade class, he knew Miss O'Brien forced everyone to do this for him, but he still thought it was very nice.

Out of his daze, he heard the teacher as she prodded, "Arthur, you could start by saying thank you to your classmates."

"Oh, sorry. Thank you, everyone! This is really nice," Arthur responded, clutching the bag of cards.

"Arthur, very good, you can take your seat now."

He put the overstuffed bag of "welcome back" cards on the floor next to his desk as he took his seat.

"Clear your desks now and put away all books. It's time for the scheduled math exam. I want one piece of paper and a pencil on each desk, nothing else! Did everyone hear me? I said a single piece of paper and a pencil on each desk," she commanded.

Arthur couldn't believe what he was hearing. He hadn't been in his seat for more than ten seconds and his teacher was pulling a sneak exam on him. He was sure Iron Finger was really still out to get him as he raised up his hand in protest, accidentally kicking over the bag of welcome cards with his foot in the process.

"Miss O'Brien?" Arthur questioned.

"Yes, Arthur, what is it?"

"This isn't fair! I don't know anything about this test, I haven't been here."

"Arthur, it's okay. You're not expected to know the subject matter. You don't have to take the test. Just sit quietly at your desk."

A wave of relief washed over him as the teacher's words settled in. He felt for the round marble in his pocket as he bent over to adjust the bag of cards that had fallen out on the floor. He noticed that one of the cards had landed upright, leaning up against the iron leg of his desk. Arthur thought that someone must have spent a lot of time making this card. He picked it up, admiring its perfect scalloped edges and hand-colored flowers that had been carefully drawn in a circular border encasing the words, "Welcome Back, Arthur." He opened the card and inside there was a picture of a big bright green marble with the caption, "Thank you, Arthur, I'm not afraid anymore. From Jill."

Arthur sat in the silence, except for the sound of tapping pencils and the muffled scraping of soft chalk against hard slate. The words written on the card seemed like a secret message sent to him from some far-off land, an imaginary place he wasn't sure still existed. It seemed so long ago. What had once seemed so vivid and dazzling was now the faded remnant of a disappearing dream, a dream where words moved mountains and thoughts became real. He read the words from the card again, "I'm not afraid anymore." He read them slowly over and over until they became part of his breath. The words moved through him like a soft comfortable stream that carried him back to that magical place of peace and light.

"Arthur, please put those cards away. I don't want you to distract the class during the test. You can read them all after school," Miss O'Brien instructed firmly.

Arthur, startled from his daydream, sat up straight and looked up to the front of the room. He shoved the card back into the bag.

"Sorry, Miss O'Brien. They just fell over and I was putting them back," he said.

"That's fine, Arthur, just put them away now. The math test is about to start," she said before addressing the whole class.

"Class, I have written five questions on the board along with one bonus question. Please do your best to answer all five. If you have time after answering the five questions and you want to try to solve the bonus question for extra credit, please do so. The time allotted for the test is 30 minutes. Please start now."

Arthur stared at the blackboard. He was intrigued by the five math problems that appeared oddly familiar, almost as if he had perhaps seem them somewhere before. He knew he shouldn't be able to, but he felt certain he knew what the correct answers were. He shyly raised his hand.

"Arthur, a test is in progress. What can possibly be the matter?"

"Can I take the test, Miss O'Brien?"

"Arthur, I don't think you could pass it. Why don't you wait until I have time to go over this new material with you?" she said.

"But I think I know the answers, Miss O'Brien. Would it be all right if I took it now?"

"Arthur, you're disturbing the class. Take it if you want, but just be quiet while you do."

15 minutes into the test, Arthur folded a single piece of paper in half and passed forward his completed exam. Mrs. O'Brien smiled politely as she put Arthur's test paper off to one side of her desk and busily reviewed that afternoon's geography lesson. Although a courageous move on his part, she was certain that the result of Arthur's test would be dismal. She wasn't sure why he insisted on taking it, as math had always proved a challenge for Arthur. Perhaps this behavior was due to the damage to his head, she mused. After 30 minutes, the math exam ended abruptly and all tests were quickly passed to the front of the room. Miss O'Brien gave a reading assignment to occupy the class while she corrected the tests. She started with Arthur's test since he had been the first to finish.

After a few minutes, she sternly said, "Arthur Chambers, please come up to my desk."

"Yes, Miss O'Brien," Arthur said walking to the front of the room.

"Would you please explain this to me right now, young man?" she said in a low but clearly displeased voice.

"What do you mean?"

"These answers on your test. They're all correct."

"They are?"

"Yes, and you gave your answers without any work. I want you to explain to me how you got these answers?" she demanded.

"Well, I wasn't sure how you wanted me to do them, so I just did them in my head and wrote the answers down."

"Arthur, did you cheat?"

"No, Miss O'Brien, I didn't cheat. Those are my answers."

"Arthur, how could you possibly know the answers to those questions? You've been out of school for over four months!"

"I don't know, ma'am, I just did."

"Did you have a tutor at home?"

"No, Miss O'Brien."

"Has anyone been helping you with math?"

"No, no one has, but my brother Charlie asks me to try harder."

Miss O'Brien's face turned beet red as she peered down at Arthur over her silver wire reading glasses and let out an exasperated sigh and declared, "Then, the only logical explanation is that you cheated."

"No, I didn't cheat on anything, Miss O'Brien. Honest. I thought up those answers and wrote them down all by myself."

"Hmm! Well, let me see if I can get to the bottom of this, right now," she said as she pulled selected tests from the stack on her desk.

"Let's look at the tests of the students that sat around you."

"I didn't look at anyone else's test. I didn't cheat," Arthur insisted.

"I'll decide that, Mr. Chambers. Now be quiet please, while I check this work.

She continued to mumble, "It wasn't Eddie. He had only two right. Mary's fourth question is wrong. Suzy had the fourth and second wrong, and Tony didn't do any better."

She looked up at Arthur and said, "Mr. Chambers, I had you at a C-minus before you got hurt. How in the world can I possibly believe you came up with these answers? You even got the bonus question right."

Arthur's eyes widened and his shoulders pulled back and straightened proudly in front of the class at Miss O'Brien's desk and said, "Wow, that's great! I didn't know I did that good."

"Arthur Chambers, I don't know how in the world you did this. You got an A-plus, but next time you must show all your work, or I assure you that I will deduct points."

The highest mark Arthur had ever received on a math test was a B minus, but that was a long time ago. It was at the beginning of the third grade, and he was pretty sure he didn't deserve it either because he had guessed on some of the questions. He had never considered what it might be like to get an A in anything at all. It was just impossible to imagine, but he felt very proud of himself as he made his way back to his seat. Jill Kalvitis was smiling at him from across the classroom and he noticed she was holding a green marble between her thumb and index finger. Jill had thick, fiery red hair in long, tightly-braided ponytails that hung down along her back and mild green eyes that reflected her pleasant temperament. She was nodding her head approvingly in praise at Arthur for what he had just accomplished. Through her gesture with the marble, she was telling him that she knew exactly how he did it.

Arthur was starting to wonder if there was something to this marble thing after all when he heard Miss O'Brien say, "I think it's a good time for our special event. Mary and Jill, would you two please bring out the special items from the back room?"

The two girls started giggling as they opened the coatroom door, and brought out balloons, ice cream, and a large decorated cake with "Welcome Back Arthur" written in blue icing.

"Arthur, everyone thought it would be nice to have a little

party to welcome you back. Now, everyone, let Arthur through since he gets the first piece of cake as the honored guest," Miss O'Brien announced.

Arthur noticed something odd about the thin blue writing on the cake and asked, "Hey, it looks like someone else's name is under mine? Happy Birthday, Maggie?"

A contagious rumble of laughter started to make its way through the students gathered around Arthur.

"Well, Arthur, we hoped you wouldn't notice that, but since you did your cake was donated by the Savin Hill Bakery," Miss O'Brien explained.

"Yeah, someone forgot to pick it up," an anonymous student voice from the back announced.

"The cake looks really great to me! And tastes just as good," Arthur replied as he stuck his finger in the white icing.

Arthur tried to recall the last time he had ice cream and cake. It was so long ago that he was having trouble remembering how it tasted. The tongue-tingling icing with the cold sweetness of the ice cream was almost too good for Arthur to bear as he hungrily dug deep into the heavy moist cake. Engrossed with devouring his unexpected treat, he didn't notice Jill struggling through the crowd of students trying to reach him.

"Arthur, I'm glad you're back," Jill said as she pushed her way up next to him.

"Thanks, are you going to have some ice cream and cake? It's really good!"

"No, my mother doesn't want me to have sweets like that. She says they're not good for me."

"Oh, are you sure you don't want to try some of mine?"

"No thanks, Arthur, but I want to ask you a question."

"What's that, Jill?"

"Do the marbles last forever?"

"What do you mean?"

"I mean can you wear them out by using them too much?"

"I don't think so, Jill. Why?"

"Because I've been using mine every night before I go to sleep and I don't want to wear it out, that's all," she explained.

"What do you do with it?"

"I just hold it and pray that the nightmares will stop."

"What kind of nightmares, Jill?"

"I wake up screaming thinking that there's someone in my room. It wakes my father up and then he gets mad at me. He says I can't leave the light on all night because it costs too much money, but I'm too afraid to sleep in the dark," she said.

"I'm not sure that the marble you have can stop you from having nightmares, Jill. You just have to know that you don't need to be afraid."

"But, Arthur, it does work. That's what I'm trying to tell you. I don't have nightmares anymore. I just want to make sure it's all right to use the marble every night. I don't want to wear it out."

"Jill, how did you hear about the marbles?" Arthur asked.

"I heard some kids talking down at the Dillboy Soda Fountain that Tommy Laucka had these magic marbles that had the power to change things to the way you wanted them to be. So I went to Tommy and asked him for one. That's when he told me how they work and how you brought them back from Heaven."

"Jill, your marble didn't come from Heaven. It came from my sister Alice and the power to change things comes from you, not the marble."

Arthur began to get frustrated with Jill. No matter what he said to her he couldn't convince her that the marble wasn't doing all the work. "Tommy has really botched things up," Arthur thought to himself.

"I won't tell anyone, Arthur, if that's what you're so worried about," Jill offered.

"Who else did Tommy give a marble to?" Arthur asked.

"The only one I know is Faith Clark. Faith was too shy to ask Tommy so I got one for her myself."

"What does she use her marble for?"

"She's been using it on Spike."

"Spike? Who's Spike? Oh, you don't mean that monster German shepherd that lives on her street?"

"Yes, Spike's that awful dog. At first, she didn't think it was working and asked for a different marble. That was when Tommy told her that he didn't have anymore of them and to keep on trying with the one she had."

"I saw that dog eat a glass Coke bottle once. Spike is the meanest dog on the planet. What happened? Did she keep trying?"

"Like I said, at first it wasn't working, and Spike would try to attack her every time she walked by, but Faith kept trying. She would walk by Spike's yard every day with her eyes closed, holding the marble trying not to be afraid. Then one day out of the blue, it just happened," Jill explained.

"What happened?"

"She felt like she could do it. She felt like she could really fill herself up with love and told herself not to be afraid. That's the day Spike stopped going after her and now she even gets to pat him sometimes on the way home from school. It's crazy, Arthur. He even wags his tail at Faith."

"Are you fooling me, Jill? No one ever patted Spike and lived to tell about it."

"Arthur, I don't understand why you don't believe me! Tommy told me that the magic is in the marbles because you found them in Heaven. Did you go to Heaven, Arthur? Please tell me."

"I'm not supposed to talk about it," Arthur said, looking at his feet.

"Why not? If you really went to Heaven, why wouldn't you want people to know?"

"Because if you tell anyone something like that they'll just think you're crazy, that's why."

"I don't think you're crazy. I believe in the marbles. Did you really go to Heaven?"

"Yes, for a while, but they made me come back," Arthur muttered under his breath.

"Why?"

"They said I had more work to do."

"What kind of work, Arthur?"

"I wish I could tell you, but I really have no idea."

"Maybe your job is to give out the marbles?"

"I don't think so, Jill."

"Why not?"

"Because I didn't find the marbles in Heaven. I told you already. My sister Alice gave them to me as a present."

"Why did Tommy say they came from Heaven if they didn't?"

"That's what I plan on asking him when I see him after school today."

"Arthur, did you bring anything else back from Heaven?"

"Not really."

"What do you mean not really? Either you did or you didn't. What is it?"

"I told you I'm not supposed to talk about it."

"I promise. I'll keep it a secret if you tell me."

"Well, I did bring back something Jill, but I could get in big trouble if I tell you."

"Arthur, I promise!" Jill paused as she tried to think of something worthy to set her promise upon. "I promise on my marble that I'll keep what you tell me a secret for the rest of my life."

"Okay. That sounds good enough," Arthur replied.

"Good. Arthur, come on, tell me!"

"Well, I was kind of told a secret in Heaven."

"How do you know it's a secret?"

"Because no one seems to know anything about it."

"What is it?"

"It's a secret about how people are supposed to live."

"Come on, just tell me, Arthur, will you please?"

"There's nothing to worry about," he replied.

"I know there isn't, but will you please tell me the secret?"

"That's it!"

"Huh?" she blurted out.

"You're supposed to live your life like you have a marble inside you all the time, but it's not a real marble, it's you. It's the power that God gave you, but you don't know you have it yet," Arthur explained.

"How do you know I don't? I'm smarter then you are, Arthur Chambers, always have been too!"

"You don't know who you truly are."

"If you're so smart then, who am I?"

"You're someone who thinks a marble can change her life."

"It did help me. I don't have nightmares anymore."

"As long as you think that marble helped you, you will never know who you truly are," Arthur continued.

Jill stood with Arthur off in the corner, randomly tapping her polished brown shoe on the wide boards of the classroom floor. She stared down at the worn floor in silence as she tried to contemplate a possible deeper meaning to Arthur's words.

"Do you mean Mary stopped Spike? And I stopped my night-mares? Not the marble?"

"Yes! That's it, Jill! You did it. Not the marble."

"Do you think God might have done it, Arthur? I prayed to him too."

"Jill, God is always there to help, but he gave everyone the power to change things in their life on their own. He gave us all the power to stop our nightmares and he gave us the power to create our dreams too. It's like God put a marble inside us so we could make things different and make everything the way we want."

"Why don't we know that? Why is it a secret?" Jill asked.

"I don't know, Jill. Maybe it was because we weren't ready to know or we weren't grown up enough, but I know it's been going on for a long time. Ancient people used to pray to statues. To them, the statues were their marbles. They didn't understand that the power was inside them either," Arthur explained.

"Okay, class! I think it's time to end the party now. Let's clean up everything and get back to our seats," Miss O'Brien declared.

Arthur returned to his seat, happy that all the other students thought enough of him to have an ice cream and cake party to welcome him back, yet he felt concerned after talking with Jill. How could he keep his promise to his family not to talk about Heaven, while Tommy traveled around the neighborhood handing out Arthur's magic marbles? He should have known Tommy was up to no good when he kept asking for more marbles. "Now I'm left with a big mess to clean up," he thought. The only thing he could think to do was to have a long talk with Tommy after school. Arthur wondered what his guardian angel George would think of all this marble business? Heaven gave him an important message that people need to know and now everyone was walking around thinking they had magic marbles. "They've got it all wrong," he thought, befuddled about how he could turn this around. Arthur felt weak as he put his head on his desk and thought, "George isn't going to like this. Heaven sure messed up when they picked me."

Chapter 20

Evil Ed

Arthur sat with his legs hanging over the edge of the long puddingstone wall that ran along the front end of the school. The early spring sun was high in the afternoon sky, resisting the call of the distant horizon. He was looking intently at a small group of light purple flowers that were struggling to emerge from the half-frozen ground. They stood bravely on a tiny patch of dirt between two mounds of blackened snow. Arthur had once told Alice they were snow flowers because they were the first ones to fight their way up through the melting snow. Deep in thought, he didn't notice Tommy approaching from behind.

"Hey, Art, I heard your class had a big party for you at school today?" Tommy announced.

"Yeah, they had cake and ice cream and everything. Why didn't you come?"

"Our teacher didn't tell us about it. I don't think she wanted us to go."

"Tommy, we have to talk about what you're doing with the marbles."

"Sure, Art, that's great! I wanted to ask you how we could get some more of them anyway. I've run out and everyone's asking for them."

"That's not exactly what I wanted to talk to you about, Tommy. I was talking to Jill at the party and she told me what you're telling everyone. It's not right," Arthur stated.

"What's not right? What are you talking about?"

"What you're saying. It's not what I told you."

"Oh, do you mean the part about them being magic marbles?"

"Yeah, Tommy, that and the part about how I brought them

back from Heaven. Why are you telling everyone that? You know Alice gave them to me. Tommy, are you selling the marbles? Because if you are, you're going to have to give all the money back."

"No! Art, honest. I'm not selling them. I'm giving them all away. I'm trying to help people. You helped me, and now I'm trying to help some of the other kids. That's all."

"That's all?" Arthur questioned.

"Well, it kind of made me feel like I was important," Tommy added.

Arthur had known Tommy for a long time and he always knew when he was lying. He was the first friend Arthur could ever remember having. He met Tommy for the first time when he was four years old. It was on a warm July day that they met. Arthur was playing on the sidewalk, hiding from the afternoon heat in the long shadow of his Dorchester triple-decker. Tommy walked right down the center of Arthur's street with a baseball bat and glove slung over his shoulder. He looked to Arthur like he was someone important and someone he would like to get to know. The rim of his dark blue Boston Red Sox cap was pushed back revealing his freckled face as he shouted, "Hey, can you play baseball?"

"I don't know," Arthur answered.

"Do you want me to teach you? You can be the pitcher and I can be the hitter."

Arthur's mother nodded her approval as she watched from the front stoop of their house.

"Stay where I can see you," she added.

That was the beginning of the friendship. Arthur had grown to love Tommy, but he would never let anybody know that, and he knew now that Tommy was telling the truth.

"Come on, will you, Tommy? You have to stop telling everyone that. You're going to get me into a lot of trouble if you don't," Arthur pleaded.

"I know, I know, I'm sorry. If your brother Charlie finds out about it you can blame me. Okay?"

"It's not all your fault, Tommy. Everyone wants to believe in the marbles."

"I know, Art. I didn't even have to try to talk anyone into it. Everybody just believed right away."

"I think that's because people need to believe in themselves, but they don't really know how. That's why they believe in things like statues and marbles."

"How do you do it? How do you get to believe in yourself, Art?"

"I don't know for sure, but I think you have to just keep practicing believing in yourself until you can," Arthur said.

The tip of Tommy's shoe sent a rusted tin can rattling down the sidewalk as he pondered his best friend's words. Somehow he knew he was right.

"So — no more marbles, Tommy, okay? Deal?"

"Shake on it. It's a deal!"

"Hey, I was going to head down to the tracks to look for coal. Do you want to come?"

"Okay, I think I'd better come with you just in case. Because well — just in case something happens."

"What could happen?" Arthur laughed.

"Gee, I don't know, Art? The last time you were down there you just ended up visiting Heaven. Don't ya think you might want to be a little more careful this time?"

"Okay, let's take it easy."

"Last one to the track carries the coal all the way home!" Tommy yelled and took off running.

A cold wind from the bay pushed Arthur and Tommy toward the tracks. As they got closer, Arthur could smell the diesel fuel and taste the coal dust in the air. Many times since his accident, he had wondered if he would ever again walk the track hunting for coal. The familiar sound of gravel crunching under his shoes made him relax, and he slowly let his mind drift back to the grayness of that late afternoon several months earlier.

"Remember that giant piece of coal we found the last time we were here?" Arthur shouted to his friend.

"Sure do. I didn't find anything like that when *I* was looking."

"Tommy, do you remember how it looked like a big black diamond?"

"Yeah, Art, what happened to it?"

"I still have it. I hid it in my room the night Charlie wanted to toss it in the stove."

"What made you think of that?"

Arthur paused knowing he could trust Tommy, and said, "I remembered seeing something that looked like it when I went to Heaven, but it wasn't made from coal, it was a giant diamond of light made with every color you could imagine. It floated high in the sky so everyone could see it."

"A giant diamond of light? What was it there for?" Tommy asked.

"I don't know for sure, but I think it was there to show everyone in Heaven when someone created a new way to reach God."

"Why would Heaven want to show that?"

"Maybe it's because God likes it when we use the power inside us to find our way back."

"Do you mean God likes it when we go to church?" Tommy asked.

"I didn't hear anything about that there, but I think God likes it when we use our power to find him because we have to look inside ourselves to do it. He wants us to find out who we really are."

Tommy came to a sudden stop, and threw his arm out to prevent Arthur from moving ahead.

"Oh no!" Tommy gasped.

"What is it?"

"Look what's up ahead on the track."

Arthur squinted into the glare of the low sun and he couldn't believe his eyes. He took off his glasses, quickly cleaned them, and then, rubbed his eyes and looked out again. Arthur could feel his heart starting to pound in his ears, and the air grow thin and tight in his lungs. Several hundred feet down on the track, stood all six feet and two hundred pounds of Eddie Skinner. Straddling the track like a two-eyed Cyclops guarding the entrance to some forbidden land, he stood challenging them. Arthur hated bullies, but he especially disliked this one. Evil Ed was what Arthur and Tommy called him, and he was the worst kind of bully. He would steal your lunch money, beat you up, and embarrass you in front of all your friends. Suddenly, Arthur felt like he was walking in slow motion with his feet glued to the gravel below. Like a terrible nightmare, Evil loomed ahead. Arthur hoped he would wake up soon. Stories of Evil told by the other neighborhood kids flashed through his mind. They were tales about how he enjoyed ripping the wings off butterflies and how he had electrocuted his neighbor's cat just for kicks. In past encounters with Evil, Arthur would not have hesitated. He would have run as fast as he could in the opposite direction at the first sight of him. The last time they ran into him ended up very badly with Arthur and Tommy just barely escaping. But now, Arthur struggled to put one foot in front of the other as he gradually approached the menacing giant. With the rhythm of his slow, deliberate footsteps, Arthur started repeating to himself, over and over again, that his fear was not real, and that he was made of a loving light.

"Art, let's get out of here now," Tommy warned.

"Yeah, maybe. I'm not so sure we should."

"Did that whack on the head make you nuts? He's gonna kill us both."

"If we run now, he'll chase us forever."

"I'd rather run now and live, Art. He looks like he means business."

Evil Ed stood a short distance away from them, pounding his tight fist into his large, rough hand. Arthur could hear the sharp slap from Evil's broad knuckles as he slammed them into his hand with a steady punishing beat. As if he was looking at a movie clip, Arthur suddenly recalled the lesson of trust he learned from the orbs of review. He saw an image of himself as a young child who was riding that giant ocean wave to the shore. Seeing that scene in his mind somehow gave him the boost of inner strength he needed, and he quietly muttered to himself, "I was just as scared then as I am now."

"What's that, Art? What did you say?"

"Tommy, we can't run. We have to believe in ourselves. The fear we feel isn't real."

"Are you nuts?"

"I have an idea; follow me," Arthur insisted, stepping up the pace and walking right up to Evil Ed.

"Hey there, Edward, great day we're having, don't you think?" Arthur abruptly offered.

"Don't call him Edward! He hates that name," Tommy admonished through his clinched teeth.

"Don't call me that! Call me by my real name," Evil Ed thundered, practically spitting out each word. His eyes seem to glow bright red as he spoke.

"Okay, okay, Evil!" Tommy replied.

Evil took one menacing step forward. He slammed his warmed-up fist into Tommy's shoulder, and yelled, "What are you — some kind of wise guy?"

"No, I'm just really glad to see you, Ed. What are you doing all the way down here?" Tommy asked, coughing and swallowing hard from the pain to his right shoulder.

"I have some unfinished business with you two from that day on the bridge. It's time we settled up, so I thought I'd come by and say "hi" and settle the score," Evil said menacingly with a sarcastic smile.

"I could wait a little longer to settle up if it's all right with you," Tommy retorted.

"Oh, yeah? Well, guess what? You're the first one I'm going to settle with, then!"

Arthur felt the pure rage flashing off Evil's giant body like red-hot blasts of heat from a steaming coal furnace. Arthur knew the root of Evil's ruthless anger was somewhere deep down inside of him as a black, cold pool of fear. He knew this fear was so thick and suffocating that it blocked out all light, making Evil violent and destructive. To save his good friend Tommy from his wrath, Arthur knew he had to act quickly. An idea came to him as his fear quickly gave way.

"Why don't you like your real name?" Arthur asked with a strange calmness.

"What? What the heck are you saying, you little four-eyed creep?" Evil shouted.

"Edward. Why don't you like your name, Edward?"

Tommy was shaking and holding up his hands in front of his face guarding against an imminent attack. Evil abruptly stopped, stumbled, and then turned around.

"Edward? Why don't I like my name, Edward? What kind of stupid question is that?" he demanded.

"Art, are you crazy? What are you doing? He'll turn your face into chopped meat," Tommy warned.

"I don't think it's stupid. I don't think your name is stupid at all. I think you have a great and noble name," Arthur replied calmly.

"I didn't mean my name was stupid, you little idiot."

"Of course you didn't. Would you like to know what your name really means?" Arthur asked.

Evil looked dumbfounded and replied, "Names don't mean anything. They're just names."

"I know for a fact that all names have secret meanings that can tell you what kind of person you'll grow up to be," Arthur responded.

Tommy had no clue what Arthur was trying to do, but strangely, he knew it was working. Arthur had more guts than anyone he had ever known, but this seemed downright reckless. He slowly backed away from Evil's grasp, strategically positioning himself on the other side of Arthur for a speedy escape.

"I've never heard of that. You're making it up," Evil said suspiciously.

Arthur reached into his pocket to retrieve his green marble, and he began rolling it slowly between his fingers before he answered Evil again.

"I'm not making it up, but if you don't want to know — well, that's okay with me."

"You little rat. Tell me, but it's not going to get you two off the hook if that's what you think."

Before Arthur answered, he tossed the marble into the air several times, catching it with one hand, and then the other so as to make sure Evil Ed noticed.

"Actually, your name, Edward, means "noble leader" like a king, or someone that people admire greatly."

Tommy watched with amazement as Evil's scowl softened into an agreeable look of simple curiosity. Like a magician Arthur continued to toss the green marble up into the air, right past Evil's long pointy nose. Evil's eyes followed the marble's hypnotic spin back into Arthur's hand. The wizardry seemed to lighten Evil's very presence, and his dark beady eyes amazingly began to twinkle.

"Does that mean I might end up being a king?" Evil stammered in a trance-like state.

"You could, but that's hard to tell right now," Arthur announced.

Evil kept one eye on Arthur as the other followed the spinning marble through the air as he said, "Is that one of those marbles?"

"What do you mean, Ed?"

"I heard that there are some kids around saying that they have magic marbles. Is that one of them?"

"Yes," Arthur replied.

"What's so magic about it? It looks like a stupid, old green marble to me."

"You can't judge a marble by the way it looks on the outside," Arthur replied cryptically.

"What's that supposed to mean? Don't try to get smart with me, you little wisenheimer, or I'll just snap you in two."

"No, Ed. I'm not being smart. I'm just saying that what makes these marbles magic is on the inside. You can't see it just by looking at it."

"If you can't see it, how do you know it's there?"

"Because it makes things different— "

"Like what? What could that green marble make any different?"

"Haven't you heard, Ed? Everyone's talking about it. They're saying the marbles can change your life."

"You're crazy! If that marble's so great, what did it do for you, four eyes?"

Arthur's glasses slid down his nose, while his calm, unblinking gaze penetrated fearlessly into Evil's cold dark glare.

"It took my fear away. I'm not afraid any more."

Evil took a menacing step forward, slamming his oversized boot down into the rocky gravel right in front Arthur.

"You're not afraid of what?"

"To start with, Ed, I'm not afraid of *you* anymore."

"Oh yeah, why not?"

Arthur flicked the marble up into the air with his thumb, sending it spinning between Evil's black beady eyes.

"Because I have the marble," Arthur replied.

Evil snapped his hand out trying to snatch the marble out of the air before it reached the outstretched palm of Arthur's hand.

"Give it to me. I want it," he demanded.

"I can't. It won't work for you."

"Why not?"

"Because it doesn't work for anyone who is mad."

"I am not mad, you twerp!"

"You don't look happy to us," Arthur responded, and added, "Why don't you try smiling? If you smiled maybe then it could work."

"Smile? Why would I want to smile? I'll smile when I snap both of your skinny little necks!"

"Do you want to try the marble? If you want the marble you're going to have to stop being angry at us, or anyone else. If you smile, it might work."

Evil took a long deep breath as if he was trying to extract some odd phenomenon from the air. His large chest expanded from the effort and his black eyes narrowed as his nose scrunched up in a contortion that made him look like he had just smelled something awful. The corners of Evil's narrow mouth struggled upward, and stopped painfully as his face started to resemble a fat chipmunk crunching down on a nut.

"What do you know? That's a great smile, Edward! That's exactly how you do it. The marble just might work for you after all."

"Give it to me then," Evil spat out, trying to grab it.

"No, not yet, you have to believe first," Arthur instructed.

"Believe in what? What am I supposed to believe in? Just give me that marble."

"I'm trying to make this work for you, Ed. You have to believe in yourself and you have to believe that the marble can really change your life."

"Could it make me turn out to be a king?"

"I think so. Sure, why not?" Arthur replied.

"How does it work? Do you just toss it up in the air? Is that how you make it work?"

"No, that's not how you do it. You have to relax and let the happiness seep in. Can you feel anything yet?" Arthur said.

"I don't know. Yeah, maybe. I think I'm starting to feel something."

"That's good, Ed. Here, you can take the marble now. Just hold it gently in your hand and keep smiling."

"Uh-huh. I'm pretty sure I'm feeling something now. Got it, I feel this king thing coming on," Evil replied.

"That's great, Edward. I think it's starting to work."

"What should I do now?" Evil asked.

"Okay, close your eyes, then hold onto the marble and think about how you want the marble to change your life, and whatever you do, keep on smiling!"

"That's it?" Evil asked.

"That's it!" Arthur responded.

Arthur and Tommy slowly backed away while Evil smiled awkwardly with his eyes shut as he held the marble in the palm of his rough outstretched hand.

"How long do you have to do this for?" Evil asked.

"About ten minutes. Don't open your eyes or it won't work. Ed, we're going to take off now, we'll catch you around. Good luck with your marble."

Deep in concentration, Evil nodded his head and said nothing. Arthur and Tommy walked steadily away from the track, breaking into a full run only when they were around the corner and completely out of sight of Evil.

"Art, that was the greatest thing that I ever saw in my entire life! I can't believe you just did that. You set that up perfect."

"Thanks, Tommy, but that was a little too close for me all the same."

"You had him just eating out of the palm of your hand. You were great!"

"I'm just glad we got by him. I just wish I didn't have to give him my last marble, that's all." Arthur replied.

"But I don't get it. You sounded like you really did believe in the marble."

"Do you really think I would have given Evil Ed that marble if it was magic?" Arthur asked.

"I guess not, but you sure could have fooled me. You looked like you believed it yourself," Tommy said.

"Look, if I had given Evil a magic marble he probably would destroy the world with it. Do you think I would do something like that?"

"I sure hope not, but if you say they're not magic, I guess I'll believe you."

"The magic is not in the marble, Tommy, it's in you. Don't believe in the power of marbles, believe in the power of you," Arthur said.

"You'd better find some of that power right now because here comes Evil," Tommy explained.

"Okay, Tommy. I get your point. Let's run," Arthur shouted.

Chapter 21

The Invitation

Betty Robinson sat alone in the still emptiness of her Victorian home at the antique desk her husband Joe had bought on a fall weekend while they were leaf-peeping along the coast of Maine. Joe had loved the maple desk with its river reeds bending against a wind that swirled up to its polished top. The carving had reminded him of the pharaohs of ancient Egypt. She wrote slowly in smooth elegant strokes as the black ink flowed across an invitation made from the finest English parchment. The name "Mr. Charles Chambers" was eloquently written across a matching envelope that was placed off to one side of the desk. She paused on the last few lines she chose to invite the Chambers family to her home for afternoon tea. As she glanced out the window, she considered how odd it seemed to be sending her finest handwritten invitation to a family of young children whom she barely knew. She reluctantly admitted to herself that her behavior over the past few months had been a bit peculiar. She hadn't written anyone at all, nor had had any guests to her house since Joe had died. She was vaguely aware that she had become a lonely recluse in her vast home, wandering from room to room searching for memories to sooth her broken heart. Nothing could console her. She felt completely lost without Joe. As the ink in her fountain pen flowed to a graceful stop, she felt haunted by thoughts of the young boy Arthur and her mysterious encounter with her beloved Joe at the hospital. Somehow she imagined that seeing the Chambers again might somehow connect her to Joe once more. Nonetheless, it all seemed so hopeless and pointless that she wondered if she was truly ready to see anyone yet. She let out a deep sigh, reluctantly placed the invitation in the envelope, and sealed it with her stamp, marking "R" in the red wax.

Several days later, Alice Chambers was walking home from school, and she saw it from two houses away. The mysterious looking envelope stuck out from the top of their mailbox. She quickened her pace. They hardly ever received any mail and Alice felt a strange tingle of excitement as she ran up the front stairs two steps at a time, quickly snatching the envelope out from the rusty mailbox. Her eyes narrowed and her heart sank when she saw the envelope was addressed to Mr. Charles Chambers. "Why can't I ever get a letter like this?" she thought as she lifted the envelope up to the light of the sky, trying to spy what was inside. The faint smell of flowery perfume drifted off the envelope as she noticed the return address of Mrs. Betty Robinson displayed in swirling ink in the upper left-hand corner. "Why would she be writing to my brother? I hope she hasn't changed her mind and wants to have her money back," Alice thought. The sound of hard footsteps followed behind Alice up the stairs.

"Hey, sis, what's in the fancy envelope?" Arthur asked looking over her shoulder.

"I don't know. It's for Charlie."

"Let me see it. It looks like it's from a girl."

"It's from that woman we met at the hospital. Remember the lady that paid all your hospital bills?"

"Oh yeah, but I never met her, did I?"

"No, but she was the sweetest old lady, Arthur. I talked with her in the waiting room when they were operating on you. Maybe you'll get to meet her someday. It was the most unbelievable thing she did, paying your bill like that. I still can't imagine how someone could be so kind to us."

"Joe was really nice too," Arthur replied.

"Who's Joe?"

"Joe? Oh, he's that woman's husband. I met him in the

215

hospital."

"Arthur, you couldn't have met him at the hospital. He died before you woke up."

"But I did meet him. I met him before he went up to Heaven."

"Arthur Chambers, you must stop that crazy talk right this instant. Charlie told you what would happen to you if you didn't stop talking like that."

"Yeah, I know. They'll put me away on the nut farm."

"That's right, and there'll be nothing we can do about it either."

"All right, sis, just forget it. Okay?"

"Why don't you go into your room and start your homework now and I'll make dinner."

Alice walked toward the kitchen table shaking her head. She held the envelope up to the light bulb hanging over the table, turning it around again trying to read what was inside, but she couldn't see anything through the thick paper. She placed the mysterious card on the center of the table, and pulled out a bowl of potatoes from the kitchen shelf.

Arthur felt the roughness of the canvas strap slide through his hand as his book-bag hit the bedroom floor. Overcome with exhaustion, he fell back into his bed. His tired eyes wandered across the plaster ceiling, following one of its long winding cracks into the far corner of the room. Sitting on top of his dresser was the black shiny diamond of coal that reminded him that it all really did happen. It wasn't just a dream. He wasn't crazy. George had told him that he couldn't stay in Heaven because he still had work to do, but for the life of him he couldn't imagine what that work might be. He clearly remembered George telling him that God liked it very much when someone used their power to find a new way back to Him. He wondered, "Maybe that's it. Maybe the work I'm supposed to do is to find my own special way back to God. Then, everyone will be happy. But I don't know. That can't be it. They're expecting too much from me. I'm only 10 years old. How can I know what I'm supposed to do?"

A sharp knock on the bedroom door startled Arthur from his meandering daydream.

"Hey, Art. Are you in there? Come on out. I want to talk to you," Charlie shouted.

"Okay, I'm coming. Just a minute, Charlie."

Arthur placed his gray stocking feet on the cold floorboards. With his big toe sticking out of one of his socks, he made his way out into the kitchen.

"Charlie, you're home early, aren't you?" Arthur asked.

"Yeah, the delivery of stone didn't make it this afternoon so they sent everyone home early today."

"Art, there's a couple of things that I want to talk to you about."

Arthur's throat turned dry. It was never a good sign when Charlie wanted to talk about things. He couldn't imagine what he had done to get in trouble so soon at school. He ran through a mental laundry list of possible offenses and came up with one thing, and one thing only. Charlie must have heard about the marbles. If that was what this was all about he had no doubt he was a walking dead man.

"Hey, Charlie, do you want to play a game of checkers?"

"No, Art. I don't think so."

"Are the Red Sox playing? Maybe we could listen to the game on the radio? What do you say?"

"Art, what's eating you? The Red Sox don't open for another three weeks. You're acting awfully strange."

"Charlie, if you're mad about those marbles I can explain everything."

"Marbles? What marbles? Art, what the heck are you talking about?"

"You're not here to talk about the marbles?" Arthur asked.

"Art, the only marbles I'm looking for are the ones that fell out of your blasted head," Charlie answered.

"Oh, very funny! Can I go now?"

"Art, it's no big deal, relax. I just wanted to tell you I got a call from your teacher, Miss O'Brien. She says that you got an A+ on a math test recently and that you're doing so well in class she's asking for permission to have you re-tested."

"Re-tested? What for?"

"She wants to see how smart you really are. They call it some kind of an IQ test.

"I just have to answer some questions?"

"That's right. There's nothing to worry about," Charlie replied.

Arthur was startled by his brother's words and thought to himself, "Did I just hear him say that there's nothing to worry about? Could it possibly be that Charlie was beginning to under-stand his message from Heaven that 'fear isn't real and there's never anything to worry about?' Wouldn't it be fantastic if Charlie really understood?" Arthur decided to investigate further.

"Charlie, do you know who you are?"

"What?"

"I said do you know who you are?"

"That's what I thought you said. Are you sure you're feeling okay?"

"Sure I am, but I mean if you had to say who you really are, then what would you say?"

"Are you starting that crazy talk again? Because if you are, we're going to have that long talk. Do you know what I mean?"

"No, Charlie. I'm not starting anything. Just forget it, okay? Taking that test sounds all right to me. I'll do it if you want."

"Okay, I'll let Miss O'Brien know. Before you run off, there's just one more thing."

At the prospect of hearing more bad news, Arthur's shoulders slouched forward and his head dropped slightly.

"We've all been invited to afternoon tea on Wednesday at Mrs.

Robinson's house. She's the nice woman who paid your hospital bill. Like I said, we've all been invited, but Ed and I can't make it because of work. So it will have to be just Alice and you," Charlie said.

"Having tea is a girl's thing. Can't Alice just go? She loves that stuff. I don't want to go to a tea," Arthur complained.

"No, you have to go. That woman was kind and generous to us. It would be very rude if you didn't go," Charlie replied.

"I hate tea! Plus, I'll probably just spill something on her fancy rug. I think you should just send Alice," Arthur argued.

"The decision has been made. You're going. That's it. When Alice gets back from the store, I'll tell her that she'd better make sure you are with her when she goes. I don't want to hear another word."

Chapter 22

The Tea Party

Alice and Arthur stood at the edge of the long driveway feeling awkward dressed in their Sunday best. In contrast to his usual carefree look, Arthur's hair was neatly combed and his typically scuffed brown shoes were polished. His Irish knit sweater was buttoned up above his neatly-pressed trousers. When he first walked out of his bedroom into the light of the kitchen, Alice commented that he looked like a picture straight out of the Sears catalog. She wore long white gloves borrowed from the lady downstairs and her only dress with a tulip print, along with her mother's old sun hat that was slightly too large for her head. The two of them looked with anticipation up toward the bend of the path that led to Mrs. Robinson's house.

"Can you imagine what it must be like to live in such a beautiful mansion?" Alice asked.

Arthur stopped. His face suddenly became pale as he looked ahead. His eyes widened at the sight of the Victorian mansion perched on top of an outcropping of Roxbury puddingstone.

"Alice, wait. I've seen this house before."

"Arthur, of course you have. You've walked by this house a thousand times."

"No, you don't understand. I mean that I know it from someplace else. I've seen it before, but it wasn't here when I saw it."

"Arthur, come on. You're making no sense at all. Please try to act normally when we get inside. If you don't act right, you'll embarrass me."

Arthur looked quickly at Alice, and then walked up the hill to the old house in silent bewilderment. He knew he had been to this house once before. Everything was the same. The ginger-bread detail hanging beneath the roof like fancy candy and the faded porch that snaked around the base of the house felt strangely familiar to Arthur. It was all just as he remembered it. But where was this place? Where did he see it before? The mental aberration slid through his consciousness like a ghostly image just beyond his reach. His sister's voice seemed far away.

"Arthur, will you please pull yourself together! We're going to an elegant afternoon tea and you're acting like a complete goof!"

"Sorry, sis, but I just know I've been here before and it's driving me crazy."

"Will you just get a grip and try not to say too much when we get inside? Please, come on! Try to act proper," Alice scolded.

In a slow, almost apologetic movement, Alice lifted the heavy brass door knocker with her gracefully gloved fingers, noticing that it was fashioned in the likeness of a lion's head. As she let go of the door knocker, it swung back down through the air, striking the oak door with a booming crack. The unexpected bang startled Alice who moved a half-step back.

"Arthur, do you think anyone is home?" she whispered.

"No, I don't think so. I think we should just go on home now," Arthur replied.

"You're just saying that because you didn't want to come to the tea anyway."

"No, this place is starting to give me the heebie-jeebies. I don't like the way it feels here. Let's just go, Alice."

Arthur could feel the sadness radiating out from the stone walls surrounding the front door. His chest started to feel heavy. Suddenly, a flash of memory came to him. It illuminated the dream for an instant. He was certain now that this strange place was the house from his dream. This was where his father had brought him. This was the house on the summit of the mountain, the dark and ominous mansion that was surrounded by a mist of loneliness. He remembered his father's last words to him,

"There's someone here who needs your help."

"Arthur, do you think we should keep trying or just go home?" Alice paused, and then continued, "I guess I could try once more."

She reached out and pulled the door knocker up, which once again came crashing down onto the brass striker plate of the door with a resounding crack.

"That should wake her up," Arthur announced.

Alice saw the lace curtain on one of the first floor windows move slightly, and then she heard a frail voice of a woman from behind the door ask, "Who is there?"

"What did she say?" Arthur asked.

"She wants to know who's there?"

"Didn't she invite us?"

"Arthur! Shush! Let me handle this."

"Hello, ma'am. I'm Alice Chambers and this is Arthur. We're here for afternoon tea,"

Alice and Arthur stood up straight, conscious of their best posture as they waited politely for a response from behind the great door. They were greeted by an awkward silence.

"You invited us here for afternoon tea, ma'am. I have the invitation right here," Alice added, holding up the envelope.

Arthur watched the doorknob begin to turn before the door cracked slightly open. The fragile voice from behind the door asked, "Where is the older boy?"

Alice shrugged her shoulders and Arthur said, "I think she means Charlie."

"Oh yes, of course, ma'am. Charlie and Ed couldn't come today because they had to go to work," Alice explained.

Just then the door slowly swung open, revealing a frail elderly woman whom Alice did not recognize at all.

"We're here to see Mrs. Robinson," Alice announced.

"I am Mrs. Robinson."

Alice was sure the woman had to be mistaken. The lady she

remembered from the hospital was elegant and stately with neatly-cut white hair, possessing a manicured appearance. She remembered feeling comforted by the woman's calm, dignified demeanor in the waiting room. The old woman who stood before them in the doorway now seemed an unrecognizable shadow of the regal lady she had met before. She was bent over a wooden cane and her unkempt stringy hair hung over her forehead. Her rumpled housedress bore the obvious signs of needing a good cleaning, and her dry, rough hands revealed fingernails that were grown out and yellowed. She seemed to lean down upon her cane as if she carried her heaviness from some unspeakable hurt. "How could this phantom of a woman be the dignified Mrs. Robinson?" Alice thought to herself.

"Is this the young boy? Is this Arthur?" Mrs. Robinson asked.

"Yes, this is Arthur," Alice replied.

"How are you feeling, young man?"

Arthur felt immobilized by the aura of sadness that surrounded the old woman. Her intense emotional state seemed to further drain her failing presence. It seemed odd to Arthur that so much grief and melancholy could be generated by such a wisp of a woman.

"I feel fine, ma'am. How are you feeling?"

"That's a fine question, Mr. Chambers. You are a direct young man, aren't you? As it seems, no one — no one at all — has dared to ask me that for some time now, but you have. I've seen better days. Maybe God will bless me soon and take me home to Him, but I'm sure you two don't want to hear talk like that, now do you? Please, do come inside. The table has been set for afternoon tea."

"Yes. Thank you, Mrs. Robinson," Alice replied.

"There's nothing to worry about, Mrs. Robinson. God likes it when we find our way back to Him," Arthur added.

"Shush, Arthur! I told you not to talk about that stuff," Alice whispered sharply.

"That's just fine, young miss, everyone can speak their mind here in my home, but that was indeed quite an odd thing to say, in fact. Arthur, what did you mean by such a funny statement? And whatever is it that makes you think I'm worried?"

The stern warning from Alice's menacing stare and the invisible pinch to the back of his arm made Arthur reply, "I have no idea what I meant."

"Very interesting, young sir. Maybe we could talk more about this over some hot tea then? Please do come now into the drawing room. I've made some special sandwiches and freshly baked cookies too. Do you like cookies, Arthur?"

"Yes, Mrs. Robinson, I love them. What kind do you have?"

"I've had chocolate chip and sugar cookies made especially for you."

"Sugar cookies are my favorite," Arthur replied.

"Is that right? My husband Joe loved my sugar cookies too."

"He did? He never told me that," Arthur said.

Alice covertly kicked Arthur's shin under the table sending him a clear warning to stop. He winced at the sudden pain in his leg as Alice said, "Mrs. Robinson, this is such a beautiful room. I think it's the most lovely room I've ever seen."

"Thank you, Alice, that's a nice thing to say to me. It's been a long time since I've had guests in my home for a visit. Nobody else has been here since my Joe left me," she said sadly as her voice trailed off.

Alice's eyes moved slowly around the formal drawing room in awe at the splendor. Heavy velvet drapes elegantly covered white French doors from the floor to the ceiling. Exquisite handmade tapestries adorned the walls and a sparkling crystal chandelier hung down from the molded ceiling. Alice imagined she was a princess in a grand castle having tea with royalty. She had never been in such a spectacular house surrounded by such fine furniture and wall hangings.

"Arthur, kindly tell me again what you just said? I'm not sure

I understood you," Mrs. Robinson asked.

"Nothing, I didn't say anything."

"Oh, on the contrary, Mr. Chambers, I'm quite certain that you did. You just said something interesting concerning my late husband, Joe? You seemed to say that he didn't tell you about liking sugar cookies. Pray do tell, exactly what did you mean by that?"

Alice started to slump down into her chair at Mrs. Robinson's inquiry, which could only lead to an embarrassing situation. Alice was beginning to feel disappointed that the elegant tea wasn't going as expected. She had been looking forward to this afternoon, and now was beginning to realize Arthur was going to ruin it.

"I'm sorry Mrs. Robinson. Ever since his accident he says the strangest things sometimes. He doesn't mean it. Please don't pay him any mind. He doesn't know what he's saying. "

"Oh, is that right? Oh my. However, I think Arthur should be able to speak for himself, Alice. Did you know my husband Joe, Arthur?"

"Yes."

"How did you know him?"

"I met him in the hospital."

Goosebumps rose up on Mrs. Robinson's arms as she remembered her shocking moment with Joe in the hospital corridor and his plea to help the young boy, the same young boy now sitting in front of her, Arthur.

"Please tell me how you met him."

"He was in the bed next to me and he talked to me."

"What did he say?"

"At first he just asked me my name and stuff like that, but when all the doctors were around him he acted different."

"How so?" the old woman asked.

"The doctors were worried that he wasn't going survive the operation and that's when Joe just kind of popped up and smiled

225

at me."

"What did he look like? I mean did he seem different in any way?" she asked.

"Yes, he kind of sparkled like a bright white light and he could fly."

The old woman was having trouble containing her emotions, and she seemed electrified by Arthur's words, which mirrored her own mystical encounter with her husband Joe at the hospital.

"Arthur!" Alice scolded.

"Did he say anything to you?" Mrs. Robinson probed.

"He said that there is nothing to worry about."

"Really! What else did he say?"

"Nothing," Arthur replied.

"Nothing else? Didn't he say anything about me?" she said sadly.

"He said nothing then, but he did say more later."

"Later when?"

"When I met him in Heaven."

Alice abruptly shifted her weight in her chair, and rolled her eyes incredulously in Mrs. Robinson's direction. Alice had grown completely weary of the conversation and desperately wanted to change the subject.

"See, I told you. He can start talking about all this crazy stuff at anytime. Like I said, he doesn't mean anything by it. We should just try to ignore him. Mrs. Robinson, I'd love to try one of those delicious cookies," Alice said.

"I do mean it and it all really happened. I'm tired of pretending nothing happened. If they want to lock me up for telling the truth, then they can come and get me. Mrs. Robinson, Joe told me to tell you that he loves you, and that there's nothing for you to worry about. Joe told me to tell you that I could be in the club, and that he was sorry he broke your green lamp. I saw him. I did. And he told me all that."

The china teacup slipped from Betty's fingers and spun

toward the floor. Her hands shot up to muffle the gasp that came out of her mouth. The spinning teacup seemed to hover in mid-air before smashing into a thousand pieces on the wood floor.

"Oh, my Lord! Oh, heavens! What? What did you say? I can't believe this. There isn't any way you could have ever known that. How did you know that?" Mrs. Robinson blurted out.

"You see, Arthur. You really did it now. Charlie is going to kill you when he finds out. Mrs. Robinson, are you all right? Arthur didn't mean any of this. He's just a young goof. Please, Mrs. Robinson, I'm very sorry about my stupid brother," Alice pleaded.

"No, it is indeed okay, Miss Alice. Please calm down, sweet-heart. I'm surprised, that's all. I'm just fine, really. I do believe every single word you said, Arthur. I most certainly do. I have no idea why I do, but I do," she answered dabbing her eyes with her linen napkin.

"You do?" Arthur asked with wide eyes.

"Yes, now please tell me some more about this. Tell me every-thing. I want to know absolutely everything my Joe told you."

"Mrs. Robinson, thank you for not being mad at Arthur, but I think we probably should go back home now. Arthur and I have a lot of homework to do for school tomorrow and it's getting late," Alice said.

"Yes, of course, Miss Alice. I'm sorry to have kept you for so long. I would like very much to ask Arthur if he would be kind enough to come back soon by himself to talk with me some more? I would like that very much indeed. It would mean a great deal to me."

"Well, I suppose, if you want him to do that he can," Alice replied, slightly annoyed.

"Would you like to do that, Arthur?" Mrs. Robinson asked.

"Yes, ma'am, thanks. I would like to."

"Grand! It's all settled then. Can you please come back to see me again this coming Saturday?

"Yes, I can do that. I just remembered something else, Mrs. Robinson."

"What's that Arthur?"

"Joe told me to tell you he's is making you a garden in Heaven. He told me how much you love gardens, and that's what he's doing now in Heaven, making you a garden."

Tears welled up in the old woman eyes as she took Arthur's hand in her own.

"Oh, tell me, dear child. Do you remember what it looked like?"

"I remember that it had the most beautiful, bright pink rose right in the middle," Arthur said as if he were still looking at it.

The old woman bowed her head down and quietly wept.

Chapter 23

Betty's Club

A chilly breeze rose up from Dorchester Bay covering Savin Hill in a hazy mist. With the coal bag slung over one shoulder, Arthur walked up the roughly-fashioned puddingstone steps to the woods at the top of the hill. The icy wind whipped at his bare neck and Arthur lifted his collar in defiance. The gray morning brought back dreamy thoughts of the stories he had heard about Savin Hill. He was told that the pilgrims had landed at the base of the hill in wooden ships in 1630. They had built a log fort on the crest of the hill to protect them from Indian attacks. Like others, Arthur believed the hill was hallowed Indian ground. He was convinced that building the fort right there must have made the Indians furious with the pilgrims. This morning, he had no time to hunt on the side of the hill for ancient arrowheads or to look for evidence of the old fort. Arthur had promised Mrs. Robinson that he would come by her house at 9:30 to talk with her again and to help clean up her yard.

Upon reaching the summit, he stepped into a halo of mist that was glowing from the morning sun. Looking out onto the area where the pilgrim fort had once stood, and to his utter amazement, he saw a crisp green $10 bill float right past his nose. He was stunned to realize that the sacred Indian ground before him was completely covered with countless dollar bills floating and tumbling through the air like dry leaves above the brown winter grass. The advancing legion of money lifted up into the air on a short gust of wind, surrounding Arthur in a green vortex of spinning money. He reached out into the funnel of paper to capture a swirling $20 bill. Arthur stared at the twenty in complete amazement because it was the first time in his life that he had ever held one. It began to occur to him that someone must have lost all this money. He ran to the edge of the hill to look, but there was nobody anywhere in sight. The sea of money continued its advance across the top of the hill as Arthur scrambled to figure out how he could save it all from blowing away. Hunched over, he ran from one bill to the next as they tumbled along. He picked each one up and stuffed it as fast as he could into his coal bag. There were ones, fives, tens, and twenties moving across the ground in a random jumble that made Arthur dizzy. He circled this way and that in chaotic pursuit. The last bill came close to sailing off the edge of the 30-foot cliff. Arthur reached out as far as he could, successfully snatching the $20 in mid-air. With all the money safely captured in his coal bag, Arthur collapsed, panting onto a nearby rock. He gazed with astonishment into his bag at the huge green pile of crumpled money. More money was tightly stuffed into his coal bag than he knew existed in the entire world. He began to sort and organize his jumbled-up pile of cash. He counted 18 ($20s), 32 ($10s), 27 ($5s), and 28 ($1s) for a massive total of $843. Arthur stared in wide-eyed amazement at the neatly stacked money between his hands. He tore a thin strip of cloth from his coal bag and securely tied it around the bills to keep them safe. He had no idea what to do next, but he knew that he must be late.

Betty Robinson heard the faint sound of the grandfather clock in the foyer chime 10 o'clock as she made her way out into the back garden lined with oak trees. A rusted green watering can filled with decaying leaves leaned against the old stone foundation. She viewed her overgrown garden full of brown bramble and weeds with a deep sigh. Turning over the abandoned watering can she dumped its decaying contents out onto the ground. "It's about time I did something with this old garden," she muttered.

Betty wondered what had happened to her young guest when the back gate suddenly swung open and Arthur came running into the yard apologizing.

"Sorry I'm late, Mrs. Robinson."

"Yes, hello young man. I've been wondering what might have delayed you."

"I came up over the hill back there. It's a short cut."

"Well, I don't think it's really much of a short cut if it delays you," she said winking.

"I know, but I found something up on top of the hill," he replied.

"Oh? What is that, Arthur?"

"Money, and lots of it."

"Money? What do you mean?" she said.

Arthur opened his coal bag revealing the large pile of neatly stacked money.

"It was just blowing around on the ground up there. All I had to do was pick it up," he said.

Betty's jaw dropped and her soft eyes widened in fear. The watering can she was holding dropped to the ground. To Arthur, her expression revealed she didn't appear quite pleased with this strange turn of events.

"Oh, my heavens! Where in the world did all that come from?"

"Like I said, right up there on top of the hill."

"You mean on the top of Savin Hill? How could all that money be up there?" Betty replied.

"It was there. All I had to do was pick it up. It was every-where, spread out all over the top of the hill. I picked it all up before it blew away. That's why I was late."

"Arthur, are you sure that's exactly what happened?"

"Yes, that's exactly what happened, Mrs. Robinson."

"Well, even if that's true, it must belong to somebody," she scolded.

"I looked all around and there was nobody there. I thought I would give it to you."

"But that's not mine and it's not really yours to give, now is it? It must belong to someone," she objected.

"I thought you could pay my hospital bills with it so you wouldn't have to spend your own money."

"You do have a kind heart, young man, and that's thoughtful of you, but I can't accept this. I think you should take it to the police station right away. I could telephone them right now."

"No, I think I'll ask my brother, Charlie, later. He'll know what to do about this."

"Okay, perhaps it is best to ask your brother. I guess you can wait to show him. Now, let's take a look at this garden. I'm glad you made it here," Betty said.

Betty stood at the garden's edge, surveying a field of twisted vines and jumbled weeds. With her hand firmly upon her hip, she shook her head.

"Arthur, have you ever seen a more disappointing garden than this one?"

"It looks pretty bad to me, but I haven't seen too many. There aren't any gardens on my street. Why does it look so bad?"

"Because it's been neglected. Lots of things around here have gone untended lately. I think my husband, Joe, would be very disappointed with me right now if he could see this garden."

"I think Joe wouldn't want things to be so bad here. I think he would want you to be happy," Arthur said.

The old woman picked up the watering can again. She knew Arthur was right. There was no difference between her and the overgrown garden. "Both of us are dying from neglect," she thought.

"Arthur, tell me about Joe in the garden in Heaven. What did he look like?"

"He looked younger than when I saw him in the hospital room and he looked happy. He was walking around planting things and every once in a while he'd stop, take out his handkerchief and wipe his face, and say, 'Boy, it sure is a beautiful day to go fishing.' That's one thing I couldn't really understand. Why was he saying he wanted to go fishing in a garden?"

"Arthur, please excuse me. Would you bring that chair over to me? Oh my dear, it's warm. I think I'm feeling a bit faint."

The flaking blue paint on the metal chair rubbed off on Arthur's hand as he carried it to her. The color reminded him again of the bright blue sky in Heaven.

"Here, Mrs. Robinson, sit down on the chair so you can feel better."

"Thank you, Arthur. I do feel better already."

"I'm sorry if what I said made you feel bad, but I'm just a kid. I don't think I know what I'm doing sometimes," he said.

"No, Arthur, I think what you're saying is really wonderful. You're helping me to feel better. It is really quite astounding that you knew what Joe would always say when he was helping me with the garden. He would take out his handkerchief, wipe his brow and say, 'It's a beautiful day to go fishing.' It was just his way of teasing me. It was his way of letting me know there was something else he could be doing, but that he liked helping me with my garden more. It surprised me a little when I heard you say it, that's all."

Arthur nodded his head and smiled. He didn't feel safe talking about Heaven with anyone, except maybe Tommy, but Mrs. Robinson didn't stop him from believing the way Alice and his brothers did. He trusted her and felt relieved he could talk with her about his experience.

"You're the first grown-up who believes me. Everyone else thinks I'm crazy and wants me to be quiet."

"I don't think you're crazy and I don't want you to be quiet. On the contrary, I want you to tell me absolutely everything my dear Joe said. Tell me what else he said."

"Everyone said kind of the same things up there, Mrs. Robinson."

"And what was that, Arthur?"

"They all said there's nothing to worry about. They said if we knew who we really are that we would never worry about anything ever again."

"Who are we supposed to be?" she asked.

"They told me we are supposed to be co-creators," Arthur replied.

"Co-creators? That's interesting! I didn't expect that. What do you think they meant by that?"

"I'm not really sure. They said that God gave us the power to change anything and that we really can create things with him, but we just don't know it yet," Arthur replied.

"Who are they? I mean who told you all this?"

"Everyone I met in Heaven, my mother and father, George and Joe."

"Arthur, who's George?"

"Oh, he's my guardian angel. He's great! He's seven-feet tall and made of light. He showed me all around Heaven."

"Oh my, a seven-foot guardian angel made of light. Is that so?" she said with a smile.

"See, you don't believe me either, no one does. Why did they tell me all of this if no one is going to believe me? It makes me mad that they made such a big mistake," Arthur said.

"Who made a mistake?"

"I wish I knew, but it was someone in Heaven. I'm only 10 years old, you know. Why tell me the message? No one is ever going to listen to me."

"Arthur, I'm very sorry that I laughed. I just felt excited by what you were saying. A seven-foot angel made of light must have been quite a spectacular sight. I believe you completely and I think Heaven made a very wise choice in picking you."

"Do you really?" he asked.

"Yes, I do, and I want you to tell me more, but first I think we should clean up this old garden."

Arthur knelt on the ground rearranging the last of its riverstone edging at the end of the rambling garden. He had dumped the final wheelbarrow of debris and turned the garden soil over exactly as Mrs. Robinson instructed. He heard the sound of shuffled footsteps approaching on the garden path. It was Mrs. Robinson carrying a serving tray sporting a tall glass of cider and a short stack of star-shaped sugar cookies.

"Arthur, you have done a grand job! The garden is coming back to life again. I think if Joe is making a garden for me in Heaven, then I'll make him one right here. How does that sound?" she said with a bright smile.

"What did you just ask me, Mrs. Robinson?" Arthur said as he hungrily eyed the sugar cookies.

"Do you think Joe would like it if I made him a garden just like the one he was making me in Heaven?"

"That sounds like a good idea to me. I think Joe would like that."

"Arthur, would you like to have some cookies and cider?"

"You bet I would. I'm starved."

Mrs. Robinson sat down watching Arthur enjoy the snack. It had been a big disappointment to her that she had never had any children, but she hadn't thought of that in many years. Watching the young boy so innocently devour his treat made her think of how it might have been if she and Joe had had children, or even grandchildren. Arthur's brown eyes even seemed to have a slight family resemblance, she thought dreamily.

"Mrs. Robinson, these are the best cookies I've ever had, really. They're so good and chewy. I wish we had these at home."

"I'm happy you like them. When you're finished would you carry that bush over there into the center of the garden? Do you see it, Arthur? It's the one in the brown burlap sack."

"Sure, I see it," Arthur replied.

"Please, place it right there in the center of the garden."

"Right here?" Arthur asked.

"Yes, that's perfect. I'll be able to see it from my window."

"What is it supposed to be?" he asked.

"It's a rose bush, Arthur."

"That's a rose bush? It looks like a bunch of dead branches to me."

"Hopefully, after it's planted it will grow beautiful pink roses," she proclaimed.

"I don't see any roses on this. Maybe you should take it back to the store and get another one."

"It's fine, Arthur. It's just lying dormant."

"Dormant? What's that?"

"Well, it's like the rose bush is sleeping and when it's planted it will wake up and grow."

"We must seem like that. Like rose bushes to God," Arthur said.

"That's an odd thing to say, Arthur. Why would you say that?"

"Because God is trying to wake us up. That's what I was told. A long, long time ago God planted a seed in all of us, and now he wants us to wake up so we can make it grow," he explained.

"Is that what your friend George told you in Heaven?"

"Sort of, but he told me a lot more."

"Do you think George would mind if you told me more about Heaven?" she asked.

"No, I don't think he'd mind. He wants me to tell people."

Betty looked at her watch and saw that the time was getting late.

"Arthur, that's marvelous. I can't wait to hear all about it, but it is getting very late and your family must be getting worried. Maybe it would be better to tell me the next time you come."

"You don't really want to hear anymore, do you? You're just saying that because I'm a kid and you don't want to hurt my feelings."

"Arthur, no, that's not true. I'm very interested in what happened to you. It's just getting so late and I don't want you to get into any trouble."

"I won't get in any trouble. Alice knows I'm here," he offered.

"Well, all right then, why don't you tell me just one thing about Heaven that you liked and the next time you visit you can tell me more. How does that sound Arthur?"

"That sounds okay, Mrs. Robinson. I guess it is getting late."

"What is the first thing you want to tell me?" she asked.

Arthur closed his eyes and lowered his head as if he was in a deep, contemplative state. Mrs. Robinson sat patiently waiting as he thought.

"The diamond! I'll tell you about God's diamond," he began suddenly.

"That sounds fascinating!"

"There's a giant diamond in Heaven. My father said they call it God's diamond. I saw it in Heaven when we were walking toward the great hall. It looks much bigger than the moon is in the sky and it's made of every color you can think of."

"Why would God want to have a big diamond?" Mrs. Robinson asked.

"Because when someone finds a different way back to him it makes him smile. God likes it when we use our own power to find our way home. When we do this, the diamond grows a little bigger and brighter. He doesn't like it very much when we use our power to stop other people from looking for other ways back to him."

"Arthur, I'm sorry, but I'm getting a little confused. What is this power you keep mentioning and how do you stop people from looking?"

Arthur took a deep breath and looked directly at Mrs. Robinson. His forehead wrinkled slightly as he tried to remember what he had heard. He began slowly.

"God put a great power in us a long time ago, but we don't know that yet. It's the reason why he wants everyone to wake up. He wants us to know that we don't need to follow anyone else to find him, but that it's also okay if we do. We can find our way back home to him just fine. He doesn't like it when we let other people tell us the way home instead of following our own hearts. And he really doesn't like it when we believe the people that tell us they know the 'one and only' way home. No one owns God and no one owns the way home. All ways are good and there are many ways. God doesn't like it when we fight each other about the right way home. He smiles each time a new way is found. And when that happens, God's diamond shines a bright light that just grows and grows."

"You know, Arthur, I believe that. I think most all of the difficulties in this world have been caused by people who think that they own the only path to God. When we stop fighting over who owns the path to God and realize that no one does — that's when the world will be a better place," Mrs. Robinson responded.

Arthur nodded as he finished the second glass of cider and gingerly pulled the last cookie off the plate.

"I think so too," he said.

"Oh my, look at the time. I really think you should be getting home now," she said taking the empty plate from Arthur.

"Mrs. Robinson, what kind of club do you have?"

"I beg your pardon, Arthur. What did you just say?"

"Joe told me to be sure to tell you to let me into your club. What kind of club do you have?" he continued.

She smiled while her wrinkled eyes filled to the brim with tears. She knew what Joe was trying to do. Even in death, he was still trying to protect her. The message was clear. He did not want her to spend the rest of her days in isolating grief. He had sent Arthur to help her, or as Arthur would say, "to wake her up." It was so beautifully simple. They both needed each other. "This young boy needs me as much as I need him," she thought tenderly.

"I'm sorry, Mrs. Robinson. Please don't cry," Arthur muttered.

"The club is just a place in my heart where I keep all the people I love. Would you like to be in that club, Arthur?"

Arthur's face began to light up as he pondered the question.

"That sounds like a great club to me," he replied.

"That's marvelous! It's settled then. You know, Arthur, if you're in the club you must come to visit me at least once a week."

"Okay, Mrs. Robinson, it's a deal, but I better get going now. I'll see you later."

Betty patted Arthur gently on the shoulders as he bent down to grab his treasure-laden coal bag off the ground. She stood watching him disappear through the gate, thinking about Joe's message to her.

Chapter 24

Lucky Charm

Charlie sat at the kitchen table tapping his new smoking pipe into the amber ashtray. Columns of thin gray smoke swirled up from the glow of the pipe, filling the kitchen with the sweet yet sharp smell of tobacco. Charlie sat with his legs crossed as he held the smoking pipe out in front of his face like an actor in a moving picture show.

"Alice, how do you think this pipe makes me look? Do you think it makes me look sophisticated?" Charlie asked.

"No, I think it smells bad and I think it makes you look stupid," she replied.

Arthur made his way up the back stairs, stopping every few steps to make sure the stack of money was securely in the coal bag. The unfamiliar scent of burning pipe tobacco drifted down the stairwell, making Arthur wonder if there was a strange man in his house. He quickly ran through the short list of people he knew who smoked pipes and there were only two, Principal Adams and Policeman O'Connor. He sure wasn't interested in seeing either one of them today. The unsettling thought that Mrs. Robinson may have called the police after he left her house quickly startled him. He silently turned the doorknob to slowly crack the kitchen door open to spy on whoever was smoking inside.

"Charlie, what are you doing smoking a pipe?" Arthur asked, swinging the door wide open in relief.

"Hey there, Art, I thought I'd give it a try. Don't you think it makes me look more sophisticated?"

"I think it makes him look stupid. I hate it," Alice blurted out.

"What do you think Art? How do you think it makes me

look?"

"I think it kind of makes you look like Sherlock Holmes," Arthur said.

"Sherlock Holmes? I like that. Now don't you think he looks sophisticated, Alice?" Charlie exclaimed, pushing out his chest proudly.

"Oh boy, he'll never stop smoking now," she laughed.

"Charlie, I need to ask you about something," Arthur said.

"What is it, Art?"

"I kind of found something," Arthur said as he reached into his coal bag.

"What did you find another interesting piece of coal?" Charlie asked.

"No, not exactly. It's something much different."

Charlie continued to practice his new smoking skills, and he drew deeply on his pipe while Arthur reached into his coal bag to retrieve the thick stack of bills. Charlie's eyes almost popped right out of their sockets and the smoke billowed out from his nose in a short powerful burst as he tried to speak through a spasm of coughing.

"Art, what—," he coughed and tried to say, "where did— ?"

He pointed at the money and started to cough again. Finally, Alice rescued him with a glass of cool tap water. Between long sips of water and gasps of air, Charlie was finally able to say, "Where in the heck did you get that?"

"On top of Savin Hill," Arthur replied.

"You found all that money on top of Savin Hill? Come on, Art!" Charlie asked.

"I did so!" he answered defensively.

"When?"

"On the way to Mrs. Robinson's house. I cut up over the hill," he said.

"What time was that?"

"I'm pretty sure it was before nine o'clock."

"Did you see anyone? I mean did you see anyone on the way up or the way down? Did you see anyone at all?" Charlie demanded.

"No, I saw absolutely no one. I looked."

"Where on the hill did you find it?"

"It was right on the flat top where the old fort used to be," Arthur said.

"Charlie, it doesn't matter. We can't keep it. It doesn't belong to us. You know it has gotta be somebody's," Alice said.

"Art, did you count it? Do you know how much money's there?" Charlie said, lowering his voice.

"843 dollars," Arthur proclaimed.

"Oh, my God! That's a lot of money. Can I touch it?" Alice asked.

"Sure, sis, you can hold it if you want," Arthur replied.

Alice held the stack of money in her outstretched hand, bouncing it slightly in the air.

"It feels heavy, Charlie. Here you feel it."

Charlie fanned the money at one end as he tried to estimate its value with the brush of his thumb. He tapped his foot nervously and he scratched his chin as he waited for the answer to come.

After a few moments of silence Arthur asked, "What do you think we should do with it, Charlie?"

"Are you sure you didn't see anyone?" Charlie said, measuring each word.

"No one at all, Charlie, honest."

"Did you cut back up over the hill on the way back home again after you left Mrs. Robinson's?"

"Yes, and I didn't see anyone then either. Not a living soul!"

"You're sure about that?" Charlie asked.

"I swear it!" Arthur replied.

"Alice, do you have a paper bag I can put all this money in?" Charlie asked.

"Yes, but we can't keep it. It's not ours," she said in a shrill voice.

"Alice, I'm not going to keep it. I'm going to find out who lost it."

"How are you going to do that?" Arthur asked.

"I'm going to take it up to the corner bar and ask Big Joe Moakley. If someone's looking for it, he'll know," Charlie explained.

One hour later, Charlie came running up the back stairs barging into the kitchen completely out of breath.

"Charlie, if you didn't smoke that stupid pipe you wouldn't breathe like that," Alice admonished.

"Alice, I only smoked one pipe-full," he said.

"Well, don't you think you should stop then?"

"Charlie, what did Big Joe say?" Arthur asked.

"He asked all around and no one knows anything. No one is looking for lost money."

"Did you give him the money?" Alice asked.

"No, he said we should sit on it for a few weeks and if no one comes forward we should keep it."

Charlie took the paper bag out from underneath his coat and put it on the table.

"Can we do that, Charlie? That doesn't sound right to me," Alice protested.

"He said that a lot of people are having hard times because of the Depression, but no family has had a harder time than us. He said we deserve this money as much as anybody does and that we should wait a while to see. Alice, I want you to take this money and hide it in a safe place where no one will find it. We're going to wait a while and just see what happens."

"Okay, Charlie, if you say so, but don't you think this is all a little strange?"

"Strange, like what?"

"Don't you think it's strange that you hit the number, and now we have all this money out of nowhere, and we don't have to move to a new place now, don't you think that it's all kind of weird, Charlie?"

"I don't know, sis, I haven't really thought about it much."

"Charlie, Arthur's school is testing him to see if he's some kind of genius. You're telling me you don't think that's strange?"

"No, Alice, I don't think that's strange. I think it's incredible and I can see what you mean. It does seem like Arthur has turned into a lucky charm."

Reaching up Alice carefully took down the single decoration in her kitchen. She held the purple vase gently under one arm and placed the large stack of money deep inside.

"I'm putting the money here in mom's vase. She'll keep an eye on it for us," Alice said as she placed it back on the pine board shelf.

"That's a good place for it, and don't tell anyone," Charlie added.

Chapter 25

The Rose

The last remnant of the moon faded into the windy afternoon sky as Arthur made his way toward Mrs. Robinson's house. He remembered how that day's morning sky had looked milky red and thought, "red sky in morning, sailor's warning." The sky now looked like a thick blanket of white as he made his way up the steep side of Savin Hill. A bitter wind rode up over the hill, sending shivers down his back. Arthur fastened the top button of his wool jacket and pulled his scally cap down over the top of his ears to ward off the onslaught of cold. It was becoming difficult to see through his glasses as they fogged up with the rapidly falling temperature. The air seemed electrified. A sudden crack of deafening thunder and a brilliant flash lit the sky in a dome of white. He trembled at how close it was as he cautiously climbed toward the top of the hill. A second louder crack of thunder shook the ground beneath him as another and even more powerful lightening bolt hit the hill. The shockwave shot up through his body like a swarm of angry bees charging up from his shoes all the way to his Irish cap. Arthur stumbled, unable to keep his balance as a thick white blanket of wet snow fell down from the sky. The heavy snow fell at such a startling rate that it covered everything in Arthur's view instantly in a thick curtain of frozen white.

The sudden thunderous clap startled Betty, forcing the carving knife in her hand to slip off the ham she was slicing for Arthur's lunch. As the sharp knife pricked her finger, she shouted "Ouch!" She pulled her hand back and thought, "This is awfully queer weather for March."

The second booming clap quickly followed which shook the

thick timbers of her house, and made the dishes in her kitchen rattle. Her heart jumped. "Oh my, that was very close," she mumbled, pausing to look out onto her garden through a thick veil of white. Peering out the window, she noticed something quite odd and exclaimed, "Hmm, this just can't be." She retrieved her spectacles from her purse and looked out yet again. Straining to see through the heavy snow she was certain now there was something most peculiar out there in her garden. "Why that's impossible," she whispered. Betty hastily put on her snow boots and wool coat and walked slowly through the heavy snow. She stopped. There to her utter amazement, blooming on the newly planted rose bush was a perfect, deep pink rose shrouded in frozen white. It looked so flawless and tender with its smooth petals unfolding in the freshly fallen snow. She reached out to touch the rose with her bare hand. Next to her wrinkled fingers, the rose looked like a baby's silky hand, innocent to its own beauty. The rose felt oddly warm and conveyed a sense of peace as she touched it gently. Joe was waiting for her in the garden in Heaven. She knew that this was his loving way of reminding her that there was nothing to fear.

"You're right, Joe, my sweetheart. There's nothing to worry about. It's just a storm with a little wind and snow."

With a sense of wonder, she plucked the miraculous rose from the newly planted bush and softly held it in the palm of her hand. A golden light danced along the perfect edge of its petals and Betty walked with the rose back toward the warmth of her home.

Arthur wondered for an instant if he had been hit by lightning as a cold blanket of snow fell down from the darkened sky. "I better get off this hill right now and down to Mrs. Robison's house if I know what's good for me," he thought. He quickly scrambled down the hill to the back gate of Mrs. Robinson's garden. He noticed a narrow path of footprints running through the snow from the house directly to the recently planted rose bush. As he looked down, he was startled by what he thought were splashes of red blood in the snow. Arthur moved closer. He quickly realized the red blotches in the snow were not blood, but odd bits of pink scattered along the edges of the broken snow. He reached down to pick up one and it seemed to be a flower petal. The outline of footprints in the snow led to the open back door to Mrs. Robinson's kitchen.

The quiet darkness of the house sent an eerie shiver down his back.

"Mrs. Robinson, are you here?" Arthur spoke into the shadows from the kitchen doorway.

A faint snapping sound followed by a louder crack came down the hall and into the kitchen, alerting Arthur to the presence inside.

"Mrs. Robinson, it's me, Arthur! I'm here for our visit."

There was no response from the distant parlor so Arthur walked down the silent, shadowed hall to investigate. In the parlor, the last glowing embers of a fire lit the Victorian wallpaper with a soft iridescent glow.

"Are you alright, Mrs. Robinson?" he whispered into the flickering shadows.

Mrs. Robinson sat silently with her head resting against the padded wing of her tall chair. She was staring unflinchingly into the dying fire in the fieldstone fireplace.

"Mrs. Robinson, it's me, Arthur. I'm here. You were expecting me, right?" he whispered again.

There was no response as he moved toward her. As he got closer he noticed beads of sweat on her face and that her right arm trembled as she clutched her chest.

She turned to look at Arthur with peaceful eyes and said, "It's fine, dear. Come closer so I can see you."

Arthur moved forward into the fading light. On the fireplace mantle a slender vase held a single pink rose adjacent to a picture of Joe.

"Arthur, it's so beautiful! My Joe was right. There is nothing to worry about. Nothing at all," Betty said.

Her face appeared pained at first, and then calm, as she asked, "Arthur, you know there's nothing to worry about, don't you?"

Arthur nodded his head in agreement and smiled.

"You have the best smile. You should smile all the time," Mrs. Robinson said as she closed her eyes. Her head fell gently down. Arthur bowed his head and kneeled by the chair. He was still for a long time and then, he thought, "God's diamond just got a little bigger."

Many years later the animated voice of a young girl blended with the lively reds and yellows of a New England autumn. Her carefully woven ponytail swung across the back of her white party dress dotted with miniature flowers. Black high-heeled shoes too large for her feet dangled from her toes as she playfully arranged the teacups and saucers on top of a folding table. Arthur walked up the driveway of his stately home, and opened the back gate to see the child arranging a tea party, thinking how very much she looked like her mother.

"Uncle Arthur! Uncle Arthur, would you like some tea?" the young girl asked.

"Betty, it's too cold to be outside dressed like that. You should put your coat on."

"We're not cold. The tea keeps us warm," she replied as she poured more of the imaginary tea for her silent, stiff-legged guest.

"Your friend looks cold to me. I think that maybe you should both put coats on.

"Ginger never gets cold, not even when she played with Mommy a long time ago. Do you?" she asked looking straight at the doll.

The doll's black saucer eyes seemed to look right through him too, and Arthur couldn't remember why the doll seemed so familiar. The memory lifted up from his heart as he closed his eyes for a moment.

"Where did you find her?"

"She was up in the attic. I think she was there for a long time because Mommy was surprised to see her. Uncle Arthur, do you want to sit down with us and have some tea?"

"That sounds like a grand idea."

The girl looked at Ginger and asked, "Maybe we should ask Uncle Arthur if he wants to be in our club."

Arthur hesitated, and for a moment he thought that young Betty reminded him of someone. He shook his head, laughed to himself, and sat down next to his niece, and answered, "That sounds like a great club to me."

Afterword

Down east on the coast of Maine, the morning fog hovered above the marshes as my dream drifted out toward sea. The cry of the gulls along with an oddly familiar voice could be heard over distant breaking waves. A young boy's voice seemed to grow louder, but there were no tangible words, just thoughts. As I remember it, the boy in my dream was walking along the railroad track picking up pieces of broken coal. There was a strange loneliness about him, but there was also an unmistakable sense of promise. The boy and his older brothers and sister had grown up together without parents during the Depression of the 1930s. One afternoon during a snowstorm, the boy had been gravely injured while gathering coal along the track. He was only 10 years old at the time, and he never told anyone about what really happened that day. As the dream flashed before me, I somehow understood he had briefly died when the accident happened, and he had met an angelic figure who gave him an important message to bring back to help others. As my awareness grew, I knew he had lived to the ripe old age of 71 without ever whispering a single word of the message to anyone. It came to me with an absolute clarity that I'll never forget. He wanted to let me know what had happened to him back then, but also insisted, which seemed strange to me, I write his story down in a book. From the picture window of my cabin, I considered all of this while I looked out on the marshes as the sunlight began to pour through the mist. I shook my head in disbelief. I had never written a single creative word in my entire life. How could I possibly write a book from only a wisp of a dream? The boy on the track was my father, Arthur, and this is his story that came to me. It is the story he wanted me to tell.

BOOKS

SPIRITUALITY

O is a symbol of the world, of oneness and unity; this eye represents knowledge and insight. We publish titles on general spirituality and living a spiritual life. We aim to inform and help you on your own journey in this life.

If you have enjoyed this book, why not tell other readers by posting a review on your preferred book site?